Orphans, Assassins
and the Existential Eggplant

A novel by J.T. Gillett

ISBN 10: 0692391665
ISBN 13: 978-0692391662
Library of Congress Control Number: 2015902922
Homunculus Press, Ashland, OR

Cover design—Ted Killian

For my parents, Skip and Sally—my greatest heroes.

PART ONE

"Good stories rise and fall like empires in the endless pursuit of happiness, like armies of lovers marching to paradise—good stories change the world."
—Last words of Hamdan Karmat

1. Unexpected Visitors

It's midnight, April 30, 1211 and Layla is sealing her last vial of belladonna vapors and wondering if she'll ever return to paradise. She places the vial carefully in a large embroidered travel bag, already packed with salves, tinctures, a small case holding a man's beard and a priest's collar, more poison vapors and several lemon-sized cloth bags filled with colored powder. She closes her travel bag, hides it inside the stone-faced furnace that occupies an entire wall, and looks across her laboratory's shelves, still covered with half-full jars of medicinal herbs and minerals, along with ingredients for more dangerous creations. Her alchemical laboratory has served her well, and she'll miss it.

This is her last night in this English wilderness outpost before setting out to capture one of the ancient world's most well-guarded secrets—the Lost Stone of Eden. For centuries, tales of the Stone's existence were carefully passed among elder shamans, including Layla's mother, who told her it was a gift from the heavens, crafted from a fallen star and capable of providing its possessor with immortality.

After serving an apprenticeship with a little-known French alchemist who passed away during a life–extension experiment and left Layla his fortune, Layla spent the rest of her life searching for the Lost Stone. She scoured esoteric and apocryphal literature, sought answers from deeply-hidden mystics, gathered dozens of clues, cultivated more than 100 informants across Europe, Northern Africa, Persia and Arabia and gave each of them messenger pigeons ready to fly to this castle if they heard even a single word about the Stone. This morning, the first of those pigeons returned with news of an old man in Alexandria, Egypt who inquired about the Stone's properties and was willing to pay 'a mountain of gold' for useful information. That was all Layla needed to mix some extra belladonna and pack her bags for a journey to Egypt in the morning.

Ever since she moved into this rundown, humble castle 10 years ago, Layla spends her days and nights waiting patiently for news of the Stone's location. She tends gardens, studies manuscripts and personal letters pilfered from Church archives and private collections, prepares medicinal salves and tinctures, and devises poison and explosive concoctions that could defeat a small army, if necessary.

Tonight, on the eve of St. Walpurga's feast, she's hoping for a sign to guide her to the Stone, or maybe a vision to point out pitfalls to avoid on her trip across Europe and the Mediterranean Sea. She knew St. Walpurga was special. A writer and alchemist, she inspired women across Europe ever since she was canonized more than 300 years ago. At this moment, on the highest peak in Germany's Harz Mountains, female mystics—many of them Layla's friends—are celebrating St. Walpurga's Night and dancing around bonfires, whooping it up and reciting spontaneous poems to the moon and stars, their voices echoing across the universe. And at dawn's first light, their shadows will stretch for miles across the valley, as if they were giants.

Instead of bonfires, Layla began her ceremony by lighting six candles, one for each direction, their shadow's leaping like hypnotic dancers up and down the laboratory's tall stone walls, shifting shapes and suggesting meaningful patterns. She sat on a carpet in the center of the room, silently called on St. Walpurga for guidance, then closed her eyes to meditate and visualized the Lost Stone. She envisions it is the size of a man's skull and almost egg-shaped with a smooth, bright surface like a great shining seed. She imagines her reflection bending around the Stone's curved ends, she can see herself holding it and rubbing it with her hands, sliding it across her face and belly, covering herself with its ethereal scent and feeling visions pouring in and out of her mind's eye, as if tracking the Stone's elusive aroma across the lands, transporting her high over the forests of England, France, Germany—she looks below for a hint of the Stone, maybe puffs of colored smoke, an illuminated highway or a beautiful dwarf waving her arms—some point of reference she can hold onto, but the scent pulls her southward, soaring like a great bird over the Mediterranean, over Moroccan minarets and the Sahara, then east towards Cairo until she hovers above Persia's Elberz Mountains, looking down at a rugged peak with a fortress containing thousands of scrolls, books and diagrams in every language—when a loud knocking coming from the main door shattered her vision. She closed her eyes and tried to go back to the Persian mountains, but there was nothing but scattered thoughts, questions about the vision and more urgently, who was knocking on the door?

Layla couldn't believe her ears. Nobody ever visits. Not ever. King John's henchmen, Pope Innocent III's heretic-hunting monks, a renegade band of Templars and even Hassan i Sabbah's trained Assassins were all after Layla at one time or another, but they'd either crash through a roof, vault over a wall or ram down a door. Nobody knocks.

Two centuries ago, this castle was Edward the Confessor's favorite outpost. Hidden deep in the English forest, far from roadways and surrounded by miles of trees and brambles, Edward's great pains to keep its location secret were successful. After his death, the fortified five-room castle remained mostly abandoned, with a few rare exceptions.

The knocking grew louder, echoing through the hallway and around the room, until Layla started for the door, still trying to imagine what sort of trick this could be. Were others waiting to break through the door as it cracked open? This old outpost had neither the luxuries nor fortifications of most castles—its remoteness was its defense.

"Please help me!" It sounded like a boy.

"Careful, this may be a trap," squeaked a small voice inside Layla's head.

Layla lit a torch, pulled her hooded robe around her waist, held a dagger in one hand and opened the door an inch or two. "Why are you here and where did you come from?" It was a teenage boy, about her height but much thinner, standing alone in the darkness.

"I came from a hamlet that's weeks away. I've been lost for days. Please ma'am? Just a morsel of food?" He looked sincere and his diction was civilized. Definitely English.

"What's the name of the village?"

"They call it Pluck's Gutter."

Layla knew the place. There was a shroud in its abbey, supposedly once used to cover the body of Jesus after his crucifixion, and according to some, you can still see his image on the yellowed cloth, crown of thorns and all. She saw the shroud years ago, when her French alchemist benefactor was in the process of manufacturing it using ancient fabrics and old coal collected from the Holy Land. It was a tedious process and took its creator years, but the final product appeared incredibly authentic and brought a high price, making it well worth the trouble.

Layla looked at the boy from head to toe and saw nothing unusual. She opened the door wider and scanned the area but saw only shadows. "Wait here," she said and stepped to her pantry, grabbed a small hard cake of rye bread and when she returned, the boy was gone. She stepped outside and called for him, but there was no answer so she walked to the edge of the meadow and still saw nothing. She climbed a few branches of a craggy old, leafless tree for a better view when a limb snapped and she fell like a sack of stones, hitting her head hard on the way down and landing in a twisted, motionless heap.

When Layla opened her eyes, the boy was sitting in front of her with the full moon behind him, like a halo. Her head was sore and her legs ached, but she could move them. Her right arm was fine, but she couldn't move her left arm, which she favored.

"You've been out for a while. I'm not sure how to help you. What can I do?"

Layla was relieved. She may be in pain and incapable of launching her quest for the Lost Stone tomorrow or anytime soon—but she was not disabled. She looked up from a bed of rocks and fallen branches at the open meadow filled with full moon shadows. Every breath ached and she cradled her left arm, which appeared to be broken, and listened for signs of others who may have accompanied the boy, but heard nothing. Layla was always concerned about being captured by one foe or another. Not that she was wanted for any actual crimes, more like she was sought by priests who wanted to burn her for sorcery, a King who wanted her taxes and a host of others, including a handful of rogue Templars, who wanted her secrets. Layla's quest for the Stone had uncovered knowledge of ancient mysteries and occult matters that made her legendary among her contemporaries, even though most had no idea what she looked like.

"Thank you for staying with me. It appears I broke my arm and I may have broken ribs," she winced again and grabbed her side, "But I'm still breathing."

The boy shook his head and rested one hand on Layla's unbroken forearm. He was very gentle and sincere, which were both odd qualities in a teenage peasant. Usually these lads were brutes at best, incapable of random kindness, but he was different, almost innocent.

"My name's Layla. What's yours?"

"Aaron. Aaron Sloopshire." His curly hair was matted across his brow and even in the moonlight she could see dirt was caked on almost every inch of his skin and clothes.

"I'm pleased to meet you, Aaron. Sit down beside me." The back of her head was pounding, but not bleeding, and even the slightest movement was painful. She could probably ride a horse, if necessary.

"What were you doing in that tree?"

"I was looking for you. You were gone when I came back with bread and water."

"I had to pee really bad." He looked at his feet as he continued, "And I didn't want to pee too close to your house, so I went into the woods."

"Thank you for being so considerate." In Layla's experience, manners and honesty were more rare than kindness among peasants and nobility in this Dark Age. She wondered who taught him these traits. Layla never had children and circulated in a world inhabited by old men and women who considered kids of all ages troublesome at best, but she was already starting to like this young man.

"Well Aaron, if you'll help me up we'll get back to the castle and I'll get you some food." Before she finished the sentence, she saw a shadow moving far behind Aaron, a dark silhouette on the castle's roof, and heard a booming sound echoing through the night again and again.

"What's happening?"

"Shhhh," whispered Layla. "Stay down and stay still. I believe that's a battering ram knocking down my door."

"What are they looking for?"

"They're looking for me—or something they believe is in the castle. There's one on the roof," she pointed, "And there may be others. Be very still, so they don't see us." Layla wondered how she could have two unrelated, unexpected visitors in one night, when she hasn't had a single guest in 10 years. She was used to strange occurrences on St. Walpurga's Night, but this night was far stranger than most.

*****

At daybreak, Aaron left Layla and weaved carefully through the woods until he came to a stand of thick brambles not far from the castle's door. He waited until three young men appeared with bags filled with plundered goods and watched as they climbed onto their horses and rode west through the forest without looking back.

"Three intruders? Are you certain there were three?" Layla thought they might be Assassins sent by Hassan i Sabbah, who was also known as the Old Man of the Mountain. The Old Man always sent a trio of Assassins for a single victim, but they usually worked silently, killing their victims as they slept. Bashing down a door was not their style. Door bashing was very European.

Once inside the castle, Layla and Aaron were surprised to see only one room was ransacked. "Nothing looks moved, but it's freezing in here." Aaron wrapped his arms around himself and looked for a fireplace, but there was only a stove in the kitchen and a furnace reserved for experiments in the laboratory. And even when the furnace was burning for days, these walls were still cold, dark and damp enough to keep almost every type of mold and mildew in England growing on every surface.

Aaron stepped into the largest room and was ambushed by a barrage of unfamiliar and mostly unpleasant aromas. Ceramic containers of saffron, blue ginger, balls of black opium, minerals like cinnabar, butter of antimony, liver of silver and philosopher's wool, vials of alcohol, green, red and brown tinctures in bottles large and small, plus alembics, retorts and crucibles—were all smashed into a pile of broken shards, powders and lumps in puddles of thick, smoking liquids covering the floor.

"What was this?"

"This used to be my laboratory." Layla's head was still throbbing, the bump swollen to the size of a small quince. She went to the furnace and pulled a long chain extending from the ceiling, opening the flu so fresh air could circulate.

In Layla's bedroom, everything was in order except for a note attached to her pillow with a long, curved dagger. "Assassins are notorious for leaving daggers in pillows while their targets sleep," she said, and read the note: *"If we want to kill you, you be dead. Stop looking for the Stone, or we be back."* Layla tossed the note aside.

"Not too big on grammar," said a small voice in her head.

"Or they don't want us to think they're English," added Layla.

*****

Layla's arm and head ached more as she moved from room to room, and she knew it was time for some serious medication. She went for her opium tinctures and spirits, but the thieves had emptied her bedroom's medicine cabinet, too. Fortunately, they didn't find her best alchemical ingredients and concoctions, which were safely hidden behind a false wall inside the furnace. She pulled a cord that opened a secret door and revealed a well-stocked apothecary and small armory filled with knives, swords, long needles, and bags of explosive black powder, along with her embroidered travel bag.

After washing down a dozen drops of opium tincture with a glass of smooth but potent liquor, she sat down at her long oak table, slowly turned her broken arm so her palm faced up, and gently felt the bones until she found the break halfway between her wrist and elbow.

"I've fixed broken bones many times, and it's not as bad as it seems," she assured Aaron. "Years ago, my partner fell off her horse and landed just right so her arm was broken and bones quite dislocated. We had to figure out which bone went where, but we did it and she used that arm the rest of her life.

"I'm much luckier. My bone broke but didn't move much, so I'll just need some splints to keep it in place." Layla could feel the tincture starting to work on the pain, sending its little agents out to wrap her in a soft blanket of numbing fog. As Layla's agony lost its edge and faded into the background, she helped Aaron collect short planks of thin wood from her kindling pile, position them on the sides of her forearm and bind them with strips of cloth. She used a violet-colored silk scarf from Damascus as a sling, tied it around her good shoulder and slipped her bandaged arm inside.

"Much better." And she poured another cup of liquor.

*****

"He smells like a dead rat," said the small, humming voice only audible inside Layla's head. "A really old, ugly, dead rat with a hint of fresh urine. And there's enough dirt on him to plant a royal garden. Somebody has to soap him up and give him a good scrubbing."

Layla chuckled and stroked the diminutive, petrified eggplant attached to a gold chain around her neck. This was no ordinary eggplant—this one was the size of a small toe, hard as polished marble, rich like a deep purple-black jewel and more than handsome—it possessed a certain intelligence, magnetism

11

and 'voice' that set it apart from the rest of the vegetable kingdom. It was Layla's magnificent little companion.

Layla agreed wholeheartedly with the eggplant and showed Aaron how to burn wood in the oven and boil water for a bath. There was a big iron tub in the garden, and they mixed the boiling water with cool creek water to get the bath's temperature just right.

"What kind of stone are you wearing around your neck?"

The eggplant perked up and immediately took offense. "A stone? Did he say a stone?"

"It's not really a stone." Layla lightly stroked the amulet as she spoke. "It's a tiny, dried eggplant."

Aaron looked at it closely. "What's an eggplant?"

"What?" shuddered the eggplant. "He's never heard of an eggplant? Did he grow up in a stable? He'll never be able to help us. I'll tell you right now…"

"An eggplant is actually a fruit, but this one prefers to be called a vegetable," interrupted Layla, rubbing the eggplant's smooth, shining skin as if she was massaging a restless infant.

"Can you eat it?"

"If he lays one finger on me…" started the volatile little vegetable.

"When this eggplant was fresh, it was extremely edible and probably quite delicious—if anyone had been foolish enough to eat it. But unlike other vegetables, this amazing eggplant was preserved to last forever. It's more than 600-years-old and there are no others like it anywhere in the world."

"It's pretty. It must be worth a lot."

"At least he has good aesthetic taste," remarked the eggplant.

"Priceless. Now clean yourself up, wash all the old dirt and grime away like sad memories." She stared at Aaron's frail little frame and his shoulder blades looked sharp enough to slice cheese. Soil, leaves, sweat and berry stains were caked on his arms and hands like layers of old, hardened skin and there was a big, diamond-shaped scab on the end of his nose.

"What happened to your nose? Were you burned?"

Aaron nodded.

"Now get in the tub and we'll see what's hiding underneath all that dirt. Maybe we'll find an apprentice hiding in there."

"What are you saying?" inquired the eggplant. "We don't need anybody, especially not a liability like that stinky spud."

Aaron looked puzzled too, and stepped away from the tub. "What's an apprentice?"

"An apprentice is a student who learns by helping his instructor."

"And doesn't cause any problems or mess with the eggplant," added the amulet, wishing it had arms and legs so it could push the boy into the tub, scrub him and douse him with rose oil.

"You bathe and afterwards we'll prepare a feast. You can start by telling me how you got those burns on your nose, and how you wound up at my doorstep." She sat back in her chair and watched Aaron dip his blackened, crusty fingers into the tub, cup his hands and bring the sweet, warm water to his face and pour it through his tangled hair, turning it slowly from matted black to curly and blonde as it was washed. He stepped slowly into the big tub and watched the clear warm liquid turn brownish-grey before he slid all the way to its bottom.

"Well Aaron? What was it like growing up in Puck's Gutter?"

"It was alright until my parents died."

"Oh my, you poor boy. When did you lose your parents?"

"They both died of the Fever about three weeks ago. The monk burned down our hut and everything in it, except my goatskin pouch."

"So what happened after the monk burned your hut?"

13

"I had no place to stay, so I followed a group of holy men for a day or two, but they had no food and were sick and bloody from whipping themselves. They argued and wailed about their sins all the time and tried to get me to whip myself. When I refused, they tried to whip me, so I left them and followed deer paths in the woods, drank water from creeks, and ate berries until a blacksmith found me and made me work for him. Maybe I was his apprentice?"

"Maybe he's brighter than I suspected," said the eggplant.

"It depends. What did you do for this blacksmith?"

"I'd spend the day filling buckets of water from a pool at the bottom of a steep gully and hauling them up a hill until the smith's water barrels were full. I wanted to run away, but the smith would've caught me and killed me. One day he grabbed a long metal poker from the fire and held it to my face. I begged him to let me go back to work and I hollered as loud as I could for help, but he just laughed. I closed my eyes and could feel the hot pole getting closer and closer to the tip of my nose—and I really screamed when it touched me and my skin sizzled. When I heard the hot poker clang to the ground I stopped screaming, opened my eyes and saw the smith's body crash at my feet with an arrow though his chest."

"It must have been horrible for you."

"He still has his nose," added the eggplant. "I'm just saying, it could've been worse."

2. The Non-Existent Knight

"A man stood at the other end of the room, bow in hand, almost invisible in the shadows. As he walked closer, I saw the archer was wearing knight's mail, a battered helmet with a King's mark and a pitted, rusty breastplate.

"He bent down to talk to me, pulled a scarf from under his mail, dipped it in the water barrel and held it to my nose. It made my nose feel a little better. He told me my nose was still intact, and would look just fine when it healed. Do you think he was right?" Aaron rubbed his arms and legs with the warm, brownish-grey water.

Layla looked closely at the distinctive, crescent-shaped indentation on the tip of his nose, only slightly discolored, like a small birthmark. "I think you'll have a scar, but it will be an attractive scar. I'm interested in this knight. Did he have a name?"

"Not really. He told me he was a non-existent knight."

"What?" chimed Layla and the eggplant. Neither had ever heard of a non-existent knight. Could it be a new, secret order? Or was it even a knight at all?

"Do you know him? Have you met the non-existent knight?"

"I don't know. Tell me more about him."

"He said he was in the village by chance and trying to stay a step ahead of any outlaws or sheriffs chasing him because of what he called, 'misunderstandings'. He said he usually avoided villages, but when heard me scream, he had to do his knightly duty and help."

"Why did he call himself a non-existent knight?"

"He said he and the Sheriff of Nottingham disagreed about an old religious Stone. When King John heard about the disagreement, he wiped the knight's name and deeds from all records, leaving him with no identity. He said in the eyes of the world, he longer existed. Yet he stood there before me and he appeared to be a knight."

"I wonder what Stone they were fighting about, huh Layla?" asked the eggplant.

Layla ignored the vegetable. "Where did you learn so much about existence?" After all, she had only met a handful of gurus and shamans who spoke of existence. The knights she knew certainly didn't gather around the fire to wallow in each other's existential crisis. They were too busy marauding through some foreign land, chaperoning a king's army en route to a Crusade, or drinking ale until they dropped.

The eggplant had a higher stake than most when it came to existence. As far as it was concerned, its self-awareness was all the proof of existence it needed. It possessed memories and was quite aware of how others felt about it—even if they had no feelings about the vegetable. But the eggplant also understood it needed others to offer credible reassurance from time to time, otherwise it could never be 100% sure if it did exist, or if it was the imaginary product of a few humans giving the little vegetable make-believe qualities, like consciousness. There were several other existential scenarios the eggplant routinely considered, but none of them provided any certainty, so it continued to think of itself as a real being who possessed intelligence, observed and interpreted the world and was recognized as an independent consciousness by at least one human at a time. Unlike the knight, the eggplant needed no official papers to exist.

"I spent a lot of time with the knight and he never stopped talking. Before we left, he told me he couldn't let me starve or die in the jaws of wild dogs or in the kettles of witches. He said, 'We must do what must be done,' and we took the dead smith's horse.

16

A non-existent person taking a dead smith's horse seemed like the right thing, don't you agree?"

"I'm afraid it's not for me to judge." Layla wondered if this so-called knight was really just a common thief who was masquerading in a knight's stolen armor.

"What would you have done?"

"Same as you. But that doesn't make it right. Telling right from wrong is usually a lot more complicated than people believe. Sometimes it's hard to tell the thieves from the heroes, Aaron."

"What do you mean?"

"What's right for one person may be wrong for the next. People in different parts of the world have completely different ideas about right and wrong."

"Have you been to other parts of the world?" Aaron was quite comfortable sitting naked in the tub of water, rubbing his hands up and down his arms, but not clear on the concept of cleaning.

"Yes. I've been halfway around the world. Now keep scrubbing. You can surely talk and wash at the same time. Use the brush and soap there beside you."

"What's soap?" He spied the soft beige lump of waxy substance in a dish beside the tub.

"Why am I not surprised?" asked the eggplant.

"People in Arab countries and some Europeans use it to clean themselves. Soap is one of the great secrets. I have many more if you choose to stay."

"What kind of great secrets?"

"The kind that can keep you alive. Soap is the first lesson of longevity. It can easily double the length of your life. Wash your hands and face and all your skin with soap and water, like this," and she rubbed the bar between her wet hands and against the skin of her arms. "More than half of the peasants and barons die from their own filth and grime they collected from others. They wipe their ass with their bare hands then wipe their babies' faces and eat with the same fingers. They touch open wounds while they're cleaning sewers, work in muck and filth all day then prepare their food in scum-coated pots, and they wonder why they get sick and die before their 30th birthday."

She held the waxy, oval-shaped lump like a golden key. "This soap will save your life again and again. All you have to do is wash your hands with soap and water after you pee or poop, before you eat, before you cook, and before you touch a wound. You'll live longer."

Aaron took the soap. "This is magic?"

"No tricks. It's real magic."

*****

"So what happened to your non-existent knight?"

"We rode together for a few days before things went bad. A band of thieves ambushed us and knocked me from my horse. I must have hit my head when I fell, because when I came to my hands and feet were bound with strips of leather. I saw three bandits surrounding the knight, and the knight drew his sword and stabbed two of the thieves but the third bandit's sword slashed right through the knight's mail and nearly chopped off his arm. Blood poured down the knight's breastplate and he fell from his horse like a canister from one of your shelves.

"The bandit lifted his dead friends onto the knight's horse, then removed the knight's mail, breastplate, helmet and boots and stuffed them in a sack. The stripped knight was shaking on the ground, his wound still bleeding and his eyes wide open. Then the bandit picked me up and heaved me onto the knight's horse between the two dead men. When he led the horse away, I could hear the lone bandit sobbing and see the non-existent knight at the edge of the road—and he wasn't moving.

"I ended up almost face-to-face with one of the dead men. He looked like he might be 20-years-old. I tried to hear my heartbeat or my breath, but there were only horse's hooves pounding when I passed out.

"When I awoke, a woman, not much older than my mother, was sitting beside me. She rubbed warm salve on my nose, and it took away the itch and the pain. She promised nobody would hurt me and left me alone in a deerskin tent. When I peeked outside, I saw more than a dozen children, many of them sick. I played with the younger children and used my father's knife to carve a small doll from a stick for a little girl who was too weak to walk. Then I sneaked away and followed the road back to where we were ambushed and looked for the knight, but there was no trace of him anywhere. So I set out on the road again, heading east, away from the setting sun.

"Weren't you frightened?" Aaron's tale was more exciting than she expected.

"Not after I got away and was traveling on my own."

"Why did you travel east? Why not follow the sun?"

"My father told me stories about London. He told me to follow the sunrise and the stench. He said thousands of people live on a mountain of shit in London, and you can smell it from miles away."

"His father was right," noted the eggplant. "At least 10,000 horses in the city, each dropping 10 pounds of manure a day for about 50 tons of horse shit plus 25 tons of fresh human poop daily, all dumped in and around the city and its lovely waterways. Of course, that's only a rough estimate."

"I walked all night, sniffing the air, feeling my way along the bushes at the side of the road until I was bumping into trees and stumps at every turn. When the sun came up, the road was nowhere in sight so I wandered through the forest, following deer paths for days, until I finally came to your castle. I looked for a window or a gate, but found only one wooden door. I pounded it with my fist at first, but it sounded dull, so I picked up a rock and banged it against your metal latch."

Layla was impressed. What appeared to be a hungry, lost boy turned out to be a hungry, lost boy with an amazing tale of misfortune, adventure and survival. "You've had some difficult times, Aaron. There certainly is more to you than meets the eye."

Aaron slipped into his new woven pants and tunic and he felt like a prince. When he stepped into the open courtyard, it was like walking into a living paradise. There were high stone walls blocking any view of the surrounding forest and a section of the river flowed through the courtyard, around boulders and under a little wooden bridge before the waters disappeared beneath another stone wall and rejoined the forest river. In the center of the yard, a red-and-blue silk canopy shaded a bed covered with plush sheepskins. Big, flat-topped rocks circled a large fire pit, moss dripped from the sides of trees and lush, green ivy climbed the stone walls. A rose garden overflowed with vivid red, pink, yellow and fiery orange flowers, tiny blossoms sprouted from succulents that crawled between rocks and elephant ear-sized skunk cabbage grew at the edge of the water.

Layla looked much different to Aaron in the sunlight. She was barely taller than him and heavier but not fat, with wide hips, full breasts and a thick blanket of curly black-and-silver hair dancing down her back. Her smooth olive skin gave way to only thin wrinkles on her neck and hands, her brown-green eyes sparkled like the brightest stars and her long and graceful nose was suited for a queen. Somehow, she looked young and old at the same time.

"What do you do here, Layla?"

"I preserve paradise."

"What do you mean? How do you preserve paradise?"

"I took a vow to preserve paradise wherever I lived. It's an old tradition started long ago by the Sisters of Lilith. I maintain gardens, like other Sisters who cultivate their own little paradise behind cottages, on islands and in the uncharted wilderness. It's our calling." Then she whispered, "This garden is my paradise," as if it were a great secret.

"Hmm. Excuse me, but this is our paradise," grumbled the eggplant. "And don't tell this kid about the apples."

"Why did you make your garden here in the woods and why do you need walls to protect it?"

"Good questions," noted the eggplant.

"I prefer the solitude of the forest. I'm usually working in the garden, performing daily exercises, preparing foods or mixing tinctures."

"Why do you have to be here to do those things?"

"You're not going to tell him…" started the eggplant.

"I need a safe, unknown place to stay while I'm trying to find something that's extremely important. And I need a laboratory. I'm looking for a Stone that is very dangerous. People have been killed because they simply mentioned this Stone."

"I wonder if it's the same Stone that got the non-existent knight into trouble?"

"It's called the Lost Stone and it may have been in the Garden of Eden at one time. Have you ever heard of the Garden of Eden?"

"Not really. Should I?"

"Be careful," cautioned the eggplant, "Don't get him started. We've seen too many minds destroyed by religious madness."

"The Garden of Eden was the first paradise in this world and the first man and woman, named Adam and Lilith, lived there."

"Where was it?"

"It was on an island called Bahrain in the Arabian Sea, far from here."

"What about the Lost Stone?"

21

"The Lost Stone was a gift to Lilith when she was still living in the Garden of Eden, and since then, it passed through several families, until it disappeared centuries ago. Now, I'm here to find the Stone and return it to the Sisters of Lilith."

"Do you know where it is?"

"No, and it may still take years, but my Stone and I will find each other, and I'll bring it back to paradise." Layla said the words with complete certainty, as if she and the Stone had a secret pact.

"Why are you in this castle in the woods instead of looking for the Stone?" Aaron thought she should be running across Europe and Africa, knocking on doors and putting up signs.

"I work in my laboratory with minerals and plants," she pointed to a common stone on the ground. "By using the right words and combining the right ingredients, I can use that rock to create an explosive and blow a hole in these walls. And I could use your help in the laboratory, if you're interested."

"Will you tell me more about the Garden of Eden and the Lost Stone?"

"I will tell you about Eden, the Stone, Lilith, Isis, Walpurga and so much more." She pointed to his goatskin pouch. "But first, you tell me about your treasures."

He opened the little cloth sack and held up a tarnished, metallic ring. "My mother's ring," he said, and pulled out two more items. "My father's knife. Letters."

"Can I see the piece of paper? I'll show you what the letters mean."

Aaron gave her the paper and she placed it on the table. "Each one of these marks is a different letter of the English alphabet. This one on top is A, this one is M and the other is S. What's your middle name? Does it start with an M?"

"What's a middle name?"

Layla wondered why his mother chose to write these letters. Was she copying them from something she found, or a message?

Either way, the letters, like everything else in Layla's world, had a thousand alternative interpretations.

"You use the letters of the alphabet to create words, phrases and books. There are only three letters here, but I'll teach you the rest of the alphabet and you'll be able to write all of the English words you want."

"The world was created from letters. That's what my mum told me, before she died."

"Your mother sounds like a very smart woman." Layla dipped a long quill pen into a small ink well and wrote, 'Aaron Sloopshire' on a piece of paper. "That's what your name looks like."

His face lit up. "Those letters spell Aaron Sloopshire?"

"Yes they do."

Aaron laughed for the first time he could remember. It sounded unfamiliar and comforting at the same time, so he laughed again, this time louder. Even the eggplant cracked a half-grin when it realized Aaron had tasted his first morsel of literacy. Already he was looking more like a young hawk ready for a high dive than a boy lost in the forest. In a few weeks, he'd be drifting across a rising breeze, reciting the alphabet from beginning to end and hunting for new words in the manuscripts from Layla's library.

Layla saw it too. Aaron was eager to learn and he seemed reasonably capable. "If you'll stay here and help me, I'll open the door to a new world for you."

"With more things like soap?"

"Much better. I'll teach you to read and write."

3. Secret Teachings

Layla's arm healed quickly. After two months she removed the splints and just used the sling, which was ideal for concealing daggers, a vial of explosives or other emergency items. Aaron handled household duties—cleaning floors, watching for incoming pigeons, cooking and collecting water from the creek. In return for his assistance, Aaron lived like Layla's favorite son. His room had its own door, window, bed, writing table, lamp and basin for washing his hands and face, which he did several times a day. Reading lessons began before breakfast each morning, writing lessons in the afternoon, and alchemy lessons before and after dinner. In less than a month he was reading scrolls and manuscripts in English, including treatises on pyramids, secret caves and European fortresses. He felt at home with the letters and books, as if he was meant to be with them the way some people were meant to ride horses or chase Lost Stones.

From the start, Aaron took to writing letters like a flying squirrel to high branches, paying careful attention to each letter's consistent size and shape, as Layla instructed. At the end of three months, he was transcribing the oldest books onto new paper while learning the basics of Latin, French, Hebrew and Arabic. Aaron had a gift for languages and an uncanny thirst for new subjects. He was content to sit and read all day, even if it meant using one of Layla's glossaries to figure out a manuscript's meaning one word at a time.

Despite the collection of reading material in the library, Aaron's favorite stories came directly from Layla. She described some of her tales with such detail it seemed like she must've been there. His favorite story was about Hamdan Karmat. Hamdan was the leader of the Karmations, an Ishmaelite sect living in 10th century Bahrain. According to Layla, Hamdan Karmat understood the perils of trying to change the world far better than most. He was only one man, but he had many loyal followers. And if changing his world meant overcoming the powerful caliphs in Mecca and Baghdad, he accepted the challenge and vowed to bend the course of history with the patience of a tiny spider spinning its web to the moon.

This afternoon, Layla told Aaron the story of Hamdan's return to Bahrain after weeks of battle. "They pounded over the blistering desert with nothing but hot sun and screaming vultures overhead for days until they came to the sea, where their boats waited. They rowed through the night while their horses and camels dozed and a warm, oyster-scented breeze filled their sails. It appeared to be a glorious day, but trouble waited in Bahrain. If Hamdan could read the buxom clouds scattered above the horizon or the delirious zebra fish swimming below, he'd know he'd be dead before the sun would rise again.

"In Bahrain, a barefoot woman named Samar climbed atop a fortress wall and waited for the first glimpse of the boats. She was the oldest dancer in Hamdan's harem, and one of the most beautiful. She watched twinkling reflections rise and fall across the water until the forms of faraway ships appeared on the horizon and the children howled. Before long, the tiny spots crawled closer, until the long boats filled with white-robed oarsmen finally landed on the pearly beaches of Bahrain.

"The fortress opened its heavy wooden gates and Hamdan was first to ride inside. Samar found a place in the shade, away from the crowd and listened to the screams, whoops and whistles blend inside the tall, sun baked walls as the great parade began. It was sweet music to Samar, who'd been waiting for this day since she arrived in Bahrain.

"She was one of the prizes Hamdan captured when he and his men defeated Amir Fuqur, a sultan from Baghdad. Fuqur was also Samar's lover and her brother's best friend. When Hamdan killed Fuqur, her brother vowed revenge. Like Hamdan, Samar's brother was a radical Ishmaelite fighting to change the Moslem world. Unlike Hamdan, her brother had no army. But he did have a loyal sister, which can sometimes be just as powerful.

"Hamdan held his hand high over his head and the crowd cheered again. Samar remembered the first time she saw him peering from atop his sweating black steed. He appeared imposing, strong and almost handsome—until he climbed off his horse. Hamdan was short and bald with a long, black beard and an overgrown moustache hiding his few remaining teeth. He had almost no shoulders, exceptionally large feet and his appetite for wine left him with an enormous belly and a bright red, round nose begging to be squeezed."

Aaron pictured this funny little ruler sitting atop a huge horse and chuckled. "He looked more like a clown than king."

"But a very courageous, generous clown. He was also a brutal warrior who led every charge into battle, risked his own life to save others, and rewarded his soldiers with more riches and pleasures than most would see in five lifetimes.

"As soon as Hamdan and his soldiers appeared, women called out sweet promises and waved clouds of bright-colored scarves over their heads. Battalions of men, each with sparkling clean, ghost-white djellabas, guided their horses and camels slowly through the living corridor formed by the adoring crowd.

"More camels and horses plodded into the court, their backs bowed with looted treasure. Gilded statues of goats, birds and fishtailed ladies poked from large woven baskets strapped to the animals' sides. There were baskets filled with rich-hued silks once meant for the gowns of sweet virgins on their wedding night, leather-bound books filled with family secrets, bracelets once worn by mothers of young warriors and slippers fit for a newborn prince. The heirlooms of an entire great city were reduced to bundles of prizes strapped to the sides of these beasts.

"Samar saw much more. She saw the people who'd been left behind, like the old widows and young children whose homes were plundered and burned. They were left in the streets, hungry and sleeping under makeshift tents, like discarded trophies.

"Young women and girls, riding two-to-a-horse, filed into the court next. The Karmation women were silent as they passed, for many of them had come to Bahrain the same way. The women were the warriors' most precious booty, clothed in pure white robes with white scarves covering their heads and exposing only their eyes.

"Samar remembered when she was captured and paraded into the fortress. It was still frightening. She knew these women felt like animals marching mindfully to slaughter, like she once did. They didn't know they'd all be free to stay or return to their villages after a few moons. If they stayed in Bahrain, they'd become dancers, servants, mistresses or sister-in-laws, depending on their fortune.

"The crowd's hushed voices turned to shrieks as the berserkers passed through the gates. These half-human, half-shark creatures could smell spilled blood across miles of desert and once they killed their first victim, they couldn't stop murdering everything in their path. Berserkers didn't suffer from mental maladies—they reveled in them. After the parade, Hamdan gave the berserkers plenty of food and shelter outside the fortress, where they'd be his standing army of ruthless killers, ready when needed."

"What are mental maladies?"

"When you start seeing and listening to invisible demons."

"Can you tell me more about the berserkers?"

"Everybody wants to know more about the creepy berserkers," complained the eggplant. "I don't know which is worse—the berserkers, or people's endless fascination with them."

"They were filthy. They smelled like steaming piles of donkey dung and hordes of flies buzzed all around them—from their black greasy hair to their grime-covered toes. Their camels carried gruesome ropes strung with dozens of amputated hands and feet. The half-rotten legs of young men, arms of calligraphers and heads with faces frozen with horror swung at their camels' sides like charms on a bloody bracelet. Most disembodied feet were rugged and dark with dirt and calluses. Occasionally, a pink, clean foot was mixed in a bawdy bouquet of limbs dangling from a camel's side. It probably belonged to a young woman who masqueraded as a man to follow her lover into battle, a young priest who couldn't find a safe haven beneath the sanctuary, or a male concubine who took a wrong turn at the baths.

"One of the decapitated heads had eyes as wide as chamber pots and a sad mouth that seemed to whisper about the girls he'd never met, mountains never climbed, music never played. This trophy contained the sadness of 10,000 farewells in a single unspoken syllable. It was the voice of a shattered heart, its sorrow spilling over the edge of every cup like tears filling great canyons and covering entire continents. Right beside it there was another strangely serene head that was resigned to its predicament and ready to ride its own flying camel through the clouds and into Allah's garden of delights. This head had the look of unconditional ecstasy, and it was most haunting of all."

Aaron could almost see and smell the horrible berserkers with their awful body parts hanging from ropes, and he felt sorry for their victims.

"Finally, desert orphans and vagabonds marched in, a safe distance from the berserker's heels. They wore soiled blankets with holes cut for their heads and rags tied around their waists, some smiling like they'd tasted sugar cane for the first time, others sick and weary from days of travel with little food or water."

"Was Hamdan kind to the children?"

"Most who survived the journey were very lucky. Bahrain was like paradise and they ate more at a single feast than they were used to eating for weeks. The feasts began with fires burning all around the courtyard, some cooking long skewers of succulent goat's meat or crackling under vats of aromatic Indian rice. The children wandered from one fire to the next, tasting little samples of food. There was a phalanx of squab served with an assortment of candied and savory jellies, pickled fruits and pools of curried vegetables. Extended families of peacocks were roasted and presented on long tables with their tail feathers still in full glory. A school of fresh-baked bass was perched merrily across a platter decorated with spiced passion flowers and pickled lark tongues. Barrels filled with luscious mango juice, syrupy, tooth-melting cane juice and dark red wine were emptied into an endless procession of colorful clay cups and painted bowls.

"Karmations had a simple rule when it came to wine, ale, kif and hashish: smoke, drink and share them as often as possible. They had a strong commitment to any shortcut to the doorstep of euphoria. This day, the courtyard was full of fun-loving diversions and perversions. Jugglers performed their most spectacular routines with balls of fire and sharpened cleavers. Comedians delivered their tried-and-true lines and improvised absurd cross-dressing routines. Contortionists stretched every limb at once, rolling across the ground like human pretzels and dangling from flagpoles with their ankles behind their ears. Cross-dressing girls and boys danced around the court, enticing warriors at every turn, their elaborate, spangled outfits accenting every curve of their bodies, yet only revealing a few patches of honey-colored skin as they twirled, twisted, leaped and lured the revelers in an erotic, spontaneous ballet.

"Long sheets of bright-colored silk waved from the tops of watchtowers while ouds, bendirs and bazoukies tuned up in groups under gazebos. Drum circles pounded out anxious preludes and trance-inducing rhythms, filling the air with an exotic blend of sounds.

"Karmations were well versed in the pleasures of love and eager to practice their specialties. Boys and girls learned the 50 most satisfying sexual positions by the time they were 13-years-old—just a bit younger than you, Aaron—including special positions with names like 'flying mare' and 'camel's trick'. Karmations developed secret oral techniques, many involving multiple partners, and devised new words to describe the 23 ways to arouse a lover with a single kiss."

"They must have had a lot of babies."

"Nope. Arab women have used herbs and sponges to prevent pregnancy for centuries."

This was a bit too much information for Aaron, who may never look at a sponge in the same way again. And he already read about several of the pleasures in more than one of Layla's books from India. It sounded like sex was extreme in paradise, and full of numbers.

"What do you think Aaron? Interested in learning more about these techniques?"

"What do you mean?" Aaron was both naïve and embarrassed, having never been around any woman or girls beside his mum and Layla. He blushed when he realized Layla wasn't joking.

*****

Layla never wanted a son. She intended Aaron to be more like a homunculus—a little man whom alchemists believed could be created outside the womb by allowing semen to ferment in a sealed vessel in the back of a dark closet until its top was brown and a toothpick came out clean. Then you remove the homunculus, teach him as necessary, and use him to perform certain delicate operations, like measuring miniscule amounts of exotic mineral elixirs, reaching down the necks of tiny vessels to extract the roots of crystals, or entering a hot furnace, with an anti-flammable suit, of course, to measure the temperature of molten metals.

Aaron proved far more valuable than a homunculus. He and Layla rebuilt the laboratory and before long several simultaneous extractions, fermentations, re-combinations, purifications and contained explosions were in progress. There was lye leaching through ashes, animal fats extracted and boiled with mint oil and poured into small, oval-shaped molds to make exquisite soaps. Herbs and minerals soaking in colored solutions were blended together in retorts of all sizes, fermented and added to medicinal tinctures to stop infection, reduce fevers and combat allergies. She extracted the essences of crushed stones with liquids bubbling slowly in crucibles until their color, aroma and texture were absolutely perfect. On the practical side, all this work left Layla with a well-stocked apothecary. Newly created jars of opiate and antiseptic salves for reducing pain and cleaning wounds were sealed and neatly stacked on a heavy wooden shelf in the corner of the laboratory, right along with hallucinogenic tinctures strong enough to kill an elephant, although she hoped that would never be required. Many of her operations had been in progress for more than a year and needed daily attention. This made it difficult to get away for extended vacations, but offered Aaron the best alchemical training in all of Europe. He became adept at identifying various minerals and their properties, and developed a keen sense of patience and precision in the laboratory. He was always at Layla's side, taking notes, measuring the progress of mystical marriages and radical

31

reductions, and enjoying it like the laboratory was filled with Turkish taffy.

Their work wasn't all about soap, medicine and explosions. Aaron also helped Layla bake buttermilk biscuits, pickle vegetables and mix special herbs and water to make a sweet drink. All the time, they were learning little rhyming songs they'd sing together, day or night. It was months before he learned the songs were important incantations accompanying delicate alchemical operations.

"Alchemy is really nothing more than women's work and children's songs. That's the secret of real magic."

"Like healing a knife wound with household ingredients," chimed the eggplant, "or singing to stop a charging camel." Once, in the Arabian Desert, Layla accomplished both of these feats in the same afternoon.

Layla's meditation time was silent, strict and began mid-afternoon every day in a small, six-sided room whose walls were covered with rich tapestries. In the center of the room was a long, flat bed made from stone that looked like it had been there longer than the castle. It stood three feet high with a large glass-covered compass embedded at each end. She rested flat on the stone, face-up, for exactly one hour with her head pointed due north. Aaron sat in a corner of the room, watching the grains of sand fall like tiny stars inside the tall, slender hourglass until its upper torso was empty. Then he rang a small, brass bowl with a wooden mallet and Layla turned, so her head pointed south, Aaron flipped the hourglass and Layla stayed there for another hour. Every day.

This was also Aaron's meditation time, but he had a different approach. Sometimes he concentrated on synchronizing Layla's breath and his own, each combined exhale creating a fabulous new creature in the air and every inhale drawing the creature back into their nostrils. Or he focused on the sand in the hourglass, every grain falling as gracefully as tiny angels taking their place on the head of a pin. Even if each grain came from a different desert, they were all meant to be here, falling now, marking the time Layla would remain in her present position, each grain possessing a conscious identity and a will to play its special role in the current drama.

Of all Aaron's experiences in Layla's castle, the meditation sessions were the most mysterious. Aaron couldn't be certain, but after meditation Layla looked younger, as if the ritual somehow revitalized her. He often wondered how she kept time during meditation without him.

Layla was happy to speak about any subject, except her meditation. "Meditation is one of our greatest secrets and one day, I may share it with you. Right now, we depend on each other during meditation more than you'll ever know."

The eggplant appreciated Aaron more each day. It wished it could speak to him, but never mentioned this desire to Layla. If it did speak to Aaron, it would tell him it gladly kept time for Layla's meditation until he arrived, and it was still keeping time for her because the meditation time was far too critical to entrust to a boy. The eggplant had been hanging around Layla's gorgeous neck for a long time and she didn't really need it like she once did. They both knew they had grown apart, but couldn't admit it to each other. That's why the eggplant couldn't let her know about its feelings for the boy. The eggplant felt unfaithful and adulterous even considering a rendezvous with Aaron.

When Layla and Aaron weren't in the laboratory or engaged in a lesson, Layla taught him the finer points of physical arts, like dancing and fighting. She helped him master acrobatic flips, twists and wire walking followed naturally by some pretty fancy martial artistry. From handling a scimitar, to throwing a knife and using instant diversions to evade an enemy, Layla wanted Aaron prepared for any adversary who may cross their path.

The most dangerous experiments at the castle involved black powder. The substance was unknown to almost all of Europe, outside of this castle. Layla first came across the explosive years ago, when a Persian magician traded his formula in exchange for Layla performing a sacred snake dance. His powder created a flash of colored smoke, without an explosion. She'd tested new recipes for years, and now she could transform the magician's colored smoke into a handy fire starter or controlled explosions launching graceful trajectories of objects never meant to fly. Spoons. Rocks. Melons. Once she shot a huge bowl of grapes soaked in red dye over the garden wall, and their splatters stained the limbs of an old oak tree almost 100 yards away.

Aaron helped her mix the basic black powder, which was composed of six parts rock salt, one part each sulfur and charcoal. They'd stuff the powder into one end of a cylinder, weave long threads of dry grass together until they formed a single long thread for a wick, then place one end of the thread into the powder and the other a safe distance away. Their most spectacular test used a hollowed out, six-foot tree trunk as a cannon barrel, and a mix of river stones and big chunks of hardwood for ammunition. They set the cannon in the courtyard, packed a few pounds of powder in one end, stuffed the rocks and wood down the hollow trunk and carefully aimed the barrel over the wall. Aaron lit the long woven fuse and joined Layla, crouched behind a large stone. Sparks raced to the powder, but there was no explosion. They waited. Still nothing. As they stepped from behind the stone, an intense blast knocked them off their feet. They peered through the cloud of smoke and saw a sizzling crater where the cannon once sat. When the dust settled, there was a three-foot hole in the wall at the opposite end of the courtyard. Layla hugged Aaron and kissed him. "We've done it!"

Layla's hallucinogenic mushroom habit wasn't as dangerous as the cannon, but it was far more extreme. For Layla, her full moon mushroom rituals were religious sacraments connecting her to other worlds. She treated her store of dried mushrooms like they were pure gold and prepared a variety of hallucinogenic tinctures, some for her own use and others as defensive weapons to disorient enemies without harming them.

Every full moon, she drank a few drops of her mildest tincture in a cup of warm raspberry leaf tea and spent the entire night in what appeared to be another world. During a typical mushroom experience, she could easily go from cooing like a baby, playing stringed instruments, writing absurd poems, chattering about visions of invisible creatures and hordes of spirits—to crawling on her belly through the corridors, crying and sobbing, speaking in tongues—until sunrise, when she'd collapse on the bed in the courtyard, and sleep through the next day.

The eggplant learned to keep its mouth shut during these rituals. Once, when it was very critical of Layla's attempt to make a stupid carrot speak, she ripped the eggplant from her necklace and tossed it into the courtyard. It took her three days to find it. Waiting helplessly and alone, stuck in the depressing void between two rocks, those were the worst three days of the eggplant's existence. It took more than a year for the vegetable to recover from the ordeal. The darkness and desperation were more than it could bear, and its mind drifted into the deep silence of a withered old vegetable, where it wished again and again it had been fried with olive oil and tossed with garlic and spices in a warm pan of moussaka, and served to a worthy man six centuries ago, when the eggplant's sibling was devoured.

It was Aaron's job to keep Layla out of harm's way during her full moon blowouts. He hid all the knives, swords and spears and kept her from starting fires, except for lighting candles. He bandaged her wounds if she did injure herself and most importantly, he was the signpost for Layla on the rare occasions when she confused reality with hallucinations. More than once she nearly left this world and took up a permanent residence on the other side, but Aaron was always there to pull her gently back. He was real, and they both knew it.

One day, after a particularly difficult full moon night filled with extreme crying and threats of suicide, Aaron couldn't help but ask, "Why do you do it?"

"I've been in this world a long time and seen many amazing things. When I drink the tincture, I see beyond myself and beyond this world. I hear gods and demons talking about me, how I'm old and ugly and a bad dancer. I hear them laugh at my big nose and wide hips. I see I'm one person among millions on this earth, and I know my existence is meaningless. I know I'm nothing in the eyes of an old stone or a tree."

"Doesn't sound pleasant."

"But that's not all. In one night I can destroy my old self and start over, recreating a new Layla, piece by piece. In one night I see the tiny worlds beneath us and the greater worlds that hover above, beyond the sun. I hear eternal songs and smell forbidden fruits. I'm both an innocent maiden walking in paradise and a suffering whore falling through hell. When it's all over, I have a new appreciation for life, death and beauty. It's like giving my soul a good, hard scrubbing."

Layla was intense. Aaron was sure she knew more secrets than the Pope, and probably possessed more real power. There may be no limit to her discoveries. He kept a journal to record the parts of Layla's mushroom voyages he could capture with words. Many of her rambling prophecies were written in long poetic verses with no punctuation. Aaron neatly and precisely transcribed these works, which were some of the strangest and most beautiful writings on her shelves. He called the journal, *Messages from Paradise*.

"Did you know one person can move the world?" asked Layla.

"What do you mean, like Hamdan?"

"It's not always kings and their armies who change the world. Just one person, at the right time and in the right place, can turn history on its head. Keep your eyes open, Aaron. You never know when you'll get a chance."

Aaron wasn't interested in changing the world. Right now, life was easy, but he knew how quickly the whole bowl of alchemical stew could go up in flames.

"Someday, maybe centuries from now, many, many people will drink this tincture, just like me. And they'll see and feel and taste and hear the things I hear now, and they'll think they're the first. But I've been there, and so have shamans and sorcerers before me. I found their signs. I left my own markers for others to find, too." Then her tone turned more serious. "If you ever hallucinate or feel like you might be having some sort of epiphany or vision, remember to leave something in that space before the experience has ended."

"How can you leave something in a vision?"

"Picture yourself standing inside your experience—by a tree or cloud or piece of furniture. Then picture yourself with a picture, a short poem, plate of food, or anything the next traveler might find. Leave a name, a song, a flag, or imagine yourself carving a symbol into something inside the vision. Maybe leave an exotic odor. Anything sensual. All you have to do is say the name or think of an aroma as part of the hallucination. It's that easy.

"And remember to bring something back from the experience, otherwise it's purely recreational. Find something in the vision you can hold onto. Hold it and never forget it. Tell others about it. You're a fine writer, Aaron. Write your visions so others can see."

The eggplant understood the attraction of the mushroom visions and believed one vegetable could change the world. And it would be ready when that time came.

Aaron had no idea what Layla was talking about. He didn't want to change the world and he didn't intend to drink, eat or smoke any hallucinatory tinctures. The world was strange enough without more visions and it seemed to be getting stranger.

*****

Aaron savored his days with Layla. They stayed together without leaving the castle for almost nine months before a pigeon arrived with a message from London. One of her informants learned of a meeting between Robert Fitzwater, a treasure-seeking Templar, and a group of Sufi mystics with a long history seeking the Lost Stone. Layla traveled to London alone, leaving Aaron to tend to the experiments.

"If everything goes well, I'll return with a surprise in four days." Aaron hoped she was right.

Everything did not go well. The first week she was gone Aaron went about his work and studied as usual. He recited Sanskrit characters and conjugated Arabic verbs, watered plants, chopped wood, measured temperatures and the volume of materials in crucibles, and relaxed in the courtyard like a true prince. After one month, Aaron feared Layla might be in serious trouble—or worse—so he prepared to leave the castle and travel to London. He gathered soap, tinctures, balms and extracts along with plenty of cloth bandages, dried venison strips, his journal, *Messages from Paradise*, several cloth bags of black powder and Layla's strongest mushroom tinctures.

With supplies in two deerskin sacks and a pocketful of gold coins Layla left behind, the most valuable objects in his bags of tricks were still his mother's rings, his father's knife and a piece of paper with the letters M, A and S scribbled on its rough, brown surface. Aaron dressed in his finest clothes and was eating leftover carrot stew when he heard horses outside the castle. He opened the door expecting to see Layla, but instead saw four horses kicking billows of dust into the air.

"Ahah! What other rascals are trespassing on the King's property?" A man in a long black cape and tall, stiff black hat called to Aaron from atop his horse, "Are we going someplace? Are you a little thief or a friend of the big thief? Either way, the festivities have come to an end. We're returning this castle and its possessions to its rightful owner, the Crown. Now, let's have a little look in your bags." Just then, two men jumped from their horses and ran towards Aaron.

One of the men stopped running and shouted, "Run for your life, Aaron! Run!" Then a cloud of red smoke burst before the men, and Aaron knew Layla was back.

Aaron dashed inside the castle, closed the door before the smoke had cleared, bolted it and ran straight for the courtyard. He could hear the men bashing through the door as he threw his deerskin sacks over the wall and jumped into the stream leading underground and back to the river. He held his breath, crawled into the culvert, and followed the rushing current beneath the wall until he bobbed through an underground tunnel, just large enough for him to crawl on his hands and knees—first neck-deep, then holding his breath underwater until he emerged on the riverbank. The King's men were still inside the castle's walls when Aaron picked up his deerskin sacks and made his way through the tall grass along the banks of the river, staying low until he stumbled upon an old rocky road covered with weeds, followed it east and wondered if he'd ever see Layla again.

He walked for two days before he caught his first whiff of London. The stench was visible in thin yellow and brown fog hanging over the city like milky clouds of mold and mildew. From a distance, it looked like a huge heap of dirty laundry, with rows of two-storied, timber-and-daub dwellings stretching as far as he could see. When Aaron started down a narrow street, a boy

39

appeared from between two houses and almost knocked him down.

"The King's men are arresting orphans!" cried the boy, and kept running.

Two men on horseback came into view, each of them chasing after a group of four orphans until they snatched one up and deposited the child in a wagon with a big wooden cage on top, where a half-dozen others were already trapped.

Aaron felt like he should try to help the orphans. He was, after all, one of them. But what could he do? The orphans didn't seem to be in any discomfort and were probably in no real danger, he reasoned, and he ducked out of sight and followed the river through London, still feeling uneasy about the kids trapped in a cage.

The sun went down by the time the first drawbridge was in sight. The bank beneath the heavy wooden planks spanning the water was cool and out of view to all but the boatmen. The Tower of London stood before him in the twilight, bigger than any structure he'd ever imagined. Compared to the squat lines of daub-roofed houses on the other side of town, the Tower looked like a giant finger poking up from the bottom of the world.

He reached into his bag and pulled out a chunk of dried venison, then continued along the riverbank until oars thrashing through the water broke the night's peace. He crouched to watch from the shore when a hand reached from the darkness, grabbed his shirt, and jerked him into a small boat. Aaron looked up ready to strike out and saw Layla, still disguised as a man with a beard.

"Shhhh." Her finger to her mustached lips, looking very serious as she pushed the rowboat gently away from the shore and they disappeared silently into the dark, swirling river mist.

"I was lucky to find you after dark."

"Who were the men at the castle? Were they holding you? Why are you wearing a beard?"

"They were King John's swordsmen. I'm disguised as a man to keep them from finding who I really am and what I'm looking for."

"Those were the King's men?" Aaron couldn't believe it. He had actually escaped from the King's men!

"They may have killed you, if they caught you. These are complicated times, Aaron. I learned the Stone never arrived in London and I was careless, trying to learn more when the swordsmen ambushed me. I used flash powder to escape, but there were too many. Now the King and Bishop think I'm a sorcerer and they planned to burn me at the stake after I showed them the way to the castle."

"Why did you bring them back to the castle? You could have escaped any time."

"I told them I had something valuable hidden inside. Something only I could find for them."

"Did you give it to them?"

"No. I made sure you ran away."

Aaron felt very secure as the small boat glided along the south bank of the Thames. Even the shadowy skeletons of boats anchored in the estuary appeared safe tonight. On the opposite shore, far behind them, he could see tiny silhouettes of buildings flickering in the darkness like cold candles on a sooty cake.

"This river is treacherous at night. Bandits feed large families from the tolls they take after dark. Be very still and careful." Layla was on her knees, both hands on the raised oars and looking all around, trying to drift in silence.

"I brought food and black powder." He opened the bag and passed her a chunk of venison.

Without warning, a dark figure closed in on their little boat and stopped dead in the water. Layla drew a long dagger while Aaron opened a bag and removed a small, tightly wrapped pouch of black powder.

41

"What do we have on the river at this hour?" A deep, rattling voice oozed from a skiff just a few feet away. "An old man and his sweet little fry cake boy. Out for a bit of fresh evening air? Or are we up to some nasty, wicked deeds?"

It was too dark for Aaron to see, but the eggplant informed Layla there were two drunken bandits in the boat, one with a knife tied to a wooden stub replacing his hand, and the other was missing a tongue. The wake splashed against the shore and the thieves' oars dipped in and out of the water, closer to Aaron each time. Aaron opened his little silver flint box and wondered why the man thought he was a fry cake boy? What was a fry cake boy?

"Don't want to talk to us, eh?" The one-handed man was much closer now.

"Our daggers will speak for us." Layla's voice was suddenly deep and raspy. "I'm sure they'll have a lot to say to brave swordsmen like you and your mate." She spoke like a ghost, each word hanging in the mist. The bandits were silent.

Aaron felt goose bumps popping up and down his spine as he positioned the bomb's fuse in his flint box.

"Words don't scare us, old man." The outlaw's voice grew shakier as their oars slapped the water and their old wooden boat was upon them.

Aaron clicked his flint box against his makeshift bomb and its wick flickered and crackled with a dim orange light exposing two scraggly men right beside them.

"Here's some sauce for those fry cakes." Aaron tossed the crackling bomb into their boat and Layla shoved them away with her oar. Seconds later, a sharp boom and flash of sparks shocked the bandits on impact, flames stretched across the length of their boat, sending the men into the river as Layla and Aaron slipped into the darkness and rowed quietly away while bystanders clamored down the banks toward the explosion.

Besides Aaron and Layla, few people in medieval England had ever seen anything burst into flames with such a booming noise as this. The bandits thought the pair of sorcerers had struck them with a lightning bolt.

The eggplant was also impressed with Aaron's little surprise. It'd seen much stronger men falter against such scoundrels in the dark, but this boy was prepared to defend Layla and himself without hesitation.

Layla had her own stash of weaponry, and was well prepared with a handful of sand to throw in their eyes, which wasn't as spectacular as Aaron's solution, but much quieter.

"Good work, Aaron. Do you have any other tricks in your bag?"

"Nothing that would fool you." He was quiet for a long time as he considered preparing more bombs, perhaps smaller variations, and use them to protect Layla whenever necessary.

*****

"First, we'll follow Pilgrim's Way to Canterbury, then cross the channel and on to Paris. Paris is a fine destination for two alchemists in exile," and Layla lightly rubbed the eggplant. Paris had always been difficult for the eggplant in summer. A young woman who Layla once loved very dearly was captured and killed by Templars in Paris, and although Layla was able to forgive the loss, the eggplant never really got over it. It still remembers the way Layla felt when the three of them were together, and the way Layla cried when they found her lover's body floating in the Seine, right where they were supposed to meet before they left for Morocco.

Layla and Aaron rowed almost a mile along the Thames riverbank before they came to a dock and tied the boat to a twisted, rotting wooden post. Aaron waited in the boat while she shuffled to an inn with a candle still burning in one window. She reappeared minutes later atop a horse, drew up beside the dock, helped Aaron to a seat behind her on the saddle, and they were on their way to Canterbury. They rode all night and half of the next day, ate their fill of blood sausage and cake at the Canterbury Inn, slept in a barn with a dozen tale-telling wayfarers, then galloped off to Dover's chalky cliffs at sunrise.

The King's soldiers walked the streets, rode horses and stood in groups drinking ale and laughing when the duo entered Dover. Layla, now dressed as an old peasant woman with a faded red babushka hiding her face, sold the horse at the first stable she found and headed to the wharves, where the guards kept a close eye on everyone moving to and from the boats.

"Aaron, it's time to do a little acting. I want you to slump down and walk with a limp. Make yourself as small as you can, so you'll be no threat to anyone." Then she hunched over and drew her shoulders inward, limping on a twisted oak cane as she guided a gimpy Aaron around the soldiers to a sloop docked just beyond the guards. It was a private fishing boat, sea worthy with a tall mast and small cabin, and it was preparing to leave when Layla approached the lone man on its deck. She spoke French, introduced herself as a widow heading back to her family in Calais, presented some papers along with half of the gold Aaron had wisely procured from her estate, and within an hour they were sailing to France.

*****

Strong winds carried their sloop across the channel's rough waters with cold, damp gusts filling the sails and 20-foot waves lashing out at the boat's hull. Aaron was sailing for the first time, and as they moved away from the dock, he grabbed the nearest barrel and never let go. The rolling waves, clouds and the sloop's sails were the same cold, hungry grey color as the last glimmer of land fading away in the distance. At the mercy of howling winds and a heaving, heartless sea, he was certain a single wave would swallow them any moment.

The eggplant was far more terrified than Aaron. Its fear of disappearing in deep water was more than any mammal could imagine. Layla rubbed it and assured the vegetable she'd swallow it before she'd let it sink alone—a prospect that encouraged a whole new set of primordial vegetable fears, even if the eggplant already experienced the wonders of the human digestive tract.

They huddled in the small, dripping wet, three-sided cabin while the sloop's owner, an old fisherman who was bringing ale to sell to the troops, stood at the wheel. Layla slept most of the trip, but Aaron held onto his little barrel of ale and winced every time a wave crashed over the sides of the boat.

Even the salty old fisherman felt sorry for the boy. "You'll be alright. This boat has never sunk. Came close, once or twice, but it never went under and we never lost anybody."

"The barrel smells like pickled hog."

The old man shook his head, "The smell won't matter if you need that barrel to stay afloat."

Without another word, the eggplant broke into a full-blown sobbing session, its barely audible pleas for mercy interspersed with truly sorrowful, soft cries working their way into Layla's recurring dream about seizing a valuable, random object. Today, it's Ramses III's chamber pot. She inevitably escapes from an assortment of would-be captors, most with eye patches and missing at least one hand or leg, and in this version of the dream they were all crying like babies.

When the three travelers approached the harbor in Calais, the winds slowed to a whisper, the water became as still as ice and a creeping fog appeared from nowhere. Nobody spoke and it felt like something very important was about to happen as they continued blindly through the fog until it finally cleared just enough for them to see dozens of huge ships right before them, anchored all around the port. A new odor mingled with the salt mist—the miles and miles of soaking wet hemp rope tied, rolled and hanging from every ship in the bay left a pungent aroma hanging in the air like some noxious gas pouring from an over-ripe potion when you first pop the cork.

"Battleships," confirmed Layla, appearing wide-awake at Aaron's side.

The sloop lowered its sail and continued into the heart of the fleet, raised the French flag of Philip Augustus and tried to ignore the sailors staring at them from ships, some with fierce faces ready to kill, others, who looked too young to fight, were frightened and sobbing at their ship's rail. Aaron never wanted to be in their shoes. He already learned it was much better to run from trouble, than to sit and wait for it.

When their boat docked, Layla and Aaron were the first to lower the gangplank, wave goodbye to their captain and hustle down to dry land, where they soon vanished into the narrow streets leading from the docks.

"Well, that wasn't too bad, considering we could have arrived after the battle started." Layla was interrupted by war cries roaring behind them like hungry beasts. "Aaron, we need a horse."

"I'll do my best," and he prepared to do what must be done, as the non-existent knight once advised. He ran into a stable and rode out with a fresh chestnut mare, used his secret knight's grip on the reins and pulled up neatly beside Layla. Two Frenchmen ran from the stables shouting, "Voleur! Voleur!" Layla jumped onto the horse with Aaron and they rode away, leaving the Frenchmen shaking their fists over their heads.

"You just stole a horse." Layla scolded Aaron as they galloped through the streets of Calais, bouncing along on the mare's bare back.

"You said we needed a horse. Did you think I was going to buy one?"

"I hope you left them a gold piece or something."

"Good idea. Someday I may return and repay him."

They rode for almost an hour, passing several columns of soldiers marching towards the coast, before they stopped when they met a small party of pilgrims en route to St. Denis, a basilica outside of Paris where every Frenchmen since the 10th century was buried. Aaron pulled up close to a pair of pilgrims, asking how far it was to the basilica.

"I've dreamed of this pilgrimage my whole life," confessed an old, wrinkled man who was bent half-over in his saddle. His skin and hair were powdery white, and he had a curious smell, like old butter. "Just imagine, a fragment of the very crown of thorns Jesus wore on his all-forgiving head."

"And a piece of the cross!" added his young companion.

"Yes, but how far is the basilica from here?" Aaron asked again.

"The blood of Christ was on the thorn. Even a piece of his dried flesh," said the old pilgrim, and gazed at Layla with wide open, glassy pink eyes.

Layla had visited the shrine of St. Denis before and there were no relics besides the bones of French royalty. Relics like splinters from the 'true cross' had been scattered all over Europe and could be purchased by anyone for the right price. Even the fakes were kept far from public view, where the abbots and monks were lucky to snatch a glance of them, in return for their life of holy matrimony to the Lord.

Religious foolery didn't stop Layla from appreciating the basilica at St. Denis. Its many stained glass portals floated impossibly between stone buttresses like sheets of weightless, colored light. She remembered sitting in the middle of the main church with spectacular rotundas and multiple radiating chapels on either side, like rooms in heaven. Outside the gates of St.

Denis, Layla and Aaron navigated their horse through a mob of traders offering souvenirs and magic cures for everything from fevers to common warts.

"Keep your eyes open for shrunken vegetables," joked the eggplant, which wasn't ashamed to admit it had considered looking for a suitable companion someday. "It would be particularly nice if one were found before we arrive in Paris," it added.

"What about fruit?" whispered Layla, while the hawkers all shouted at once, waving their wares high over their heads, pressing as close as possible to their horse, which was growing nervous.

"Pure St. Denis wine. Holy wine! It's sweeter than honey." One aggressive seller was running beside the horse with his greasy hands holding up a half-empty bottle of transparent, red-grey liquid for Layla's inspection.

"There is no food or water in the shrine, you need to buy your supplies here, my holy friends!" A man masquerading in mismatched monk's clothing repeated again and again.

Inside, the commune was huge but almost empty. Shop stalls were closed and only a few monks stood around the perimeter like watchdogs. When they heard a crowd cheer at the opposite end of the complex, Aaron and Layla hustled through a long, open-roofed corridor, entered a courtyard and saw a young boy who was preaching from a rickety platform with dozens of peasants and children gathered in front of him. He looked like a normal 12-year-old child with ragged old clothes and filthy, matted brown hair. Layla led Aaron closer, so they could hear what made this boy so special. He spoke in French, which Layla recognized was from a northern province. He was complaining about the same old things—everybody was sinful and wicked and needed to be saved. They worked their way through the dirty, travel-weary audience until they were close enough to hear him clearly and look in his eyes.

"Crusaders before us traveled to the Holy Land, but the temptation of evil kept them from taking back the sacred place. They lined their pockets with gold and slept with harlots. Now, the devil has taken our Lord's birthplace in his evil claws." His voice grew louder and more desperate as he slowly raised his hands over his head and squeezed his fingers into tight, shaking fists. Suddenly an old woman who was standing beside Aaron raised her hands in the air and began to tremble.

Perhaps this boy was some kind of prophet, but Aaron was most impressed with the boy's command of the audience. Every time the boy threw his hands up to the sky, the audience did the same. It was crazy. But it wasn't the message or the boy capturing Aaron's attention. It was the girl who stood beside the boy. She was the most beautiful girl he'd ever seen—even more beautiful than Layla. Taller than the boy, she had long, straight, shiny dark hair falling halfway to her waist, with big, almond eyes and a smile so sweet it made him forget about the boy's ridiculous rant. Aaron couldn't help but gaze at her, his body almost weightless, like it could float away if he looked at her too long.

"And I say the doors of heaven won't be open until civilized, Christian people take back the tomb of the Lord." Then the boy slowly raised his right arm with his index finger pointing at the audience, "Not you, not me, nobody here will be saved from the horrors of damnation until the Lord's land is free!" The crowd shuffled closer to him, nodding their heads and urging him on.

Layla had never seen a child captivate an audience so completely. This boy was just spouting the same capture the Holy Land routine as every other religious fanatic in Europe, including the kings of England and France. But why would people listen to a boy? She feared something dark was behind his bizarre magnetism.

Aaron couldn't take his eyes off the girl. No matter which direction he turned his head, he saw her. Her statuesque posture, wide shoulders and slender waist were more perfect than any goddess in any of Layla's books. His heart was writing fantastic poems in unspoken languages created just for her. He could feel the words vibrating through parts of his body he'd never felt before. He was overcome with waves of weightlessness starting in his toes and rippling wistfully up his torso, through his shoulders and out the top of his skull, as if he was connected directly to heaven for the first time in his life. He wondered how this girl could make him feel this way? Why was she different? There were other pretty girls in this courtyard. Why was she so irresistible?

"Why should we believe you? Whose truth do you serve?" It was Layla, disguising her voice as a man. Everyone became very still, as if waiting for something to burst.

Aaron wanted to walk right up on the platform, take the girl by the hand and walk her into the sunset of Paris or Rome or Istanbul. It didn't matter. He wanted to sleep with her atop the Great Pyramid and swim with her in the Ganges. He wanted to spend every hour by her side.

The pontificating boy stood on the platform glaring intently at a suddenly bearded Layla, as if preparing to strike her dead on the spot. "My name is Stephen, and I serve only the Lord. I was in Chartres on the feast day of St. Mark, and watched the monks carry the black-shrouded crosses through the streets to honor Crusaders who died trying to free the Holy Land. When I returned to my home, my sheep had laid waste to my mother's entire spring planting. I grabbed a stick and was ready to beat the animals, but before I could strike, every single sheep bowed down before me, as if begging forgiveness."

The words 'miracle' and 'divine child' were buzzing through the crowd. These pilgrims came to glimpse a relic, but they were getting a first-hand revelation of an actual miracle. They pressed even closer to Stephen to hear all the details. Aaron moved closer too, until he was close enough to touch the girl.

"This is no miracle," said the eggplant. "It's just a boy giving the bible crowd what they came for—a good show."

"I think you're right. But I don't believe this Stephen is acting alone."

"Then something very wonderful happened. Our Lord Jesus appeared among my sheep."

The crowd gasped, and some began to openly weep.

"He spoke of the Holy Land, and the suffering of pilgrims who could no longer worship at the Lord's holiest shrines. He said he searched the world to find the one person who could lead a new Crusade—one pure in spirit, and he found only the innocent children can truly free the Holy Land. This will be a Children's Crusade and Jesus gave me this letter addressed to the King of France, asking for his blessing." Stephen held the letter above his head for all to see. It was rolled into a skinny scroll, like a miniature magic wand, and tied with a purple ribbon.

By this time, Aaron was almost unaware of Stephen's presence. All his attention was fixed on the girl when he took a deep breath, turned to her and said, "You're the prettiest girl I've ever seen. Really," and he lightly held three of her fingers in his hand. She smiled, blushed and looked confused, and Aaron's heart turned into a planet revolving around the stars shining in her emerald eyes, but he didn't say a word and she didn't move. Surely she wondered whom this stranger was and what he was going to do next.

"Praise the Lord for this miracle!" cried an old woman, and the audience joined in with hallelujahs and blessings, and the girl with green eyes pulled her hand from Aaron's and moved closer to Stephen.

"Quite a story the young boy weaves." Layla was fully aware Aaron melted like a slab of warm wax every time he looked at the girl. "And quite a pretty little lady you've found. Should I be jealous?"

Aaron looked at Layla and smiled, but he was too busy devising a plan to get closer to the girl to answer.

"The girl's very sweet, Aaron. But Stephen's another story. Don't you find it odd a young peasant boy would lead children into a battle the bravest knights couldn't win?"

Aaron shrugged. "I don't think they'll make it far," He was still gazing at the girl, who stood beside Stephen like a fresh bouquet next to a noisy old shoe.

"He's mad and his plan is mass suicide. An army of European orphans wouldn't last one night amongst the Arabs, if they made it that far." Layla was angry that she couldn't stop this dangerous enterprise and surprised to see Aaron so moved by the girl. He'd never been particularly interested in the opposite sex. But despite her appearance, Layla was too old to remember the secret bond between children, their innocent wish for a better world, their insatiable fascination with the unknown, and the pure dynamo of uncontrolled emotions they use to crumble any obstacle.

"Call me crazy, but I don't think Aaron wants anything to do with the Lord, the Crusade or Stephen," advised the eggplant. "It's all about the girl."

Stephen stood with his arms outstretched, ready to embrace the throngs or climb to his position on an invisible cross. "Who among you will follow me to the Holy Land?"

A boy who appeared to be no more than 10-years-old climbed on the stage and knelt beside Stephen. "I will follow," the words were barely audible, but the crowd cheered as youths of all ages made their way to Stephen. Old women cried, parents sobbed and sent their sons and daughters to go to Stephen's side and take the Crusader's oath.

"God help you if you should break this oath," warned Stephen. "For if you don't serve in the name of our Lord until we reclaim the Holy Land, you'll be excommunicated and your soul will be damned to eternal suffering in the lowest pits of hell."

"I've seen and heard enough. Let's go. We can still make it to Paris before nightfall." Layla turned away to leave, but Aaron only heard his heart begging for the girl.

"I want to go with her. I want to follow her to the Holy Land."

"What? Are you mad?" Layla's voice was still husky behind her beard, and loud enough to turn heads. "There are plenty of girls who'll be quite satisfied to stay here in France. Or England. We've come a long way together, Aaron. Have I ever steered you down a harmful path?"

"Layla, I've always trusted you and I always will. But everything inside me wants to follow her."

"I advise you to stay away from this folly and come with me to Paris."

Aaron wished she understood. He had to follow this girl. At the same time, he couldn't just leave Layla, so he rode with her to Paris, at least for now. They left St. Denis without saying a word until they were halfway to Paris, when Layla asked, "What do you know of Crusades?"

"I know Crusaders fought to win the Holy Land and hundreds of knights and even King Richard died in the Crusades. I read it in your books," replied Aaron.

"I doubt many of the children who volunteered know the Holy Land is thousands of miles away. You must cross France, then find boats and sailors to take you across the sea. And once you arrive in Africa or wherever they take you, you'll be greeted by men who'll commit unspeakable sins to protect their homes and families, just as we would. In one battle alone, more than 3,000 Crusaders had their heads cut off. And those were grown men who were trained soldiers."

"Why are you against me following this girl?"

Layla was surprised Aaron would suggest she was against the girl. "I have no problem with the girl. I have a big problem with a child's Crusade. I don't believe sending innocent babes to their deaths serves anyone." Layla paused to let Aaron respond, but he was silent.

Layla didn't want to lose him. He was loyal and bright and honest and the only person she knew who could read and write multiple languages—most of them just enough to get by in a pinch. Finally, she threw her best pitch. "If you stay with me, I'll do my best to protect you. You'll have food and fresh water. We can travel. I'll teach you more about black powder and real magic. I'll introduce you to a dozen girls like the one you saw today. Even prettier girls. I'll take you to the Holy Land myself."

"But I don't want a dozen girls, I don't need to go to the Holy Land and I appreciate being protected and well fed, but I want to make my own choice this time. I really like you and want to help you, but right now I want to be with this girl, even if it seems wrong and impossible."

"But you don't even know her!"

"Not to mention she's already on close terms with the top dog in the circus," reminded the eggplant, who really didn't want to lose him, either.

"You taught me anything is possible, Layla. I love you like my own mother and I don't want to leave you, but I have to find my own happiness, my own Lost Stone. You'll always be in my heart. But I can't imagine anything happier than running across France with this girl. I have to go with her."

Layla's heart was broken, but Aaron wasn't the same helpless boy who banged on her door almost one year ago. Maybe it was time for him to find his own way in the world. She always hoped it would be with her. Or at least his exit would be a bit more graceful—perhaps she could have helped him plan his future.

"The choice is yours." Layla climbed from the horse, sad he chose to go with Stephen's Crusade, but there were many dangers ahead for her, as well. She knew Templars would be tracking her soon, and they wouldn't hesitate to kill Aaron if the two were captured together. He may be safer crossing France and helping these children than risking a rendezvous with angry Templars.

"I'll miss you more than words can tell, Aaron. Use your provisions wisely. You'll need them. I'll do my best to keep track of you."

"When I return from this Crusade, I'll repay you for everything you've done for me."

"You owe nothing. I wouldn't be here without your help when I broke my arm. I'll always be grateful. Just stay safe. You're welcome at my table anytime, my friend." She leaned to Aaron and kissed him on the forehead, then removed the eggplant from her neck and placed it over his head. "Here, take this. It'll remind you of me and bring you good fortune. Then she moved closer and whispered in his ear, "Someday you'll tell me all about your adventures." She kissed him once again on the cheek, mounted her horse and rode like a warrior queen towards Paris, leaving the eggplant gasping as if its best friend just dropped it in a pot of hot oil.

4. The Orphan's Crusade

When Aaron returned to St. Denis, Stephen was giving last minute instructions to 30 or 40 children gathered around him outside the gates. They were dressed in rags, some of them already shivering. "We'll make it to Paris tonight, then meet with the King tomorrow. Once I present the letter from the Lord, he'll give us food and a place to sleep." The girl was standing behind Stephen, with another girl half her size standing at her side.

Aaron walked straight to Stephen and made his offer. "I want to join you. I can read and write English, French, Spanish, Arabic, Hebrew...."

Stephen never knew anyone who knew any language besides French. "I don't need translators, I need soldiers," and he gazed at Aaron's blonde hair. "What's your name?"

"Aaron. Aaron Sloopshire." He nodded first to Stephen, then to the girl.

Stephen sized him up, beginning with his handmade, buckskin boots, all the way up to his tailored green cotton pants, white linen shirt, and stared again at his shining mop of curly blonde hair. "O.K., Aaron. My lieutenants are recruiting children from all over France. We're going to meet in Vendome at the end of June. From there, we head to Marseilles, find boats and sail to the Holy Land."

"What's your name?" interrupted Aaron, smiling at the girl.

She blushed and looked at her bare feet.

"This is my sister, Eunisia."

Aaron's heart skipped a few beats. "Nice to meet you, Eunisia." The words came out in a mumbled blob, which was miraculous, considering every other part of Aaron's body seemed to suddenly freeze solid.

"Hello, Aaron." For Aaron, her voice sounded like it had long, curved wings made from immaculate clouds. He really liked her voice.

"You'll make a great lieutenant, Aaron. I'll see you in Vendome at the end of June," said Stephen, and started away.

"Good luck," called Eunisia, and followed her brother.

Aaron's temporary ecstasy was replaced by confusion. He didn't like this idea of meeting anyone in Vendome. At 16, he was older and stronger than Stephen and he saw no reason he couldn't stay right here with Eunisia.

"I believe you misunderstood," called Aaron. "I'm not a recruiter." Stephen stopped, turned around and cocked his head. "I'm offering to assist you and your sister in this Crusade. I can help you with these kids. Most of them look too young to care for themselves. It might not be easy to get them all the way across France. It's almost 500 miles from Paris to Marseilles."

Stephen looked at his sister and she agreed. "O.K., Aaron. You'll be our assistant. But just because you're older doesn't mean you're in charge. There are many older than you who already follow me. You'll see," and he turned and marched away.

Eunisia was one year younger than Aaron and flattered with his attention, even if she didn't know what to do with it. She had other concerns. Like Aaron, she didn't really care about the Crusade or understand it. She's here to watch out for Stephen, her younger brother, who may or may not be a prophet.

Aaron mistook her natural sweetness for affection. He thought she was attracted to him from the start, just like he was drawn to her. He felt like the luckiest person in the world. It wasn't long before he realized she had a sweet smile and a kind word for everyone. Without thinking, he stroked the shining eggplant hung around his neck.

"That feels good," whispered a strange, high-pitched voice inside his head. Aaron looked around, but he was alone. "We've never really been introduced, so you probably don't recognize me," winced the voice. Aaron had heard voices inside his head before, but they were always his own. This was a new voice—a little metallic, like the soft, whistling sound of quicksilver just beginning to boil—comforting and exciting at the same time.

"Where are you?" And then he looked down and held the eggplant between two fingers.

Eunisia and Stephen both stopped and looked at each other. "Who are you talking to? Are you mad?"

"I'm, I'm sorry. I was thinking aloud about someone else."

"I hope you find that person," offered Eunisia, trying to look concerned.

"It's a pleasure to finally meet you, Aaron Sloopshire," announced the eggplant. "I didn't mean to startle you."

Aaron swallowed hard and tried to think of a faraway place, hoping the voice would simply go away, but it was no use.

"I'm pleased to be in your service," continued the eggplant. "Nobody can hear my voice except you, and you don't have to speak out loud because I can hear your thoughts as clearly as you can hear my voice."

"How can I hear you?" You're a little vegetable!"

Aaron didn't know if he liked this idea. He took some deep breaths and remembered what Layla told him when she gave him the eggplant, "Protect it, and it will take care of you."

"How well do you know Layla?"

"I know all of my past possessors quite well. Layla and I have been intimate most of her life—I was in her family precisely 282 years. One of her ancestors took me from the neck of an Arab ruler, who happened to be dead at the time."

"Where did you come from? How can you speak?"

The eggplant made a sound that was like air squeezed from small, deerskin bellows and began speaking slowly, so it wouldn't have to repeat anything. "I was grown by an old woman in the Arabian Desert more than 600 years ago. She was a midwife who people chased from villages every time a baby died, and one day she was tired of being chased so she moved to the desert, where she lived alone, grew a sparse crop of vegetables each year and raised a few goats. She lived quietly until a thief burst into her hut one night and demanded jewelry he thought was hidden in her tent. When she explained she had nothing but two eggplants and three goats, the thief killed her goats and threatened to kill her if she didn't give him her jewelry. But before the thief could raise his knife, an archer—much like your non-existent knight—shot a single arrow into the tent and killed the thief.

"The old midwife gave the eggplants to the archer, and wished she had more to offer him. They shared one of the eggplants for dinner, my only sibling, along with fresh goat stew. After their meal, the archer pulled a small golden globe from a pouch at his side, opened it and revealed a shiny salve he rubbed over my entire eggplant body, then instructed the midwife to carefully dry me in the shade and protect me as if I was her only child. He told her he charmed this eggplant, and I would keep her company and provide for the old woman and whoever possessed me thereafter.

"She dried me with great care, making sure I was always in the shade. And I slowly became smaller and harder and shinier, keeping my eggplant form and smooth skin until I looked like the tiny, polished stone you're now wearing." The eggplant paused to be sure Aaron was still listening.

"What happened to the old woman?"

"Three months later, she made a pilgrimage to Mecca with yours truly, and was promptly given a house on the outskirts of the city as a gift from the local merchants, who believed the old midwife was a good omen. For the rest of her years, she was well cared for by her neighbors. And before she died, she passed me to her daughter, who was blessed with similar abundance."

"Then what happened? How did Layla get you?"

The eggplant snorted, still stunned and hurt by Layla's sudden departure. The last thing it wanted to do was tell stories about the good old days with her. "Not now," moaned the vegetable. "There'll be a better day for stories," at least it hoped there would be better days ahead, but doubted Paris would bring much pleasure to anyone in this party.

Aaron didn't see how the little eggplant could provide for anybody. Besides being a bit grumpy for a charmed vegetable it could barely take care of itself. At this stage in their relationship, the eggplant just wanted Aaron to give it a chance.

"As long as we are aware of ourselves, we are absolutely alive. We exist," announced the eggplant.

"What's that supposed to mean?"

"It means that as long as I know you are real and you believe I am real, we know we're alive. And that's a good place to start."

Aaron thought about the prospect of a very, very old, dried up vegetable actually being alive, having compassion and happiness and....

"And centuries of experience may provide valuable assistance," finished the eggplant.

Before they arrived in Paris, Aaron's stream of consciousness was mingling with the eggplant's thoughts and he was conversing with the eggplant like an old friend. He and the amulet would discuss anything popping into his head, just as those before him had discussed battle strategies, potions and their problems with men or women. If Aaron ignored the eggplant, or treated it like a child, the little vegetable would grow crankier and mumble disgusting insults beneath its humming breath. It paid to keep the amulet happy. He rubbed the shining vegetable like he was trying to release a genie from a magic bottle or reward a faithful companion. The eggplant shimmied its slender shoulders, cooed its appreciation and watched the lights of Paris approach from the hairless chest of Aaron Sloopshire.

*****

The 10th-century Syrian poet Kushajam, whom Aaron's eggplant met on more than one occasion, had a peculiar fondness for eating eggplants, despite the vegetable's notorious reputation for causing everything from freckles to genital warts to blindness. Kushajam said, "The doctor makes ignorant fun of me for loving eggplant, but I will not give it up. Its flavor is like the saliva generously exchanged by lovers in kissing."

For many, the eggplant is the most seductive of all vegetables—its sleek, smooth deep-purple skin mysteriously absorbs light and reflects a beautifully curved, salient glow—like a woman's breast or womb, the welcoming nape of her neck or gentle slope of the small of her back. The eggplant is sensuous, mysterious and delicious.

First cultivated in India thousands of years ago, eggplants spread to every Middle East cuisine and beyond. The Turks alone have more than 1,000 recipes calling for eggplant. When the Moors brought the big purple delicacy to Spain in the 4th century, the Spaniards believed they were powerful aphrodisiacs, and called them "apples of love."

Italians loved eggplants, the French adored them and even the Germans welcomed them into their cuisine, until one day when Layla was visiting Albert Magnus while he was teaching in Cologne. It all started just fine, with Albert serving a delightful dinner, but when a long plate of roast baby eggplant was placed in the center of the table, the little vegetable around Layla's neck went into a hysterical fit. No matter how much she rubbed it, the eggplant's protests grew louder and angrier.

61

"This is an outrage! Who would cook someone's babies or someone's kittens and serve them? I can't believe the audacity!" the eggplant continued without a breath.

"What seems to be the problem, Layla? Are you trying to rub a hole in your necklace?" asked Albert.

The other guests at the table laughed, but not Layla.

"Is that a little eggplant you're wearing?" asked the short, stout man seated beside her who'd already drank three pints of ale.

Before Layla could answer, Albert broke in. "Is your little eggplant upset because we've cooked its relatives and we're serving them for dinner?" He chuckled, surveyed his guests for approval, then picked a piece of eggplant from the plate with his fingers and popped it into his mouth.

"Yes," and the whole table began giggling and raising their glasses.

"How do you know it's upset?" Albert thoroughly enjoyed the spectacle.

"Because it told me." Everyone quieted down as Layla walked around the table to Albert, placed the eggplant over his head for no more than five full seconds—just enough time for the vegetable to make its position perfectly clear.

"I've been on this planet for centuries and have more power than you can imagine," screamed the eggplant into Albert's head. "I could have you, your mother and your dog Blitz cooked and eaten one-by-one if you don't remove the tray of eggplants from the table immediately."

When the expression on Albert's face turned from jovial to looking as if he just learned Blitz was the entree, everyone at the table knew the joke was over. Layla pulled the necklace from around his neck and she stepped away.

"This eggplant is insane!" cried Albert, and picked the tray of roasted eggplants up from the table and threw it across the room. "There. Now are you happy, you insane little fruit?"

Actually, the eggplant was quite pleased with itself, but Albert couldn't possibly know it. The eggplant could never harm Albert or his family—it simply wasn't that kind of vegetable. But Layla wasn't thrilled with the outcome, considering she hoped Albert would provide the connections to the patrons she needed to finally seize the Lost Stone. She kissed that opportunity goodbye as she sneaked away before matters got even worse.

"You're nothing but a mad apple! A mad apple!" Albert repeated as Layla fled through a side entrance, the eggplant babbling every step of the way.

"Damn right I'm mad!" laughed the eggplant. "I'm mad as a box of bees, but I'm no fruit. Nope, no fruit here."

By the time the story made its way beyond the streets of Cologne, there was not even a footnote for a necklace or small, dried eggplant. It was the roasted eggplant Albert ate that caused his temporary madness, according to the preferred, popular version of the tale. For a couple of centuries, the Germans and other northern Europeans believed eggplants caused insanity and called them "mad apples."

Love apples. Mad apples. Garden Egg or Guinea Squash. Our eggplant is vast and contains multitudes of metaphorical commodities that've grown since the day it uttered its first syllable, and love and madness seem to follow it like shadows under a full moon. Our eggplant accompanied many incredible characters on epic adventures over the centuries, but it never imagined joining a love-struck 16-year-old boy following a girl on an absurd quest in treacherous times. This was a tall order, even for an everlasting eggplant.

*****

Orphan camps that were once scattered outside the city joined Stephen's brigade and soon more than 100 children were marching into Paris. The city was quiet, sleeping and barely lit with dim street lamps when they arrived after midnight, so they slept close together, in the street at the entrance to the King's Palace.

The next morning, orphans of all ages spread out to raid garbage cans, scavenge scraps from fruit and vegetable stands, and steal chicken's food from troughs. When they returned, they shared first with the youngest, before the teens ate the leftovers.

When the Palace Guard finally arrived at the main gate, the children all cheered, until he said, "It's time to go. C'mon, clear the area. You're not getting inside."

"We're here to see King Philip!" protested Stephen.

The guard laughed, "And I suppose you have urgent business with His Majesty."

Stephen produced the letter from Jesus, signed by the Savior himself, but the guard just shook his head and chuckled.

"He couldn't read it, even if he wanted to," pointed out the eggplant.

The guard smashed the holy letter in his hands and threw it back at Stephen. "Go away. Find another place to make your beds or I'll call out the hounds!" threatened the guard. Stephen pleaded to speak with the King for just one minute, but it was no use. Hundreds of orphans in Paris were nothing unusual. With nowhere to turn, they left the city without food, blankets or a royal blessing.

The mood was somber until they were a good distance from the foul smells of the city, marching on the open road to Vendome when Eunisia began humming a sweet melody. Stephen and Aaron joined in, then more and more voices began humming and whistling along until they all felt like they were part of something special. For the first time since their march began, the children were smiling.

It took Stephen and his followers almost a week to reach Vendome, with more orphans and benefactors joining the cause in every town and hamlet they passed through. They were 1,000 strong when they arrived and had enough provisions to last for a week. Unfortunately, they were the only group there. It was the end of June and no other lieutenants had arrived with their recruits. Stephen decided 1,000 was a good number for his Crusade. It was a number God must have chosen.

At night they built fires and Stephen held court, moving from one fireside to the next, telling fantastic stories of his private meeting with Jesus, embellishing it a little more each time. Jesus became physically larger, his light more dazzling and the length of time they spent together increased proportionally. Stephen ended by predicting a wonderful trip across the sea, their heroic arrival in the Holy Land and the glory of a painless victory. It was medieval prosperity training at its best. "The rewards will be enormous," he promised. "Enough riches for all of us."

Aaron was tired of Stephen and his Crusade chatter. His holy idea had already turned into a greedy scheme. He didn't know how a perfect girl like Eunisia could have such a foolhardy brother.

"This Stephen reminds me of a man I once knew," mumbled the eggplant. "And I suppose he'll have the same fate."

"Was he mad?"

"Depends whom you ask," smirked the eggplant, "but all men are mad, if you ask me. Do you remember Layla's tale of Hamdan Karmat, the Arab who tried to change the world a few centuries ago?"

"Sure, the clown king."

The eggplant never thought of him that way. "Very few have ever heard of the true giants of history who truly moved civilization forward," scoffed the eggplant.

Aaron noted a difference in the eggplant's voice, as if it was suddenly worried. "Did you talk to Hamdan?"

"Yes, I was around his neck in Bahrain. It was one of the most beautiful places on earth. It was paradise."

"Layla's paradise?"

"Perhaps, considering Bahrain was the site of the original paradise."

"The paradise in the Hebrew Torah or the Hindu Epic of Gilgamesh?"

"Both," replied the eggplant. "It was also the capital of the Dilmun Empire and a favorite market for Babylonian and Persian traders. Christians, Arabs and Asians all rubbed shoulders in Bahrain at one time, but since Mohammed extended a personal invitation to its leaders in the mid-7th century, it all changed."

"Did Hamdan change the world?"

The eggplant chuckled. "He changed some practices for a short time, but not in the way he planned. There were finer gardens, bigger parades and more gold with Hamdan, yet he never really understood the perils of changing the world."

"What perils didn't he understand?"

"When a person tries to change the world, they become prey for others with even larger ambitions. Believe me, there are predators waiting in the shadows to benefit from Stephen's Crusade, even though he probably won't make it anywhere near the Promised Land. Hamdan's story is a little different. He was killed before his time and left his island in the hands of a reckless son who spoiled his legacy. His tragic story is written in many books," sighed the eggplant. "There are more pressing matters at hand, don't you think?"

Aaron was mesmerized by the story of Hamdan. To think this amulet once belonged to a man who ruled an island made

Aaron feel like the eggplant was a worthwhile possession after all. The eggplant, on the other hand, was more concerned with Aaron and the doomed Children's Crusade than the impression his stories made on the boy. If it was difficult to feed 100 mouths, it couldn't imagine feeding 1,000 traveling kids for months.

Aaron didn't care about the Crusade enough to recognize imminent failure if it crawled up his leg and bit him on the balls. He lived for his moments with Eunisia. He divided his time between helping children in need and finding food for others, always with Eunisia at his side. The eggplant hoped it was only a matter of time before this Eunisia infatuation blew over and they could return to Layla, whom it dearly missed.

On the third day in Vendome, when Stephen considered breaking camp and leaving for Marseilles, a huge surge of young Crusaders swept into the city. There were at least 300, waving their makeshift crosses high as they came over distant hills. Not long after, another band of child recruits rolled in, and another and another. As they approached, their songs could be heard clearer and louder. They arrived from different provinces, with different dialects and flags. Some had banners with religious symbols like crosses and haloes, others were adorned with names of farms and local taverns, but most consisted of nothing more than colored rags on a stick.

The Children's Crusade was thousands strong before the largest company arrived from Paris just before dark. A lieutenant had scoured the city and more than 15,000 eager recruits followed him to Vendome, not one of them over 12-years-old. The fields, streets and woods of Vendome were bustling with an army of excited, hungry, filthy, homeless orphans. Campfires dotted the landscape and the buzz of young voices covered the city like a colony of high-pitched insects.

That night, an old man visited Stephen for the first time since Aaron joined Eunisia on the Crusade. He wore loose, shiny clothes that ruffled with every breeze and he spoke to Stephen in his tent for hours. Aaron and Eunisia waited outside the tent for the old man to leave, and wondered who he was and what he could be talking about. They listened closely, but only the eggplant could hear Arabic accents in the man's voice above Stephen's grunts and muffled laughter.

"The old man's voice sounds familiar," whispered the eggplant. "I certainly recognize the smell coming from the tent— it's hashish."

When the man finally threw open the tent's door, a great billow of pungent smoke poured out and the old man looked down on Aaron and Eunisia as if he was going to strike them.

"Tell the old man to go back to his desert," whispered the eggplant. "Quick! Say it!"

"Go back to your desert, old man," declared Aaron, although it sounded more like a suggestion.

The old man stepped back, his hood covering his face, then cackled softly and vanished into the darkness with a few long strides.

"Did you know him?"

"I recognized the accent, but I'm not certain about the man. He sounds like an Arab I met more than a century ago," declared the eggplant, "And he died not long after, as far as I know."

"So it couldn't be him, right?"

"He was a very powerful man," continued the eggplant. "Maybe it was his grandson."

"What was his name?"

"Hassan i Sabbah," said the eggplant.

"The Old Man of the Mountain? The one in Layla's books?"

"The very same," replied the eggplant. "Couldn't be him. Could it?"

*****

Crouching deep in the shadows and disguised as an old peasant woman, Layla watched the scene with Stephen and the Old Man unfold. She'd followed the Old Man since he arrived in France from Egypt. It was Hassan i Sabbah, but he must be well over 200-years-old, if it was truly him. She wondered if he was already using the Stone to extend his life.

Layla was just as surprised to see Aaron's journey intersect with her and the Old Man. She didn't believe in accidents, and wondered what secret geometry was waiting to unfold. Layla saw Aaron was still foolishly in love, but she knew he was also quite capable of finding his way—even in dangerous times. And with the leader of the Assassins visiting this Children's Crusade, the situation for Aaron was stranger and more dangerous than she imagined. But she had no time to waste. The Old Man was already on the road and she had to hurry to catch up. She limped away on her cane, following the Old Man from the Crusader's camp, leaving Aaron and the eggplant behind.

Layla usually excels in her awareness of the moment, her attention to the details of her surroundings, the minutiae, nuances and discrepancies in near-field landscapes, and has a particularly keen eye for distant anomalies, such as an approaching catastrophe. Perhaps she was distracted by Aaron, the craziness of the Old Man meeting with Stephen, or an innate sensation she was closing in on her prize—whatever the reason, she failed to recognize a trio of Assassins, each of them watching every move she made—one in a tree, two behind nearby bushes, their hands on scimitars, just in case she moved to threaten the Old Man. When Layla mounted her horse to follow Hassan, his Assassins followed her, one behind and two racing ahead, riding between this strange woman and their Master.

Aaron looked inside the tent and saw a very disheveled, wasted Stephen. His eyes were half-opened and drool ran down his chin as he passed a list of instructions to Aaron and expelled a sour-smelling burp.

"What are we supposed to do next?" Stephen asked, and burped again.

Besides making rude sounds, Stephen looked terrible. The Old Man had introduced him to hashish, ale and sex in one extended lesson in debauchery, leaving Stephen sick but smiling like a newborn pervert. Aaron took the instructions and stepped outside, but Stephen's foul odor seemed to follow him.

Eunisia stayed in the tent with her brother. "Who was that man? What did he do to you?"

Stephen mumbled and looked away. "He was a friend of Jesus. He told me he'd handle all the details of the Crusade, I need only ride along to Marseilles and enjoy myself. The more I enjoy, the more likely we are to succeed."

"What do you mean enjoy yourself?" asked Eunisia.

"Aaron knows," and he held the bottle high over his head. "Drinking ale, smoking pipes, kissing girls and other things I haven't tried yet," he laughed and unintentionally spewed a mouthful of ale on his sister's dress.

Aaron helped Eunisia clean her dress and wondered what Stephen was talking about. He never drank ale, never kissed a girl and he supposed he never tried the other things, either.

"That's terrible!" cried his sister. "Are you crazy? You're supposed to lead these orphans to the Holy Land. Do you remember the Crusader's oath?"

Stephen shrugged. "Eunisia, I'm just taking orders here. I'm not a saint." He expelled a loud fart into the pre-dawn air, and Eunisia left the tent to join Aaron, who was reading instructions by their campfire's dwindling light. The orders were scribbled in French and precisely numbered: 1. Appoint 100 lieutenants who will meet each morning for marching orders. 2. Leave Vendome at dawn. 3. Cross the Loire and walk three days to Blois...and so on.

"The old man is directing every step of this underage expedition," said the eggplant. "He's the one who'll gain from this fiasco."

Aaron and Eunisia watched the sun rise over 30,000 anxious children and considered breaking up the party. "What do you think the old man wants?" asked Eunisia.

Neither Aaron nor the eggplant could imagine one good reason to send an army of children to the Holy Land. "On the other hand, these children will bring a high price on the African slave market," said the eggplant. "Especially the young girls."

"I think we should stop this whole silly game right now," confessed Eunisia, and started to sob.

"If you want to go back to Chartres, I'll go with you," offered Aaron. "This isn't my Crusade. I'll follow you wherever you go."

The eggplant groaned.

Eunisia crawled into Stephen's tent and shook the hung-over junior prophet until he sat up and opened his eyes. "Listen to me, Stephen. We need to go back to Chartres. There are too many mouths and no food. We need to send everyone back where they came from."

Stephen rolled over and glared at Eunisia. His eyes were red and his face was pale and sickly. "We can't go back. I'll be killed if I take one step back. The old man is a sorcerer. He put a spell on me. If I go back, I'll die before I reach Chartres."

Eunisia stared in disbelief. "Are we delivering these children to the devil?"

"You can go back, Eunisia. I'm going to save the Holy Land." He rolled over, pretending to sleep, but wept softly into his pillow, afraid to go forward or back.

Eunisia stomped out of Stephen's tent angry and worried for all of them. She couldn't leave her young brother as long the old man terrified him. But she didn't want to stay here, either. She wanted everybody to go home, but too many had no homes. She feared it was hopeless.

Aaron was still too love-struck to appreciate the problem's full magnitude. He'd created a sparkling world insulating him from the harsh darkness all around him. Orphan's camps stretched across the fields of Vendome like a giant ring of dirty rags and the smell of human waste and loud, squealing din was almost unbearable. He could only smell Eunisia's sweet breath and hear the wind dance through her hair.

The eggplant sensed big trouble, but Aaron paid little attention. It didn't take ears, eyes or a nose to understand this Crusade was going from bad to worse. In fact, the Crusade looked like a plague of giant locusts spoiling the countryside. Vendome's elders were ready to chase the misguided city of children away or burn them out if they didn't leave soon. The whole show was getting a bit shaky when the lieutenants constructed a makeshift platform from a broken cart and Stephen climbed atop like a shabby king to offer morning blessings.

"My fellow Crusaders!" A great cheer erupted like a wave all around the fields. "This is a historic moment for all believers. Today we begin our march to Jerusalem. May our journey be blessed by the Lord's grace, and may we return when we win the Lord's birthplace back for all good people!"

"We'll march all day to Blois and make our camp there. Onward to the Land of our Lord!" Stephen looked at the sky and held his arms up like a big empty funnel. The yips and yells rang all across the throngs as they marched down the road, six and seven abreast. Half the inhabitants of Vendome left their homes to make sure the parade vanished into the hills.

The pre-pubescent army wandered southward, chattering, singing, and skipping for miles before their stomachs began to growl and their feet began to hurt. The groups traveling to Vendome remained together like tribes for the first few days. At night, they gathered around fires to share old bread and dried pork they carried in their sacks. Others procured vegetables from fields along the way and cooked them over hot coals with long sticks. The nights were warm and most slept under the stars while the young teens made tents with blankets and broken tree limbs. Every morning, lieutenants would report how many children the Crusade had lost or gained, then Aaron read new orders from the old man's instructions.

It took six days to arrive at Blois, and Stephen was growing into his role like a real leader. It was hard for Stephen to believe he was herding his sheep across the hillsides of Chartres just a few weeks ago. Now he was the chosen savior of a different flock and he had different needs. It was time to fulfill his promise to his old patron and have some fun. At the next morning's meeting in Blois, Stephen instructed his lieutenants to get him a horse. He'd seen others with horses, so he ordered a horse-drawn chariot at the next meeting. He covered the chariot with colorful carpets he procured from villages and rode at the head of the procession with his sister and Aaron walking beside him. His taste for ale and girls had also grown. By the end of a month, his chariot was transformed into an apartment of ill repute. He invited several girls a day into his chariot, some as young as 10 years-old, pulled the carpets over the top, and kept them there until he tired of them or they ran away. He was a child in years, but quickly became very accomplished in vice.

"Stephen is a scoundrel," grumbled the eggplant. "The girls climb into his chariot for all the wrong reasons." Aaron was naive. He thought they were playing harmless games in the

73

chariot and remained oblivious to the world outside of Eunisia. "Some of the girls probably think he's a real prophet and they're screwing for the Lord," continued the eggplant. Some returned more than once, but mostly they stumbled out of the chariot, confused and disoriented. "I'll bet most leave this Crusade after a session on his couch with a good dose of fire crotch," added the eggplant.

"What are you chattering about? A solo vegetable can't possibly understand."

"Open your eyes, boy! There's shit everywhere and you're smelling nothing but roses!"

Aaron sighed and wished the eggplant could find another dried vegetable and fall in love. Maybe a nice turnip or beet.

"I hate beets," commented the eggplant. "But another eggplant would be nice."

*****

Layla followed the Old Man for miles until they came to Via Francigena, a well-used pilgrim route connecting Paris to Rome. The Via Francigena was neither paved with stone blocks, like many Roman roads, nor was it a single route. Instead, it offered travelers a choice of several different courses, which shifted with the popularity of shrines along the way. Layla stayed a safe distance from the Old Man, moving with small groups of pilgrims on the road. By nightfall, she spotted an Arab teenager whom she also noticed when she left Aaron at the Crusader's camp. If this Arab was one of the Old Man's Assassins, she knew there would be two others nearby.

After dark, Layla hunched over and limped like an 80-year-old woman, right past the Old Man, who'd already made camp beside the road for the night. After the long day's journey, she was tired but she could've hustled along the road as fast as any young traveler, if there was a need. And right now, she needed to lose the young Arab, so she waited for the right moment and darted onto an alternative road leading back to Pontarlier, on the Swiss border.

As she slipped silently off the road and hid behind a fallen log, she remembered drinking absinthe in a Pontarlierian Pub almost 10 years ago and waking up with green lips and a sack of gold. She gave half of the gold to the abbey in the morning, and procured an armful of church-mandated cassocks, habits, and other priestly garments before leaving town, never to return.

She waited patiently for the young Assassin and he finally appeared, lurking in the shadows, almost invisible, except for the sound of pebbles and dirt being crushed beneath his desert boots. When the Arab turned back toward the Via Francigena, Layla crept farther from the road, deep into the brush, pulled the collarino and neckband from her bag of tricks and returned to the main road as a priest. She walked upright holding her cane like a holy staff, passing by each camp, offering blessings to all travelers and gaining scraps of food in return. When she came to the Old Man's camp, she stopped and said in a deep voice, "I offer blessings to you, fellow traveler. May good tidings follow you all the way to Rome."

The Old Man sat by his small fire and never looked up to see the priest. Instead, he opened his robe and pissed on the fire, leaving the hot coals hissing like a pool of angry snakes. While the Old Man relieved himself, Layla identified two more Arab boys watching her and she needed a plan to take care of the trio, or risk being killed in her sleep. She limped away, hid deep in the brush beside the road and dashed a thimble of rhodiola under her tongue to help her stay awake. She quickly prepared 3 small containers with a blend of her strongest opium and hallucinogenic mushroom tinctures, fixed sharp, hollow, 6-inch needles to the containers' tops with a mixture of mud and thin straps of wool she tore from her tunic.

But before the last needle was fixed to its container, Layla heard the bushes rustling seconds before the first Assassin burst upon her with his scimitar drawn. Layla firmly stabbed him in his backside with a needle and backed away before the teen stumbled and fell to his knees, when the second Assassin ran at her with his scimitar high over his head. Layla dodged his charge, stabbed him with another needle and turned to prepare for the third attacker, who never came. Instead, the Old Man stepped from the shadows and stood before Layla, alone.

Layla thought it was a trick and the third Assassin would leap at her at any moment. But the Old Man just stared at the priest, who stood straight up and returned his gaze.

"What kind of priest are you?" the Old Man finally asked.

"The kind that can defend himself, if necessary. And was it you who sent the boys to kill me?"

The Old Man was silent as he looked down at the boys, their eyes were barely open as they curled up on the ground, shivering occasionally as they wandered between opium dreams and sleepy mushroom hallucinations, with very brief stops in reality.

"What did you do to them?"

"They'll be fine in a day or two. Why did they attack me?"

"You should get away from here before they regain their senses and try to kill you again," and he vanished.

Layla was not far behind. Beneath her tunic she kept an opium needle in one hand, strolling briskly along the Via Francigena, headed to Rome.

After walking for less than an hour, Layla circled back to find the Old Man had procured a horse and was already on his way to Lausanne, on the shores of Lake Geneva. Layla turned back towards Lausanne and hustled down the trail, hoping to find a horse along the way. It was 500 miles from Lausanne to Rome, and she'd never keep up with the Old Man without one.

The Via Francigena was well-travelled by the poor masses who believed a simple view of the Pope's new home and the tombs of apostles Peter and Paul would be rewarded with a free pass through the Pearly Gates. In the summer of 1212, the countryside was relatively peaceful, and the shrines of saints along the route were safe, compared to the days when they attracted bandits and worse, making it easier for Layla to hitch rides on the occasional passing wagon. Once in Lausanne, she traded two silver pieces for a horse and was on her way, trying to catch up to the Old Man.

The road crossed the Alps and the Apennines and she relied on abbeys for occasional shelter, water and inspiration from a favorite miracle maker, each with its own specialty. St. Maurice's Abbey, for example, was located in Switzerland at the entrance to a mountain pass leading to the upper part of the Rhone valley. The Abbey was built on the cliff-side ruins of a 1st century Roman shrine honoring Mercury, the god of commerce, communication and travelers. Layla had been here twice before and she knew St. Maurice's was famous for two things: its connection to a Theban Legion's martyrdom and its practice of perpetual psalmady, in which chants were sung day and night, by several choirs in rotation, without ceasing. The psalmady business began at the Abbey in the early 6th century and continued there nonstop, 24/7 until the early 9th century. They resumed again a couple of centuries later, mostly to attract donations from travelers, and they were still singing as Layla rounded the final bend in the winding mountain road before the Abbey was in sight.

The martyrdom issue wasn't quite so clear. The Abbey was named after Maurice, who led his Theban Legion to their deaths at the spot where the Abbey is located. According to a St. Eucherius vision, Maurice refused Emperor Maximus's orders to harass a Christian community in the 3rd century, leading to the killing of every 10th member of Maurice's legion. The legend didn't stop growing for centuries, and before long 1,000 soldiers were killed, then one-half the Legion, until all 6,600 soldiers gave their lives to save local Christians from harassment. One thing led to another and by the early 6th century, St. Maurice and his men were all martyrs and the shrine was built.

Layla stayed at the Abbey long enough to ask the friars if they had seen the Old Man and any young Arabs who may have passed, but they'd seen several old men and teenage boys, so she fed and watered her horse and moved ahead, still traveling as a priest. The Great St. Bernard Pass through the Western Alps was next, and at more than 8,000 feet it's always slow going and can be treacherous any time of year. Layla rode through the night, taking rhodiola drops to stay alert.

By morning, she reached Aosta, Italy, on the other side of the pass, and Ivrea, a recently emancipated commune outside of Turin. There were five lakes around the town, and Layla found a secluded spot by a small creek where she slept for hours under a willow tree. When she awoke, her horse was rested and she was determined to ride straight to Rome.

She rode through Vercelli and Pavia, where she stopped and traded her horse for another, fresh steed. Next, she passed along the outskirts of Poggibonsi and Viterbo and finally came to Sutri, about 30 miles from Rome. Perched on a narrow hill and surrounded by deep ravines, the commune was not only beautiful, it also had a Roman amphitheater carved in the stone hillside, dozens of rock-cut tombs and an actual Mithraeum—a cave for followers of Mithraism, a short-lived religion named for the Persian god Mithra and practiced in Rome until the 4th century. Layla was in several Mithraeum during initiations into secret teachings, but she was never in this one. She walked into the church of the Madonna del Parto alone and made her way down to the crypt, where a tall figure stood in front of colorful woven blankets at the cave's entrance.

"Are you waiting for me?" Layla was certain it was the Old Man.

The man turned around and asked, "Are you talking to me, Father?"

Layla blushed above her priest's collar. "I'm sorry, I thought you were someone else," and continued into the cave and down its long, carved walkway.

"Were you looking for the Old Man?"

Layla stopped and turned, examined the man, located his weaknesses, considered alternatives and glanced around the hallway for escape routes. "Who are you?"

"I'm the caretaker of the Mithraeum and an acquaintance of Hassan i Sabbah, the one you call the Old Man." He walked towards her as he spoke, holding his palms open at his sides. "He told me you'd come here, and asked me to tell you he has nothing for you. He's only looking for answers to questions, just like you."

"And who has the answers to these questions?"

The caretaker paused. "I fear nobody has the answers to all of Hassan's questions."

*****

The road was crowded on her 30-mile ride to Rome. Pope Innocent III had summoned monks representing Italian and French abbeys for a special meeting, and many of them were on the road today, along with their companions.

Pope Innocent III was no slouch. He claimed supremacy over all of Europe's kings, called for Christian Crusades against Moslem rulers in Spain, the Holy Land and Albigensian heretics in southern France. For his 4th Crusade, his armies invaded and sacked Constantinople, a Christian city and capital of the Byzantine Empire, which the Eastern side of the Christian family never forgave. Now, as Layla learned from pilgrims along the road, Pope Innocent was really pissed at his monks.

But that wasn't Layla's business. Nevertheless, she followed the flow of traffic right to the Vatican, and the Pope's new palace, which was built very close to the spot where Emperor Nero had St. Peter crucified upside down. When she stepped off the road to take in the whole chaotic seen, she saw a large door open at the side of the palace and the Old Man walked out and vanished into the crowd. Layla bolted after him, still in priest's garb, hustling past bystanders and peering through the faces, trying to catch a glimpse of his long white hair and beard, when she was grabbed from behind and shoved to the ground.

Without looking, Layla flipped around and swung her cane first at her attacker's head, followed by two quick jabs to his groin, which easily put him down. Layla turned and looked for another attacker, but saw none.

"You're very quick, for a priest." He was already on the ground and flat on his back. "Why are you following me?"

It was the Old Man, and he was much weaker than she thought. Layla extended her hand, helped him up and brushed him off. "You and I have a common interest," she said. "We're both looking from something that may not exist."

The Old man was astonished. "You're looking for the Kusanagi Sword?"

Layla never heard of the Kusanagi Sword, which was used in Japan during ascension rituals for centuries, until it was supposedly lost at sea 50 years ago.

"That's not all you're looking for. You were looking for the Lost Stone in Alexandria. Did you find it?"

"So you want the Stone," he chuckled. "No, I didn't find a Stone that doesn't exist."

"How do you know it doesn't exist?"

"There's only one holy Stone and it's in the Kabba, where it belongs."

Layla stared at him for a long time. She knew he was lying. What she didn't know was the Old Man had just met with Pope Innocent and traded a small wooden box containing St. Peter's bones along with a sealed certificate of authenticity from 1st century Pope Linus, along with Jesus' actual burial cloth called the Shroud of Pluck's Gutter, for King Solomon's Seal.

King Solomon's Seal was a signet ring used to cast a hexagram shape—the Star of David—in soft wax and other materials. The ring also allowed its wearer to control genies and weather elementals, speak with animals and vegetables and tell truth from lies. Stolen from under the Temple Mount by Knights Templars who tunneled for years searching for Solomon's treasure, the Seal ended up with Pope Innocent, who was more than happy to make the two-for-one trade and return European relics to their home.

Despite his denials, Layla continued watching the Old Man, changing her appearance as much as twice a day as she followed him away from Rome. She never wore the priest outfit again, but did appear as a bearded friar, a mustached soldier, a toothless old farmer and even a pretty young lady of the night. Finding new disguises was easy, since washing clothes in a river was common and she could always pick up a tunic, dress or even a uniform from someone's pile on the riverbank. The Old Man continued all the way to the Mediterranean coast and she followed him all 600 miles.

The trip was long, but the Italian and French coastlines were beautiful in summer. Miles of long, sandy beaches, sweeping vistas, amazing sunsets and delicious, fresh local food readily available at shops along the route made this journey more comfortable than most. And with the Old Man traveling at a steady, unhurried pace, she meandered casually out of sight, tracking him all the way to heart of Marseilles.

The second largest city and most important trading center in France, Marseilles was bustling with men arranging passage on outgoing merchant ships, buyers waiting for boats to arrive with new clothes and supplies, importers hawking their wares and prostitutes on every corner, all waiting to add a few more francs to their coffers. Layla followed the Old Man to the offices of the Daedalus shipping company, where he stayed for hours. While inside, Layla saw a one-armed knight standing against a building, across from Daedalus. He was surveying the scene, just like her, until he marched quickly across the street and directly into the same door the Old Man had entered. Layla moved closer to the door and heard the two men arguing, then the knight was pushed outside the office and into the street, followed by two men with swords making sure he stayed out.

"Excuse me, non-existent knight. I believe we have a mutual friend."

The knight stopped, turned and looked right into Layla's eyes. "Are you addressing me, kind lady?"

"Yes, I am." Layla was dressed as a prostitute and fully aware no other knights were in the vicinity.

"And whom would that mutual friend be?"

"You saved a young boy's life about one year ago. You killed a smith who burned his nose with a hot poker."

The knight looked at her and said nothing.

"I came to know the boy, and I want to thank you for saving him."

"How is he?"

"He's very well. Following a girl in the Children's Crusade now"

"Oh no. That's very bad business. They're on their way to boats waiting here to take them straight to slavery and worse." The knight was visibly moved. "I tried to intervene and stop the madness, but the Old Man paid for the ships and couldn't be budged. I don't think anybody can stop it."

Now Layla knew why the Old Man was in Marseilles, but why was he at the Vatican? She understood Aaron was in danger and no matter how many ways their destinies continued to intersect, they were each on their own quest: he was chasing love and she was after the Stone.

"You're a noble man. I know you'll do your best to help those kids."

"Thank you, kind lady. But as you already seem to know, I'm a non-existent knight with no choice but to do what must be done."

*****

The child Crusaders suffered from blistered feet and withered hopes, but the worst was still ahead. The summer had turned unusually hot and humid and water was scarce unless a river was nearby. Too many children were sick from drinking bad water and many had already died. Aaron used all of his tinctures and did what he could to help the weakest, but there were just too many sick kids. He and Eunisia boiled water and made fresh bread in makeshift ovens, but that wasn't enough to save lives. Weeks passed and the days grew hotter. Aaron's medical supplies were exhausted. Those who survived buried the dead in shallow, hand-dug graves and moved on.

The Knights Templars, who usually protected and assisted pilgrims were absent from the Children's Crusade. Aaron saw a knight bring supplies to Stephen once, but never saw another. Without knights to protect them, thieves and pedophiles prayed on the young pilgrims, giving them wine and ale, molesting them and even selling them like slaves. Aaron and other lieutenants chased the derelicts away when they saw them, but there were too many to catch them all. There were stories of a one-armed knight who rode alone and protected children from perverts. Aaron hoped his old non-existent friend was still at work.

The Children's Crusade marched through central France, crossed the Rhone at Lyons, and entered Burgundy like a band of sick, dirty, underage outlaws. There was neither sympathy nor assistance from the people they encountered. Not even the sweetest melody could help them now. By the 10th week, Stephen no longer led the march. There were no morning meetings and no more blessings. No more talk about glorious redemption. No more prophesy. His muse had dried up, he stayed drunk from morning until night and no girl or boy would go near him, except his sister. He was always naked in his chariot, carpets splattered with dried semen and vomit, playing with himself, picking lice and crabs from his crotch and mumbling obscenities to invisible demons.

Then one day, Eunisia snapped. She heard someone crying in Stephen's chariot and when she pulled the carpets away she found him trying to have sex with a sobbing girl who couldn't have been more than five- or six-years-old. Eunisia screamed at Stephen, pulled the girl from the chariot and threw a blanket over her, then began beating her brother with a stick until he jumped and lashed out at her, swinging his arms wildly and striking her in the face. Aaron heard a scream and when he saw Eunisia's nose bleeding he grabbed Stephen and pinned him on the ground in one swift motion. Stephen was spitting and cursing and wriggling beneath him, but Aaron held him tight.

"If you ever touch another child or Eunisia again, I'll tie you with ropes like an animal and drag you behind the others as an example." When Aaron released him, Stephen charged like a bull and scratched at Aaron's face, but Aaron took him to the ground again, and held him there with one foot on his chest until Stephen had enough. From then on, the chariot was used only for sick and weak children, and Aaron made sure Stephen was always one of the people who pulled it.

When they reached Provence, the Crusaders took up residence in elegant moss-covered ruins. They played in the broken aqueducts and crumbling buildings for two days. He and Eunisia wished the Crusade would end right here and they could make their summer home in this dilapidated temple. But the game grew old for the others, and they marched ahead.

Almost 10,000 children had already been lost to homesickness, disease and death. Many who remained with the Crusade were either hardened or mad. Some wandered naked in the heat, their faces painted with dried mud. Boys and girls who left Vendome with their innocence intact now marched as sex partners, carried makeshift spears and daggers, made love in the grass, ate bugs and stole their food and water wherever they could. As the colony of wayward misfits moved closer to Marseilles, they were constantly fighting among themselves. It didn't look like they'd last another day when the first wave of orphans came to a hilltop and saw Marseilles and the sea for the first time. Like a heavenly vision, its magnificence instantly stopped their quarrels as they rushed down to the city, falling and laughing like packs of young wolves returning to the den. From the top of the hill, Eunisia and Aaron could see the others dashing toward Marseilles, its white buildings with red rooftops and great shipyards beaming in the sunlight below—boats of all colors and sizes anchored along its coastline and tied to heavy wooden docks in the bright, blue Mediterranean. Aaron could smell the rich salt air, the fish markets, wet lumber of new boats and hear the din of horses and wagons rumbling, money-changers chattering and builders pounding out a million different rhythms in the city below.

While they admired Marseilles, Stephen climbed back in the chariot and was bowling down the hill, out of control. Aaron and Eunisia ran after him and watched him crash into a tree, sending Stephen and his horse tumbling. He landed on a heap of thimbleberry bushes and his horse thrashed its neck against the hillside a few feet beneath him, then stood and ran back over the hill, away from Marseilles.

"That horse may be one of the most intelligent creatures among us," noted the eggplant, and wished it were tied around the mare's neck.

"Stephen! Do you hear me? Can you speak?" Eunisia was at his side, her hand resting on his forehead.

Stephen felt like he finally reached the end of a summer-long binge and his body and soul were sour and aching from too much alcohol and debauchery. "Looks like we made it, Eunisia. The Holy Land."

"It's Marseilles," corrected Aaron, and he and Eunisia helped him down to the magnificent city.

*****

Marseilles was too large and busy to be overcome by 20,000 orphans, especially if they were just passing through. The city and its churches absorbed them like a sponge. They took the orphans into their homes, pulled lice from their knotted, infested scalps, scrubbed and fed them until they looked like children again. The same orphans who squirmed through the mud in wild, drunken orgies a few days earlier, now passed their time singing hymns and crowding into churches for absolutions and blessings.

Eunisia and Aaron were separated into different parishes and it took him two days to find her. Once he did, they spent days going house to house, asking for medicinal supplies, on the advice of the eggplant, until they had an assortment of salves, herbs and bandages. He and Eunisia saw fellow Crusaders everywhere, but never Stephen. They hunted in every den and alley, but nobody had seen him. In fact, the Old Man had taken Stephen to a large villa overlooking the sea. He congratulated Stephen on his successful crossing of Europe, fed him exotic food and introduced his young prophet to a fine smoking mixture he'd discovered in the East. By the end of the evening, Stephen had found a new weakness, opium.

The Old Man arranged for seven ships from wily merchants named William of Posqueres and Hugh the Iron, or Porcus and Ferreus as they were commonly known—and the boats would be ready to sail in two days. There was only room for 5,000 children, but the Old Man was content. He gave Stephen his final instructions, written in French and with King Solomon's Seal in bright red wax, and sent him on his way. Stephen turned up at an opium den the next day, where two lieutenants found him and brought him to the cathedral, where he was granted an audience with the bishop's assistant.

"I have ships taking 5,000 orphans to the Holy Land. We'll leave Marseilles in two days and I want the bishop to bless this Crusade." Stephen slurred his words, still nodding from the opium and not completely certain this encounter wasn't a dream.

The priest watched the boy swaying back and forth, eyes half-closed, smiling and occasionally shivering, and he wanted to stop this ridiculous endeavor before it turned deadly. The church was prepared to give these Crusaders an entire orphanage, but it wasn't going to bless this folly. "Who gave you these ships?"

"Porcus and Ferreus."

The priest wondered why these two greedy merchants would offer their ships to these orphans. "Richard I of England met Philip of France here in 1190 and asked the bishop for his blessing before they left with 114 ships. Richard and his army and most of the French were killed. Philip barely made it out alive. You plan to sail with children on seven poorly-equipped ships, and you want the bishop's blessing?"

"We've come a long way. It's a small request." Stephen's eyes were like two dark glass balls. The priest attributed this unusual behavior to exhaustion. After all, they'd walked across France.

"How can we bless a fleet of death ships? If you don't die at sea, you'll be killed as soon as you make it to the shore. Those are not friendly lands, my son."

"We'll sail with or without your blessing. We're on a Christian Crusade and your words are important to these children. Aren't the children important to you?"

The bishop knew there was nothing he could do to stop them. They had the ships and the crew. He'd see to it their boats had ample provisions and pray for them. "Either the bishop or I will offer blessings before you sail."

"I have to ask another favor," and Stephen passed the priest the envelope with the list of instructions.

The priest opened the seal and felt like he had just spilled wine on his finest white cape. The list wasn't for food or medicine. It was for wine and ale and opium. The priest read the list and wanted these vile orphans out of Marseilles as soon as possible. He had no intention of giving them anything but old food and fresh water. "My monks will take care of this, but you'll have to sail tomorrow. I'll be at the docks to make sure."

At noon the next day, about 2,000 boys and 3,000 girls were divided into seven groups and rowed out to the huge wooden ships. Boys and girls were on different boats, and Aaron tried desperately to keep track of Eunisia's skiff, but it was no use. The sea was choppy, everyone was huddled down in the boats and he lost her before he was even on deck.

There was no cheering on the shore. The people of Marseilles knew crossing the sea was serious business. Everyone on the docks had lost loved ones in these waters, and the orphans weren't too young to die at sea.

When the ships were full and their ports were closed, there was a grave silence on the shore before the sailors pulled in the anchors' chains and began to chant an old hymn, "Veni Creator Spiritus."

O Finger of the hand divine
the sevenfold gifts of grace are thine
true promise of the Father thou
who dost the tongue with power endow

The verses went on and the sailors' rugged voices blended with the children who hummed along as the ships sailed away one at a time. Some spectators cried and others left the shoreline long before the song faded over the water. They wouldn't hear another word about those boats or the children for 18 years.

*****

Before the ships sailed, the Old Man brought Stephen back to the villa. They each inhaled from a braided hose attached to a tarnished hookah and together watched the seven boats vanish over the distant horizon. Stephen felt nothing as they disappeared. He wasn't sure if he was temporarily out of fuel or if he had lost his soul forever. His Crusade was gone. His sister was gone. His youth was gone. Even his bottle of ale was empty.

"Don't worry, Stephen. You've served history well and there's nothing to fear. You're free to move about the world." The Old Man kept his word. Stephen watched the empty horizon until he fell fast asleep. And when he awoke, he was riding with a non-existent, one-armed knight, who'd been asked to return the boy safely to his sheep in Chartres.

*****

Layla watched the villa from afar, waiting for the Old Man and a fresh batch of Assassins to leave Marseilles and weighing whether she should follow him or return to Rome, where she may learn what the Old Man really wanted at the Vatican. Looking out over the sea and hoping Aaron and the others would cross the Mediterranean safely, she realized the Old Man was using those children for his own personal gain and her mind was made up. She silently slipped through bushes to the villa's back entrance, snuck inside then bolted across the main room and held a dagger to the Old Man's neck.

Before his Assassins could raise their scimitars, Layla spit out a small glass vial containing a tiny chunk of sodium and special mixture of black powder, which she was holding between her teeth. The mix of her spit and sodium caused the powder concoction to burst into thick, yellow clouds as soon as it hit the stone floor. She pulled the Old Man from the smoke, out the door and dropped a second bomb emitting a blackened screen of noxious belladonna vapors, holding the Assassins at bay long enough to drag the Old Man behind a thick stand of thorn bushes on the hillside.

"Why did you go to Rome? What did you want?"

"I was visiting friends on my way..." The Old Man was shaken by the surprise.

"Shhhh! No more lies!" She pressed the blade tighter against his neck. "I should kill you right here for sending those children to their deaths."

"There is no Lost Stone," he repeated.

"Yes there is, and we both know it. There's a Lost Stone and somehow it was stolen from its keepers by a magician named Falukki Babazini."

"Hassan! Hassan!" Layla heard the Assassins calling for the Old Man from the villa.

"The next time we meet, you'll tell me everything you know about the Stone, or you won't be so lucky." She released the Old

Man, vanished into the brush and began the journey back to her laboratory in England.

*****

The children were crammed into three floors under the ships' decks. Most had never sailed before and were horribly sick. When three or four started to vomit, they all began to blow their mush across the hull. It was days before their bellies settled and they found their sea legs, but the stench of curdled bile never left the ship's deck. Aaron tore off pieces of his shirt, doused them in peppermint oil and kept one piece stuffed up his nostrils for the entire voyage.

The eggplant didn't like this sea-faring business at all. Personally, it feared sailing more than anything. Seasickness wasn't an issue. Boats, in general, were fine. It was the idea of falling to the bottom of the sea giving it the chills. Eggplants are land vegetables, and being lost in deep, dark, strange waters was the worst end it could imagine. It would rather be diced and sautéed, boiled, kippered, chewed and digested by a cow with seven stomachs, shit, smashed into the good earth and eaten by worms. It would rather die by any other means than falling to the bottom of the sea.

The ship's crew stayed to themselves during the voyage and rarely spoke to the young passengers. When the sea was smooth, the children played on the deck, climbed masts and threw scraps of rotten food to the birds and fish. When the sea turned dark and waves heaved against the ship, the orphans were stowed below with other cargo.

Aaron spent his smooth-water days climbing the tall main mast to look for other ships. Some days, he could see all six of his fellow Crusader's vessels, sometimes only two or three. On rough-water days he sat alone in the hull, dreaming of Eunisia, recalling every touch, her smiling, green eyes and shining dark hair. He'd find her as soon as they arrived, he promised, and rubbed the eggplant gently between his fingers.

It was always dark beneath deck, making it difficult to see people's faces. But during storms it became pitch black, and Aaron and the eggplant were as scared as the other orphans, who hung on to anything they could as they were tossed about like corks in an empty wine barrel. They sang and prayed and cried. They called out for their mothers. They curled into fetal balls and sobbed.

There was one storm far worse than all others. It arose from a perfectly calm sea and the crew was taken by surprise, and not all of the children made it beneath the deck before it struck. Aaron had climbed high up the mast and spotted two Crusader ships heading close to a rocky island when the gale winds came out of the north and ripped the sails all around him. He hurried down as 30-foot waves rocked the boat and crashed over the sides. The crew rushed to take down what was left of the torn sails. The wind blew them closer to the other boats, but Aaron could barely see them or the rocks through stiff blankets of rain.

Lightning lit up the dark daytime skies and thunder pounded like 10,000 horses stampeding across a field of hollow bones. Aaron lashed himself to the main mast with a thick rope as waves crashed over him and the wind drove the rain through his clothes. The ship was pushed closer to shore when the horrible sound of cracking wood cut through the storm. Aaron saw two other boats caught on the jagged, steel-faced boulders lining the beach, waves crashing and pounding on the helpless vessels. The ships' hulls were beaten until they burst open and hundreds of writhing little bodies were scattered against the rocks, like tiny, fragile dolls spilled from a bucket, their desperate cries silenced when the first wave crashed over them as they vanished in the cold, dark water. Aaron was never big on prayer, but he had never seen so many die with such violence. Nature was unforgiving. He wasn't sure which god would listen to his prayers. And then he remembered Layla's favorite, Lilith, and he folded his hands and prayed those kids didn't suffer long. He prayed Eunisia was not on those boats. And he prayed Lilith would protect his Eunisia, wherever she was. Finally, he asked the eggplant to help Eunisia, and it promised to do what it could.

Unfortunately, the eggplant knew fate would determine whether Eunisia lived or died, just like fate had determined the events bringing it to Aaron, tied to the mast of this ship. It was the same fate bringing the archer together with the old midwife who planted the eggplant, and the same strange force introducing Samar to Babazini. "What were the chances?" whispered the eggplant.

"The chances of what?"

"I was just recalling the strange fates leading to our current circumstance, and I want you to understand there are many things in this world I cannot change."

"I don't expect you to work any miracles." He softly massaged the eggplant, and shed a tear for the children in those boats.

"Have you ever wondered how I became separated from Hamdan and ended up with Layla?" asked the eggplant.

"I always thought Hamdan passed you on to his son or daughter, and somehow you were passed to Layla's mother, who passed her to Layla. Isn't that right?"

"Not exactly," chuckled the eggplant. "Hamdan's son and I never shared a single thought. His name was Tahir, and he was nothing like his father. Tahir was shallow, like a puddle of urine in the desert that disappears before you walk way. Unlike his father, Tahir was tall and handsome, and he knew it. He combed his long black hair with an abalone brush, manicured his fingernails and looked for his reflection in every passing pool of water or polished stone. Tahir knew nothing of my unusual abilities. He couldn't understand why his father cherished me. Hamdan had so much gold and so many jewels, yet he wore no rings or bracelets, only a dried vegetable. Tahir imagined I was some sort of silly good luck charm.

"Hamdan loved many things in the world, but most of all he loved women," continued the eggplant. "He really, really loved women. Not just their bodies. He exalted the metaphysical concept of womanhood. Their form, function and spiritual perfection were all part of a feminine ideal Hamdan couldn't resist.

"Hamdan's appreciation for women extended to his people. He never allowed his soldiers to harm a woman, even in the midst of battle. He insisted Karmation women be treated with honor and severely punished any man who violated his wife or another woman. As a result, Karmation women had more personal freedom than any women in the Arab world, and they knew it. They could dress as they pleased, dance and sing whenever and wherever they wanted, pound drums when the moon rose over the water and smoke the hookah in the teahouse beside any man. For traditional Moslems, giving women this kind of freedom was blasphemy. But it was also one reason I'm with you today."

"What do mean?" Aaron couldn't see the connection between women's freedom and his possession of the eggplant.

"It happened one evening after Hamdan returned from battle. He and Tahir were in their private courtyard and Tahir wanted to hear every detail of the army's victory. He never saw a battle, but his father's stories always made him feel like a warrior. Hamdan obliged and recalled the final slaughter in a tone women would use to describe a day at the village market, giggling at all the wrong times. He described the Karmation's 700 horses riding through town on a moonless night, pulling men from their houses and killing them without breaking stride. No women, children or elderly were harmed, but they trapped a mosque-full of men, beheaded them all and piled their heads in a mound that nearly reached the ceiling. Hamdan said the blood and screams of those men would never leave the mosque, and some say you can still hear them to this day, as he unsuccessfully tried to hold back a bursting dam of inappropriate laughter."

Aaron pictured the bearded heads in a mound and imagined their eyes searching for their missing bodies, nostrils reaching for a heavenly scent and ears bending toward angelic choirs. The image was both revolting and perplexing to Aaron. "Why did Hamdan put the heads in a pile?"

"There's no logic in war," commented the eggplant. "It's like guessing why a camel cries in the courtyard or trying to carry quicksilver with a pitchfork. Shall I continue?"

Aaron nodded. "Yes, please. This is one of your best stories."

The eggplant loved compliments. It continued its tale of Hamdan and Tahir with more expression and a little less grumbling. "When a servant entered the courtyard and announced a magician had arrived from the West and wished to entertain them, Tahir told him he didn't invite any outsiders and told the servant to send him away. Hamdan interrupted, and asked to see the magician, then giggled and looked out the window at the red sun dipping its toes into the cool blue water stretching all the way to Arabia.

"Hamdan had a special interest in surprises, and explained to Tahir a wandering magician's tricks may offer more adventure than a restless virgin. And if they didn't like the magician, they'd throw him to the crocodiles.

"Tahir hated surprises and feeding crocodiles," explained the eggplant. "He preferred to hear the ugly battle gossip, like atrocities or booties of gilded trinkets and girls. That was Tahir's idea of a good time. Magic was nothing more than cheap tricks and misdirection. Gold and girls, on the other hand, could be squeezed, tasted and adored like Allah's most luscious creations. Tahir wanted to devour them all tonight. He knew if he had to sit through a magician's act he'd be lucky to taste the fruits of one dancer this evening. He forced a respectful smile, then ordered more tea and bread for their magic guest.

"The magician followed the servant through a dim-lit maze of corridors, up limestone stairs and into the royal courtyard where Hamdan and Tahir sat on lush wool carpets beside islands of oversized pillows. The magician had no bags and wore a loose, silk robe and pointed silk hat faded by desert sun and wind until their colors ran together in a blend of dehydrated pastels. Instead of the obligatory sandals, his goatskin boots were covered with jade beads and had metallic heels that clicked on the stones as he walked. The magician addressed Hamdan and Tahir as the great one and his young general, offered them the warmth of 1,000 fires in the desert night and the most sublime comforts of all worlds, then knelt and kissed the cold stone floor before he began staring first at Hamdan's huge feet, then at his ridiculously large nose.

"Hamdan started giggling and couldn't stop. Finally, he asked the magician who would provide these comforts?

"The magician told him he could receive the reward from anyone he wanted, and smiled politely at Hamdan, who was still chuckling through his fingers.

"When Tahir answered they wished to receive payment from the Caliph at Baghdad, the magician closed his eyes, took several slow, deep breaths, then opened his eyes and said it would be done.

"Hamdan held his breath and gazed in disbelief, then burst into piercing, staccato laughter. Parrots roosting in a kumquat tree flapped and shrieked louder and louder, until the magician glared at the birds, waved his hand slowly overhead and stopped the squawking. When I saw him quiet the birds, I knew this was no ordinary magician," added the eggplant.

"The magician looked into Hamdan's eyes and told him magic was like a restless virgin who can surprise you at any time, then winked at his host, as if they had arranged a special inside joke.

"Hamdan smirked at the coincidence and wondered if the magician had a device allowing him to hear through walls. Surely he didn't look into his mind and read his past thoughts. Still, it seemed to me this was more than coincidence," said the eggplant.

"When Hamdan asked the magician's name, he said it was Babazini the Magnificent. Hamdan laughed again and told him he was no Babazini. Ali Babazini could make vegetables speak, and he died long ago.

"The magician said he was Falukki Babazini, a descendant of Ali, but Hamdan wasn't impressed.

"Tahir was ready for a show. He wondered how the magician intended to perform with no cards, no cups and no devices whatsoever. He demanded he surprise them immediately, if he could surprise them at all, then stared at the magician as if waiting for him to quake in his jade-beaded, goatskin boots.

"Babazini asked if Tahir would like a spectacular surprise or a subtle surprise? Before he could answer, there was a sudden flash of red smoke and the magician vanished.

"Tahir stood and peered all around the courtyard looking for the magician and demanding he reappear. Hamdan grinned like a patient gambler and reminded Tahir he asked for a surprise. Still, Tahir pulled his dagger from its sheath and circled the room.

"Babazini spoke softly from the shadows, offering his apologies and assuring Tahir he wasn't roaming around the fortress. Then another burst of smoke, this time purple, filled the center of the courtyard, and the magician stepped from the cloud and stood beside Hamdan, cautiously smiling for mercy.

"Hamdan ordered Tahir to put his dagger away, then turned to Babazini and winked. Hamdan thought it was a marvelous trick and imagined being able to vanish when in the midst of battle.

"Now this wasn't magic, Aaron—it was just a cheap parlor trick," said the eggplant.

"What's the difference?"

The eggplant was surprised. "After a year with Layla, you still don't know? It's very simple, Aaron. Magic is real, not a trick. Like soap. It really can save people's lives. Tricks are just illusions and never more.

"Babazini understood the difference, and offered Hamdan and Tahir another illusion. He rose to his feet and appeared taller and wider than when he first entered the courtyard. The tattered robe once draping over him like an old curtain barely covered him now. He closed his eyes and rubbed his rippled abdomen in small clockwise circles, then parted his flesh with his fingers until drops of dark blood rolled down to his groin and he pulled a green cord from his belly. As more of the green cord became visible, they could see it was a living snake. He gave it a final jerk, and pulled the head of a six-foot cobra from the hole in his stomach. He chanted a Persian verse, gripped the cobra behind its jaws and exposed its glistening fangs. Babazini looked into the snake's mouth, whispered a few inaudible words, then thrust the cobra downward. A great cloud of red smoke rose from the floor and the cobra vanished.

"Hamdan was very pleased. He was certain this magician was a good omen. A gift from Allah, he thought and ordered the servants to bring more food and wine.

"Babazini reclined and sipped his mint-and-honey tea. Tahir's long moustache dipped into his cup and attracted a trio of flies dancing like dervish around their new feeding ground. Tahir watched the flies with increasing interest, and dipped his moustache in the sweetened tea again to attract more black, buzzing dancers.

"Hamdan smiled and tipped his wine goblet towards Babazini, who looked rather small now. He told him he understood a magician was never supposed to reveal his secrets, but if he told him how to perform the vanishing trick, he promised he'd never tell another soul.

"Babazini said he'd lose his tongue if he were to utter the first word of the secret of vanishing, but offered to give Hamdan something more valuable.

"Hamdan shifted on his pillows and cleared his throat. He'd take more than a tongue, if Babazini didn't give him the secrets he wanted. He poured more tea for the magician and asked him where he came from and what could he have that Hamdan would value?

"Babazini drank his tea in one swallow and explained he was born beyond the Red Sea in a town called Timbuktu on the edge of the Sahara Desert. His gift for Hamdan, on the other hand, came from the prophets, and it was a priceless story that would change their lives and the world forever.

"Hamdan bobbed his head and refilled his goblet. There was no story powerful enough to change Tahir's life. He rolled his eyes, clapped his hands and called for the musicians. A man with a dumbek and another with an oud appeared from the doorway, sat near the kumquat tree and started with a soft instrumental duet. Babazini hummed the melody along with the oud, throwing in a few words for the chorus.

"Hamdan recognized the tune. It was from Persia, and his mother used to sing it to him when he was a child. The magician knew it was a very old song, but decided it was better not to tell him he had first learned it from a Nubian slave. The song was laced with foul lyrics describing a young man's disappointment with women and desire for his goat. Instead, Babazini wove some psychoactive drama into the evening. He opened a small tin and offered it to Tahir. Tahir sniffed it suspiciously. It was a blend of kif and hashish and the magician claimed a mullah from Palestine had given him the mixture.

"Hamdan asked if the kif helped him tell the story, or help the listener believe the magician's words. The magician said the story lived alone and would be the same on the moon or in a camel's belly, just as your ears would hear the same words no matter where you choose to sit.

"When a servant arrived with a hookah and embers, Tahir took a wholesome pinch of the sticky mixture, placed it carefully in the center of the hookah's brass bowl, dropped a spoonful of glowing embers on top and pressed a stone to the red hot coals. Each of the men picked up one of the hookah's braided hoses and inhaled the smoke a little at a time."

Aaron remembered Stephen smoked kif and hashish during the march across France, but he had no idea how it made a person feel. "What does kif do to you?"

The eggplant happened to appreciate the effects of both kif and hashish, but knew they had varied effects on people and vegetables. Maybe it was because it was member of the plant kingdom like himself, but the eggplant felt like hashish could actually speak to it.

"There is an old saying that a bowl of kif in the morning gives a man the strength of 100 camels in the courtyard," continued the eggplant. "It brings happiness to some and scares others, but this blend made Tahir's head swirl with soft, pleasant visions as he smoked.

"Tahir clapped his hands and two young women entered with silver bowls and pitchers of water. The three men held their hands over a bowl and the women poured water from a silver pitcher over their hands. Another woman followed with dry towels, followed by another with a large woven basket filled with neatly cut chunks of dark, steaming bread. The musicians quietly played while sumptuous silver trays overflowing with roast lamb, fresh fish, rice salad, pickled mangoes, and stuffed olives were paraded into the courtyard and placed on the floor between the men. The magician thanked Allah every time another tray was presented and inhaled the sultry aromas of the spiced foods. Tahir and Hamdan sat up with big stoned grins and began to scoop the savory rice salad into their mouths with their hands before the last trays touched down, and their guest followed.

"Tahir clapped his hands again and three beautiful dancers appeared with another drummer and a flute player. The dancers were completely covered in scarves and careful not to have eye contact with any of the men. Two of the dancers were very tall, slender and young, but the third was older and shorter with a full, round figure, heavy breasts and wide hips swaying like they were circling a secret sun as she lit candles and took her place beside the musicians. Her name was Samar, and she was surprised to see the magician seated across from Hamdan.

"Samar," repeated Aaron, recalling the story Layla once told him.

The eggplant paused and asked, "Do you remember her?"

"Sure. Samar was captured by Hamdan in Persia, then became his favorite dancer."

"That's right," and the eggplant went on with the story. "Hamdan picked a long, plump piece of peppered lamb from a tray with his fingers and moved closer to Babazini. He asked why the magician had really come to Bahrain, then stuffed the entire piece of lamb into his mouth, stretched his short legs out in front of him and clapped his gigantic feet together like two huge flippers.

"Right now, Babazini wanted to do nothing more than reach out and squeeze Hamdan's nose. He wondered what kind of noise it would make. Would it honk like a goose or just sound like pressed flesh? He leaned very close to Hamdan, looked directly into his eyes and told him he risked his life to deliver this story for a great mullah. He meant no harm and asked for nothing in return.

"Hamdan heard the words, but his mind was soaring. Ten million hashish images opened their gossamer wings and Hamdan was floating outside his head, sliding along some invisible curve in space. His body was numb, but he was still in control.

101

"The music continued into the night with one drummer shifting to a slow, deliberate beat, while the other wandered through a series of rhythmic adventures and melancholy solos. The oud player accompanied with a series of rich, full chords and waited for their sound to fade before strumming another, while the flute gradually climbed an exotic scale, fell into a melodic little phrase and then floated up the scale again.

"The young, slim dancers turned in tight, spinning circles, their feet barely leaving the ground as the music played. Samar danced beside them, her red and gold scarves waving like orchids blooming in the wind, metallic bangles quivering with each suggestive motion.

"Tahir interrupted and demanded one more trick before the magician told his story. Babazini obliged and pulled a long silver nail from his pouch then showed it to his hosts. He held his left hand out before him, palm down, and pressed the point of the nail against the back of his hand until drops of blood welled up at the base of the spike. Then, he pushed the nail all the way through his hand and turned it over, so Tahir and Hamdan could see the metal shaft sticking though the center of his palm. Next, Babazini painlessly pulled the nail out and wiped the blood from his hand with the edge of his robe.

"Tahir was most impressed with this trick. He knew the secret to withstanding pain would be very useful. He couldn't imagine how so many men could suffer with deep wounds for weeks after a battle. He feared the pain he'd someday have to endure more than death itself, and silently vowed not to allow the magician to leave the fortress until he shared this secret.

"Hamdan laughed. He knew men and women who enjoyed self-inflicted pain. This was not magic. This was madness. He examined both sides of Babazini's hand closely, but could not find a hole amidst the streaks of dried blood.

"Next, the magician took the nail between his middle finger and thumb, and slowly bent it like a green twig until its ends touched. He placed the circular nail between his hands and rubbed it furiously. When he opened his hands, a hummingbird flew out and landed in the kumquat tree.

"A wide grin crossed Hamdan's face and his few remaining teeth looked more like a baby's rotten incisors than capable of a warrior's bite. He clapped for a servant and pointed to the hookah. The servant returned with embers, and after Tahir pinched more of Babazini's kif mixture into the bowl, Hamdan relaxed on his pillow, sucked on the embroidered wand and listened to the water bubbling inside the tall bronze water pipe.

"Babazini sat perfectly still with eyes closed, the drum playing softly in the background when he started his story. Do you want to hear it?"

"Yes! Please go on." Aaron was eager to hear the magician's story, and also wanted to hear more about Samar. The boys in the boat were sleeping all around him, some restless, but most were enjoying the happiest moments of their day, dreaming about a better life on the other side of this water. Aaron was wide-awake, listening to a first-hand account of a secret history, and it was wilder and stranger than any dream.

"Babazini said this was the true story of the Lost Stone, and it began when Allah gave Adam and his first wife, Lilith, a Stone carved in the heavens from a single shooting star. Lilith was Adam's equal and they quarreled day and night, until she took the Stone and left him to live on her own.

"Hamdan listened and tapped his finger on his nose. It sounded like a soft, loose-skinned drum. He told Babazini if this Lilith was truly the original wife of Adam, there would be many stories in her honor, but he'd never heard one.

"Babazini politely noted the mullahs and priests were afraid of Lilith and censored her stories along with those of Baal, Ishtar and the others. But Lilith was different. Unlike Adam and Eve, who fell out of favor with the heavenly host, Lilith was never expelled from the garden, so she kept her immortality and still walks the earth today."

"Is it true?" Aaron interrupted. "Is Lilith still alive today?"

"It depends whom you ask," replied the eggplant.

"What do you think? Is she still alive?"

The eggplant paused for a long time. It wanted to be honest with Aaron, but it also wanted to be prudent. Finally it answered, "I really don't know. At one time I thought Lilith had survived since the very beginning, but I've only been here six centuries, so I could never be certain. It doesn't seem possible, but there are many impossible things in our world."

"Like talking vegetables."

"Exactly," replied the eggplant. "Some people say the world is round and we're spinning in a great circle around the sun. Crazy, eh?"

"Very crazy."

"I even thought Layla was really Lilith," confessed the eggplant.

"Is she?"

"I really don't know. Anything is possible. Hamdan was also very curious about Lilith," continued the eggplant. "He considered some of the women he'd known and thought of a few who may be Lilith. But he was more interested in the Stone Lilith took from the Garden."

"Was that Layla's Lost Stone?"

"One and the same," affirmed the eggplant.

"The mullah who passed this story to Babazini said it came from the world's first book, called *The Book of Secrets*. Angels gave Adam *The Book of Secrets* before he died, and it contained everything that ever happened in the world—past, present and future. *The Book* accompanied Adam's body after it was embalmed, and was guarded by the eldest son of each generation of Adam's offspring, until it was passed on to Noah, who learned of the flood and how to survive it from *The Book*. After the flood, no one knows where they wound up. Some say the sons of Ishmael kept *The Book*. Some say Isaac, the son of Sarah, kept the body. They're both probably forgotten on dusty shelves in Pope's library.

"The Lost Stone stayed with Lilith and her followers for many centuries. And when Abraham rebuilt the Kabba, the angel Gabriel gave him a second sacred Stone, identical to the first. In the old story, a strange heat came from the Stone, as if it was filled with living blood, and it charged Abraham with energy. The stabbing pain in his twisted fingers instantly disappeared and his weary old body gained the strength of a virile young man. Gabriel commanded Abraham to put the Stone in the wall at the southeast corner of the Kabba, and it still resides there today.

"Babazini explained the Lost Stone—the one Lilith kept in Eden—still has the power to heal. And as long as you possess the Lost Stone, you'll never grow old.

Tahir's eyes lit up. Eternal life and unlimited power were more than he could resist.

Hamdan was confused. "And where do we find this Stone nobody can find?" he asked.

Babazini said he came to them because he learned the location of the Stone, and he was willing to share it with them."

"At what cost?" asked Hamdan.

"What is eternal life worth to you?" replied the magician.

"Do you think I'm a fool? Or do you think I'm a coward?" asked Hamdan. "Only a fool would believe your fishy story and only a coward fears death."

"Where were the dancers? Where was Samar?" asked Aaron.

"One dancer was asleep on the carpet and Samar was awake, her eyes closed and head rested on the pillow beside the magician. Hamdan sent the musicians away, but decided to let the dancers stay, and he glared at Babazini as if deciding how to kill him.

"But the magician still went on, and told Hamdan the old mullah who'd passed this story to him had asked if he'd ever heard of Hamdan Karmat. Hamdan shook his head and Tahir was on the edge of his pillow. Then the magician said the mullah had told him Hamdan Karmat's name was in *The Book of Secrets*. He told him Hamdan Karmat would find the Lost Stone and return it to Mecca.

"Hamdan was neither a thief nor an explorer—he wouldn't waste a minute looking for a Stone. Tahir, on the other hand, was ready to wake his men and begin his search for the Stone at daybreak.

"Hamdan stood and paced across the courtyard, picked up a scimitar and chopped a kumquat branch in one furious stroke, then warned the magician he could slice off his arm or his tongue just as easily. Instead of begging for his life, the magician pleaded to Hamdan, for the sake of all Karmations and Ishmaelites, to allow him to finish the story before he took his tongue.

"Hamdan glared at Babazini and relaxed his sword then told him his story was over and prayed Allah would forgive them for listening to his devil's tale. He ordered Tahir to get the magician's secrets and take his tongue, then turned nose-to-nose with the magician and told him, 'Good stories should rise and fall like empires in the endless pursuit of happiness, like armies of lovers marching to paradise—good stories can change the word,' and he left the courtyard giggling.

"Hamdan found his bed, closed his eyes and his mind soared straight to the stars. The floor vanished beneath him and the night sky opened up. A raw black meteor shot through space, rumbled, then broke into two dark, distinct Stones, both spinning like shining stars. Their dance reminded him of Samar. There was a big blue planet in the background, but he didn't recognize it. Dreams are funny that way.

"After Hamdan was in his chambers, Tahir sent the dancers jangling down the hall to the harem. Harem means forbidden and holy in Arabic, and for Samar, it was neither. She planned for this night for weeks, but not for a magician, especially one who was willing to risk his life with his story—unless he had a great deal to gain. She'd follow him later. Now, she had business with Hamdan.

"Samar left the harem and slipped into Hamdan's quarters, her dagger at her side, but it was too late. He was already stiff and cold. She pulled the sheet from his body to look for blood or a blade and found a cobra between Hamdan's legs, coiled and ready to strike again. She yanked the sheet back over Hamdan at the same instant the cobra darted at her face, caught the snake in the sheet and whipped it off of the bed. The snake escaped into the shadows and Samar turned to Hamdan's body, pulled my gold chain over his head, gave his irresistible nose a gentle squeeze, then left the fortress and waited for the night to unfold like a marvelous black flower.

"What did it feel like when you were pulled from Hamdan and slipped around a stranger's neck? Was it scary?"

"No, not scary. Very unsettling and lonely. Worrisome, too. I'd grown to like Hamdan and I didn't know much about Samar," explained the eggplant.

"What about when Layla passed you to me?"

"That was different. I knew you, in a way, and actually considered contacting you," confessed the eggplant.

"Why didn't you?"

"I thought Layla may be jealous," said the eggplant.

Aaron thought about Layla's patience and pictured her smiling face. "Was Samar related to Layla?"

"Yes. Samar was like a mother to Layla, in some ways."

"But didn't you say you've been in Layla's family for more than 200 years?"

The eggplant hesitated. "282 years. And I said Samar was like a mother, because they were very similar."

"Alright. Now what happened when they found Hamdan dead?"

"It was a complete shock to everyone—especially Tahir. The news of Hamdan's death traveled fast and people mourned his passing for weeks. They wondered who would fill his shoes, fight the battles and replenish their treasure chests? And who would protect the island? Every person on Bahrain cursed Babazini the magician. But it didn't matter. The magician needed no protection from their curses. They were only words. A real curse combined words and smells and pictures. A strand of Babazini's hair would have added extra punch to any curse. The Karmation's curses were weak and fell in little pools at their feet far from Babazini, who had already crossed the gulf on a small boat he borrowed from his host and vanished into the Arabian Desert.

"By afternoon, the Karmations noticed Samar was also missing, and surmised she had been kidnapped by the magician. After all, she was a beautiful dancer and could bring him a good price. But Samar also found her way to the mainland in a different vessel and was following the magician like a distant shadow through the nights, hoping to learn more about the powers of the Stone."

"Did she ever find him?" asked Aaron.

"Not while I was with her."

"What about the Lost Stone? Did Tahir find it? Did Samar ever get it? Who has it now?" Aaron was eager for an ending.

The eggplant made a low, disgruntled sound, as if the Lost Stone brought back bad memories. "I told you I honestly do not know," barked the eggplant. "I can tell you this for certain: Samar never stopped thinking about the Lost Stone. She was obsessed for years, even after she had a daughter. Finally, Samar removed me from her neck, gave me to her teenage daughter, left both of us alone in the streets and went off to find Babazini. We never saw or heard from her again."

*****

The five remaining ships sailed across the Mediterranean for a Moslem port in Algeria. The days and nights passed slowly, and Aaron was as eager as the eggplant to get his feet on dry land and escape the stench of the cabin, the perpetual rolling of the waves and the winds howling through the tattered grey sails. More than anything, he wanted to rush to the girls' boats as soon as he could and make sure Eunisia was safe.

Aaron and the eggplant both lit up when they heard a loud cheer from the crow's nest and land came into view. The other Crusader's ships were already anchored in the Bay of Bejaya when Aaron's ship arrived. They watched as 20 skiffs launched from a long timber dock and rowed to the side of a children's ship in the bay. Dark-skinned men with white turbans and black beards climbed on board the ship and marched the Crusaders down the rope ladders. Aaron could see their swords drawn as they hurried the boys into the skiffs, rowed them to shore and returned for more.

"This doesn't look good."

"As your elder advisor and with only your best interests in mind, I recommend you escape immediately," urged the eggplant. "These Moslems aren't here for a welcome party."

"I don't know if I can swim," confessed Aaron. The eggplant thought for a moment. "Use your black powder. All of it."

Aaron had about 10 small bombs and three large ones. He emptied the three largest into a waxed rag, which he used to keep the powder dry since the trip began, and wound the rest of his bandages around the large ball as tightly as he could. When he was done, the bomb was almost the size of his head. He packed them all into his sack and returned to the main deck.

Boys were bustling everywhere, gathering up their sparse belongings, some chattering about the Holy Land, others crying with fear for Moslem blades. The lieutenants tried to calm the boys, but the young Crusaders were preparing to fight their first battle. An older boy climbed a pile of rope and gave the order, "It's time to take arms against the infidels!" he cried. "We shall not give up this ship," and he drew a sharp wooden dagger from his belt.

Aaron took a position on a mast arm in the lower sails, his Assassin's dagger at his side, sack full of black powder bombs and flint box ready for action. The Moslems approached the ship and the boys threw anything that wasn't attached at their invaders. Ropes, empty supply boxes, cabin doors and lanterns were all hurled down on their skiffs. Aaron waited until the abductors threw new ropes up the ship's side and started climbing, then lit a small bomb and hurled it. It exploded in the air, and the attackers fell from the ropes and splashed below. Aaron threw another and they cursed him in Arabic. He remembered enough Arabic to know they called him an infidel, and he returned a few Arabic insults describing their mothers' relationship with camels. The boys cut away at the ropes, but the Arabs continued to climb until they were onboard. Aaron threw the rest of the small bombs at the Moslem boats, but it was too late and there were too many. Their swords were drawn and the boys quickly surrendered. So much for winning the Holy Land with innocence.

Aaron moved to the ship's bow with his last bomb. "Use it on the skiffs," suggested the eggplant. "Destroy their skiffs and jump overboard. It's our only chance."

"What about the other kids?"

"Their destiny is different than yours, Aaron Sloopshire."

Aaron lit the big bomb and tossed it into the center of the attacker's boats. It exploded with a huge blast splintering the nearest skiffs, sending chunks of burning wood hurtling through the air and ripping a hole in the side of his own vessel, stunning everyone on the ship. They stopped fighting as the sound echoed across the water, their ears rang and they feared some god or demon had intervened. A few Moslems jumped overboard, but enough remained to corral the frightened boys.

The ship was taking water and flames grew up the side where the skiffs were still burning. Aaron saw chunks of charred wood floating away, and decided to jump. "Swallow me," said the eggplant.

"What?" Aaron must've misunderstood.

"You didn't misunderstand anything. Take me from the chain around your neck and swallow me. I'm not kidding here. Layla swallowed me once and it was quite interesting. It's the only way I'll be safe in the water and you won't lose me. Swallow me now, before you jump." Aaron popped the little vegetable in his mouth and swallowed it down with a mouthful of water. Then he tied his goatskin sack around his waist and jumped from the bow of the ship, dog-paddled to shore and hid in the brush. The Moslems saw him, but he was only one boy. They had their hands full with a burning ship filled with 700 others.

Aaron stayed in the brush and watched the young Crusaders paraded from ships and put in chains when they reached the shore. Years later, Aaron learned the older boys were either sold to the Governor of Alexandria in Egypt, where they became field slaves and servants, and the youngest boys went to the Old Man of the Mountain in Persia, while many of the girls were sold on the slave market in Baghdad.

It took the young Crusaders nine months to travel from Paris to Algeria. Thousands of children had died and Aaron could only hope Eunisia was not among them. Thousands more were sold into slavery and the eggplant, floating down to the first stages of Aaron's digestive tract, wondered if it all boiled down to France dumping its orphans on the African slave market. Whatever the reasons, the Children's Crusade was over and Aaron's search for Eunisia was just beginning.

5. Arabian Odyssey

The Crusaders' ships left the bay and Aaron stayed in Bejaya for two more days, watching for a sign of Eunisia or any other European girl, wandering from tent-to-tent, using his broken Arabic to ask merchants about children taken from ships, but no one had seen anything unusual.

"There are always children taken from ships," replied a silk merchant, and rubbed his dark, calloused hand across a long roll of bright red silk. It made a soft, whistling sound irritating Aaron, but seemed to attract other customers, who knew such music could only be produced from the finest silk.

Aaron left the marketplace each evening with a broken heart and a little less hope for a reunion with Eunisia. He watched camels move in long lines in and out of the city, some heading along the coast to Algiers, others into the desert and he wished Eunisia was on one of them, safe and alive. More than never seeing her again, Aaron feared she was dead.

The eggplant had already given up hope. "I know it sounds cold Aaron, but you have to face the facts. If she didn't die in the storm, she's probably been sold into slavery. Now let's move on. Morocco is beautiful this time of year."

Aaron wouldn't listen. She could be dead, but until he knew for sure, he had to look for her. After all, he left Layla's side to follow Eunisia. He already deserted one good friend, and he didn't want to lose another.

The eggplant knew exactly how he felt. It lost more than its share of best friends over the years—a sad chapter in its destiny—and it learned to accept its persistent loss as inevitable as death is for others, but that didn't make it any easier.

The next day, Aaron walked through the market to the camel stables and spotted a long line of children moving towards a cluster of makeshift tents. He chased after them, looking all around as he dashed through thin walkways and ran around tents until he came face to face with a man leading the line of children, who were all dressed in grey tunics with hoods covering their heads. When one of the children turned to him he saw they were girls.

"Eunisia! Eunisia is that you?" Aaron tried to squeeze by, but the man knocked him to the ground, pulled a long dagger from his djellaba and held it to Aaron's throat. Other men were hustling the children away when Aaron turned and caught a glimpse of a dark-haired girl who might have been Eunisia.

"Don't say a word," advised the eggplant, and a group of local children ran from their tents with their mothers to investigate the crazy European boy. The man withdrew his knife from Aaron's throat, warned him to stay away in clear Arabic, and he vanished between the tents.

"Was that her? It had to be her!" Aaron watched for a glimpse of the Arab, already eager to follow them and rescue Eunisia.

"I don't know, Aaron. It doesn't sound like you're too sure," replied the eggplant, doubtful it could've been Eunisia. "There were only a handful of girls. So many girls have dark hair. They might not have been European," continued the eggplant.

"But it's possible. It could've been Eunisia and she could be heading toward a caravan right now." Aaron hustled to the camel stables where he waited for the girls until nightfall, but they never arrived. The next morning, a red-haired boy was standing beside a twisted wooden fence, feeding a long sugar cane stalk to an old grey camel. Aaron learned he was from Marseilles, his father traded camels for a wealthy man in Algiers and the boy knew

114

these stables well. Most important, the boy was certain he'd seen the European girls leave the night before with a long caravan.

"Where were they going?" Aaron was already calculating how he'd follow.

"East," said the boy, and pointed towards the hills and the desert beyond. Aaron asked him for help finding a caravan headed east and by nightfall, Aaron was riding his first camel into the desert.

There were 23 camels in Aaron's caravan, all laden with rough, sun-faded wool sacks bulging with aromatic spices, fresh-spun tunics, Spanish leather, Moroccan hashish, tin pots and pans, skins of water and other basic provisions for the journey back to Persia. Several men walked beside the beasts, and Aaron was with one of two riders at the rear of the procession. All the men wore only loose djellabas and thin gutrahs with braided bands to protect their heads from the sun and sand. The riders laughed and spoke Farsi, the language of Persia, which Aaron had never heard spoken by anyone, except himself. He could read and write a little Farsi, but this was different. The eggplant translated as best it could, although its current circumstances inside Aaron's curvy small intestines didn't make it any easier.

The caravan moved slowly through the valley and turned across a wide, desolate landscape strewn with stones. The moon was rising and Aaron could see the ghost-like outlines of sand dunes ahead. He wondered where all this sand came from.

"There's an Arab legend that says the whole Earth was once a beautiful green garden," said the eggplant. "Men and women were honest and the word 'lie' didn't exist. The first lie was a small one, but still Allah noticed it and called everyone together and warned every time they told a lie, he'd put a grain of sand into the world. People didn't think much of it. After all, a grain of sand was next to nothing. But the lies continue and the deserts are still growing."

*****

They traveled through the night, followed the Hoggar route along dune's ridges and watched the moon cross the brilliant night sky. Aaron was cold. His butt ached from bouncing on the camel's back and he had to shift his weight and struggle to keep his legs from falling asleep. Sometimes the camel drivers would shout a few quick phrases, but mostly there was silence. The eggplant knew they were discussing who would take Aaron into the dunes first, and it intended to interfere. Both men had slept with their share of boys, and when they were boys they slept with many men. The eggplant witnessed its share of deflowering, and listened closely as Mohammed cautioned the boy may be too thin and they may hurt him. Yosef said they might have to cut his throat if he's hurt, and finally they agreed he might be worth more if they kept him alive and sold him.

Except for the camels, the desert had its own vacant aroma, like the inside of bones or an empty jar of salt. But the odors floating on a desert breeze were far more vivid and intense than city, sea or forest smells. They were older and more refined. Everything was closer to bare existence in the desert than elsewhere. Right now, the desert smelled like a baked, white, stone when the wind whistles across its curved surface.

The eggplant told Aaron stories of Layla as the sun climbed over the sand. They were exciting and amazing and unbelievable. It didn't matter if they were true or partly true or completely false, most of them made Aaron wonder if Layla was greater than he imagined.

"If Layla is so wise, then why is it taking her so long to find the Stone?"

"You're assuming she hasn't found it yet," cautioned the eggplant. "And it's more than a Stone she's after. The Stone was in the original paradise and it's been used to transform the world more than once. Baal possessed the same Stone to commune with elementals and become the goddess of all nature. Ishtar used it to explore legendary love, war and sex. The Stone helped Isis bring Osiris back from the dead," explained the eggplant. "Lilith wants to bring the Stone back to Eden, and she'll probably change the world when she does."

Aaron imagined what it might have been like if he stayed with Layla. Perhaps he'd still be on a camel's back, chasing mythic dreams across the dunes. Life was strange.

"And getting stranger," added the eggplant.

*****

When the sun was almost overhead, flooding the world with vast, pure equatorial heat and light, the dunes flattened and what first appeared as a bump in the thin, grey liquid line on the horizon turned into an island of palm trees. It was their first oasis. There were no people, except for their caravan. The anemic, pale palms were so limp and sparse they offered almost no shade. The sun seemed to occupy the entire sky like a solid dome of intense light. The camels dropped to their knees, grunting and spitting, then fell to their bellies, sending a cloud of dust into the super-heated air and making a spot of shade for sleeping. Aaron and the riders went to the well and peered over its low stone sides. They hoisted up the bucket and tasted the water. It was warm and sweet. Aaron sat against a palm trunk and washed his hands out of sight as the servants pulled rugs and provisions from the bundles, then started a small fire with fallen palms and boiled water for tea. They all sat on thin, faded wool rugs for a meal of dried goat meat, dates and biscuits. The meat was black, tough as tree bark, and more heavily salted and spiced than anything

Aaron ever tasted. There were oily black peppercorns pounded into the meat making his tongue feel like he'd eaten poison, and he scrambled for the water bucket. One of the camel drivers laughed at Aaron, then explained he should eat a sweet date after chewing the meat, which instantly cooled his mouth with a moist, sweet flavor that rinsed away the salt and spices. The biscuits looked, tasted, smelled and bounced like rocks when they were thrown against the ground. Nevertheless, the men all broke the bread with their teeth and managed to eat the biscuits every day. After the meal they spread their rugs in the camel's small shadows and slept through the rest of the afternoon's heat and incessant flies.

Aaron soon understood why Arabs hold camels in the highest esteem. They're much more than transportation. They're shade-makers and a source of hair for tents, clothes and carpets. They're waterfinders, their meat and milk tasted great and their dung made excellent fires for cooking. They're an all-in-one desert caravan survival kit. Aaron listened to the Arabs talk for hours about their camel's fine colored hair, elegant looks and Herculean strength. He could see they weren't exaggerating.

The camel drivers awoke and introduced themselves as Mohammed and Yosef, brothers from Persia. The eggplant cautioned Aaron, but the boy bowed to the men and said, "Aaron Sloopshire," and the men tried to repeat the name, but ended up calling him "Sloopy," which was close enough. Aaron straightened his gutrah on his head so the white fabric flowed down his back and adjusted the long, double-coiled black cord around his forehead until it was snug. Mohammed gave it a final slant to one side and slapped him on the back. The drivers smiled with approval. "This desert garb suits you well," noted the eggplant. Aaron looked like a real Arab.

Mohammed pulled the reins attached to a ring in the camel's nose and the noble beast begrudgingly rose to its knees with a gurgling snort and a long moan. The drivers climbed aboard, and the caravan plodded into the transitive nightfall of endless dunes. Aaron pulled the gutrah over his face so only his eyes were exposed through a gap in the cloth, making him indistinguishable from the others in the caravan.

And so the days and nights continued in much the same way until the dunes all began to look alike and Aaron wondered if they were making any progress. He wasn't even certain how long they'd been gone. The eggplant, which had been resurrected from his bowels and now sparkled beneath Aaron's djellaba, had temporarily lost its sense of time. The digestive experience was so deeply spiritual it gave the diminutive vegetable a powerful psychic hangover. It grumbled now and then, lost between a deep existential crisis and marvelous aesthetic realization that beauty is truly absolute, and as it continued wrestling with a resolution to its potentially tragic dilemma, the vegetable didn't speak for days.

The monotony finally broke when they left the dunes for a road leading through a dead, stony expanse to a ridge where they could see small fires in the valley below. They made their camp and walked into a village later that morning. There were open markets on either side of a street, tents scattered across the outskirts, and a few hundred baked mud and stone huts built against a steep hillside in rows of thin alleys. Aaron looked everywhere for a sign of his fellow Crusaders. He scoured the streets, peaked into silent tents and asked children and old men if they'd seen the French girls. Then a surly man selling dates and olives said he'd seen a caravan with French girls two days earlier. They were heading east, he said, on the Hoggar route. Aaron was elated. He knew Eunisia was one of them.

When Aaron returned to his caravan, the drivers were engaged in a loud argument. Aaron couldn't understand the dialect, but the eggplant translated. Mohammed wanted to sell the boy or trade him to a street merchant. Yosef wanted to keep the boy until they returned to Persia, and sell him there. The argument continued over the afternoon meal and Aaron and the eggplant agreed it was time for them to find a new caravan. He stood and walked away, hoping they wouldn't notice. But Mohammed grabbed Aaron, threw him to the ground behind a tent, jumped atop the boy and tried to pin his shoulders down with his knees. Aaron wrestled away and fell through the side of the tent, ripping a wide hole in the material and waking a sleeping baby and its mother inside. Soon their screams and cries had everyone outside their tents, looking for the source of the commotion. Mohammed cursed and chased Aaron through the close-sided alleys dividing the tents from rows of clay huts. Aaron dodged into a low, rough-hewn entrance and covered himself with blankets.

"Don't move," advised the eggplant. "Don't even blink your eyes." The sand floor was soft and smelled like rose oil. Aaron imagined Eunisia lying beside him on the scented floor. He closed his eyes and heard Mohammed's footsteps shuffling outside the hut. When he peeked from under the blankets he saw drums, flutes and stringed gourds with long necks piled around him. Rich burgundy, bright blue and shiny yellow, bespangled costumes were stacked on the dirt floor in the corner, leaving only a small circle open in the center of the hut. Aaron consulted the eggplant, agreed he might be able to elude Mohammed and Yosef if he wore a disguise, and these costumes were perfect. He removed his djellaba and gutrah and slipped into one of the costumes—a bright violet and yellow dress with shiny coins and shells fastened in long horizontal lines across the chest and around the waist. He pulled the dress over his head as quietly as he could, but it still jangled no matter how slowly he moved. The bottom of the dress dragged along the ground, so Aaron took a long, tasseled belt from another pile, tied it twice around his waist, and doubled the dress material into the belt until it hung to his ankles. He found a bright red gutrah for his head and a checkered red-and-white scarf he wrapped loosely around his neck. He scrapped his old, rotten leather boots for plain, open-toed sandals. Everything he wore carried the scent of distant roses mingling with his own baked perspiration and camel hair cologne.

Aaron left the hut and retraced his steps down the alley. He jangled and shimmered his way to the edge of the village in his purple dress, bought hard biscuits at the market and was surrounded by children pointing and chuckling at his costume. He smiled and nodded, then walked to a spot of shade beneath a struggling duet of palm trees with a good view of the route east, where the caravans would soon be heading. The kids followed him, laughing all the way, then left him alone when he sat down and stroked his friend, the eggplant. He gazed over the lonely desert, watched the tops of dunes turn red under the setting sun and the eggplant reminded him the desert would swallow them both in the blink of a jackal's eye.

It wasn't long before the first travelers appeared. There were only three camels with one Arab driver and two men dressed in knight's mesh with white gutrahs. Aaron sashayed out to the threesome in his noisy dress with his goatskin sack under his arm. "Do you have room for a boy who carries his own food and water?"

"You don't look like an Arab. Where are you from?" asked the red-bearded man with a mesh breastplate.

Aaron stared at the knight, not certain if this was the same knight who had saved him from the smith almost four years ago.

"Are you a non-existent knight?"

"Excuse me?" said the knight.

"What?" echoed the eggplant.

"I'm sorry," apologized Aaron. "I thought you might be…"

"Are you mad? What gives you the impression I don't exist? And why are you wearing a dress?"

The eggplant was eager to hear this one.

"I mean no harm. I'm from England and I knew a non-existent knight once, before we traveled across the sea with the Children's Crusade."

"What do you mean, we?" asked the knight. "Are there more of you?"

"Let the poor soul come aboard," called the other knight. "He's been through hell already, by the looks of him," he grimaced, and offered Aaron a place with the Arab driver. The driver helped Aaron up on the camel's back, and grinned at the knight's crude jokes as they bobbed into the desert night.

"Are you headed to the Holy Land?" asked Aaron.

"We're going to Persia," answered the knight. "And why are you crossing this forsaken desert?"

"I'm looking for a girl who came from France with the Crusade. She left with a caravan and I'm afraid she's been kidnapped."

"Oh-ho-ho! A mission of love! How sweet in this sour, stinking desert," chided the knight.

"And tragic," added the other. "She's probably sold into slavery and sleeping with a silk merchant on the coast."

"Doomed," they agreed.

The eggplant could feel Aaron's heart sink. "They don't know anything," it whispered. "And if they're right, then she's better off than us, stuck on camels, drifting across this waste land, sleeping with beasts in the sand."

Aaron said nothing, but knew the eggplant was right. Eunisia was not doomed. Not as long as he was searching for her.

The village appeared small and bleak behind them. Black tents dotted its rim like dead insects. The clay huts were clustered like fleas on the smooth skin of the desert. He imagined Mohammed and Yosef crossing paths with a woman looking for her purple dress, leaned back on a bundle heaped behind him and let the camel's even, rolling, boat-like motion put him to sleep.

Aaron was awakened by a battalion of flies circling his head, landing on his nose, lips and in the corners of his eyes. He brushed them away again and again, but there were thousands of them. Then the caravan stopped. Both knights were standing on the side of a steep dune. It was daybreak, and the sun was poking its blazing skullcap into view. He looked ahead, but saw no village or oasis. The knights started up from the side of the dune and Aaron saw two children in their arms, and he ran to meet them. They laid the small bodies in the sand and Aaron saw they were European girls who appeared almost dead. Both younger than him—maybe 10- or 12-years-old, their lips blistered and their eyelids sticky with thick green crust.

"Muyya! Water!" cried Aaron, and the Arab driver brought him a water skin. The girl's clothes were ripped and they had scrapes and bruises over half of their frail bodies. Aaron went to work cleaning their eyes and dabbing water across their lips. They were too weak to raise their own heads, so Aaron lifted them one at a time and poured little pools of water into their parched mouths.

"You look like you've done this before," remarked one of the knights.

"I've helped the sick in the past. I have no choice."

"What do you mean?" asked the knight.

"I can't sit and watch people suffer. I have to help. It's a knightly duty, isn't it?"

The knight said nothing and strode back to the others.

Behind him, the camel driver was arguing with the other knight about the girls. The knight didn't think the girls could be saved, so he wanted to leave them to die. "They're not going to live and there's nothing we can do for them," insisted the knight. The Arab thought the girls would bring a good price in Cairo.

"You can't leave these girls and you're not going to sell them," objected Aaron. "The girls can take my place on the camel. I'll walk and feed them from my rations."

The driver agreed and the knight told Aaron to bring the girls. He put hard biscuits in each of their little hands, ripped long sheets of purple and yellow fabric from his dress, wrapped their heads and necks to protect them from the sun and flies, then boosted them behind the driver on the camel's back.

Aaron struggled with each step in the hot sand, trying to keep up with caravan for hours until he gradually fell behind. He walked head down, eyes on the prints of the camel's hooves in the sand as the caravan sailed ahead and the sun was high above. When the knights made their camp, Aaron finally caught up by the time they finished tea. He helped the girls down and gave them most of his water, putting a few drops at a time between their blistered lips.

"Merci," said the oldest girl, and the younger one forced a smile.

"Don't worry, I'll stay here beside you and take care of you both. But you must eat," and he broke stony crumbs from a biscuit and fed morsels to each of them until it was gone.

The girls slept all day and were able to sit up and talk to Aaron by the evening meal. They were sisters named Natalie and Donatelle, who'd joined the Crusade in France.

"The girls on our ship were divided as soon as our ship arrived on land, some went with men on camels, others on boats," said Natalie. "We walked beside the camels, and the girls who rode with the men were treated very badly whenever we made camp."

"Some were killed right in front of us," added Donatelle. "We knew them."

"We never had enough food or water, and were too weak to keep up with the others, so they left us to die," said Natalie.

Did you ever hear of a French girl, a bit older than you, named Eunisia? She has long black hair..."

"There were lot of girls who looked like that, but I never heard of Eunisia." The girls were certain.

Two days later, when they arrived at the next oasis, Natalie and Donatelle took their meal with Aaron, away from the knights and driver. Aaron's biscuits were gone, so the three of them ate dates from one plate and talked about their failed Crusade as if it was a game they'd lost. Then Aaron heard the knights talking about selling him and the girls to the next caravan. They agreed they deserved some payment for their hospitality, then laughed like feral cats that could bite any time. Aaron wasn't going to let them sell him or the girls. Aaron's dagger may be enough to stop one man, but both would overpower him in no time. He opened his goatskin sack and looked at the little bottle of mushroom tincture.

"Are you thinking what I'm thinking?" asked the eggplant.

*****

There were other caravans at this oasis, including a band of dancers and musicians. The knights ignored the music until the dancers filed out of their tent and began weaving around the fire. They looked strange, too large to be in their girlish costumes. Then it struck Aaron: they weren't girls. These were men and boys dressed like exotic female dancers. He could see their close-shaved faces and thick makeup in the firelight. Their costumes were bright with stuffed bras and exposed bellies. The dancer's thick, hairy wrists and ankles were loaded with bracelets and more bangles, and the youngest boys wore big, silver earrings and tall purple turbans.

The elder dancers formed a semi-circle around the fire and took turns stepping forward to mimic lewd acts, then the others joined in one-by-one, adding their own acrobatic, licentious gestures until they were all engaged in a wild orgy of moving, tangled taboos. Some of the elders in the audience scorned them between tokes on their kif pipes. A group of camel drivers dressed in red burnooses watched the boys intently, their rugged, bearded faces reflecting the fire blazing before the pale dancers.

125

Then Aaron noticed one of the young cross-dressers staring at him for an entire dance.

"I think he likes you," said Donatelle.

"I think he likes your dress," corrected the eggplant.

"I think it may belong to him," and Aaron covered the purple dress with a burnoose and moved into the shadows, behind the girls.

The knights had never seen such strange men. The driver was explaining the attraction of these desert performers when a hush fell over the oasis, the music stopped and everyone heard barking hounds coming towards the fire. It was Wahhabi missionaries, the equivalent of Moslem police, and they were after the dancers, who ran from the fire, tossed their pots, pans, carpets, and provisions into camel hair sacks and scattered into the desert. Everyone at the oasis was on their feet, watching the Wahhabi's charge after the effeminate dancers. The knights and driver moved closer for a better look and Aaron slipped over to their blanket, added a giant dose of the mushroom tincture to their teapots and made his way quietly back to the girls. After the dancers escaped, the Wahhabis moved on and the commotion ended, the knights returned to their blanket, filled their cups and sipped tea while Aaron and the girls waited by the well.

One of the knights grumbled, then sat up and walked straight to Aaron and the girls. "What are you three plotting over here? If you're making any trouble, you'll be very sorry!"

"No! Oh no," corrected Aaron. "I was just telling the girls how a non-existent knight once saved my life."

"What?" asked the knight, whose teeth suddenly felt like they didn't belong in his mouth. "Of course he was non-existent. All of the knights I know exist and are either too drunk or too busy to save a scab like you."

The eggplant started chortling softly at first then muffled his voice before he broke out in uproarious, shiny-skinned, deep-purple laughter making Aaron laugh out loud, too. Then the knight started laughing with a faraway, glazed look in his eyes while the other two men sat still and silent as stones. The first knight's eyes remained transfixed on some distant vision of sapphire camel droppings covering strawberry sand dunes, while the Arab camel driver watched in awe as 10,000 insects moved across his expanding universe, eclipsed the entire sky and kept closing in on him until he ran into the dunes, thrashing his arms in the air as if chasing away flies. The knight who was beside the driver felt like a quivering bag of flesh in the dwindling daylight, babbling about more freedom as he tore away his mesh breastplate, stripped naked and wandered off, into the night of a million shining teeth. The laughing knight followed close behind, but now his laughter sounded more like the cries of a man being chased, until he too disappeared.

Aaron and the eggplant said nothing, but watched and listened in the direction of the knights, even when they had vanished and their cries were too distant to be heard. When they were sure the knights and driver were far away, Aaron and the girls tossed a few provisions into sacks, climbed aboard the lead camel, and continued east, following the eggplant's directions. When Aaron opened the camel's bags, he found three burnooses along with a half-dozen full water skins and almost a full pound of dried goat meat.

"All we'll need to cross the desert." There was something else beneath the food and water. He felt deep in the rough-sided sack and pulled out a wooden box. He opened the top and found it packed with snowy white bars of what appeared to be soap. "Soap in the desert?"

"Strange cargo for two knights," commented the eggplant.

"What is soap?" asked Donatelle and Natalie.

A few hours later a young male dancer returned to the oasis on foot. He wore a dark burnoose over his tattered lace dress as he stomped from camp to camp, looking for the boy with his new purple dress. His mother made that dress for him from material she'd bought in Damascus. He'd only worn it once. Finally, he spotted a fire in the desert and ran to it. There were two nearly naked men staring into the flames, silent and unmoved by the dancer's presence.

"I'm looking for a boy wearing a purple dress."

Both men turned at once, and each saw a different figure asking the question. For one knight, still wearing only a codpiece and covered with sweat, the boy appeared as a six-headed, furry squirrel. But the other knight was shivering violently, watching salamanders crawl across the landscape, and barely able to speak. "We know the b-b-boy. He's a s-s-sorcerer."

"Sloopy," sobbed the cod-pieced knight. "Let him go."

"But he stole my favorite dress!" demanded the young Arab dancer.

"You're a b-b-boy, right? You don't need a d-d-dress," advised the shivering knight, and returned to watching salamanders in the fire.

*****

Aaron and the girls traveled around the clock for the first two days, taking turns sleeping as the camel bobbed eastward, leaving their foes far behind. They were babes in a vast, insatiable desert, on a route often disappearing into blank, open landscapes with no reference points beyond the dunes. They depended almost entirely on their camel's instinct and this camel was prone to daydreams. He was part of a long line of great camels beginning with his ancestor, Doormatmaker, winner of the Arabian camel wrestling crown for 10 solid years back in the early 10th century. Caliphs and amirs bred Doormatmaker's proud lineage ever since, but this descendant wouldn't have lasted long in the ring, and without a good driver, could easily be lost in the desert.

Aaron knew they were off course. Instead of following the caravan routes southeast to Cairo, they followed the sunrise, and headed northeast, missing the oasis at Al Jaghbub and loping their way into the treacherous Sand Sea of Calanscio.

Days burned past until Aaron lost count. The bread and dried meat were almost gone and there was only one skin of water left—enough for a few days at best. He still thought about Eunisia, but now he was more worried about Natalie and Donatelle. They looked stronger, with their blisters almost healed and faces relatively clean.

The eggplant knew Aaron and the girls needed more food and water, and it hoped an idea would arrive soon. As a former water-loving vegetable raised on the edge of a desert, it still remembered the dry, empty, light-bodied feeling when its leaves withered from the heat and its roots stretched in the baked soil—and there was nothing more grand and delightful than cool rain splashing against its smooth skin, washing away the dust and leaving it shiny. The desert built the eggplant's character and the little vegetable cherished every memory.

Aaron and the girls slept for a few hours during the hottest part of the day, then rode through the evening and the entire night, taking only a few breaks to rest the camels. They didn't catch up to any slow-moving caravans, come upon an oasis or see fires in the night. Everything around them seemed the same, day after day. Same mirrored sky. Same scorching sun. Same sound of camel farting and plodding. Same sad, ivory scent of emptiness.

"Are we dead?" asked Donatelle as they shared the last of the water. They were sitting atop a tall dune and could see nothing but more dunes in every direction.

"Do you feel dead?" Aaron had to ask, knowing that in the middle of this terminal landscape, it was a good question.

"I can't tell because I don't know what it's like to be dead, but it might be like this. Just nothing," Donatelle shrugged.

"Death is much different—and much luckier," guessed the eggplant.

Aaron hoped the eggplant was right, but he chose a different answer for Donatelle. "Whenever I'm not sure, I listen for my heartbeat. The pounding inside me says I'm alive in this world and even though we're in a dead place, we'll survive. We'll find something soon, or something will find us."

Something took the form of a humming dark cloud on the horizon. They watched as it grew darker, stretched across the dunes and started to roar like steady, rolling thunder.

"What do you think it is, Aaron?" Donatelle gazed at the cloud, still faraway but getting louder.

"I don't know. Some kind of storm, I suppose."

The eggplant confirmed it was a sandstorm. "As long as we don't get buried, we'll be alright," advised the vegetable.

Aaron pulled three heavy burnooses from the pack and the wind really started to blow—his dress's bangles rang louder and louder and grains of sand pricked their faces like tiny darts.

"Put these on, pull up the hoods and cover your faces with the gutrahs." Aaron handed each a burnoose and they headed southeast, away from the howling sandstorm raging at their backs. Soon the sand was whipping through the air like swarms of sharp-toothed flies. The camel lowered its head and moved forward, even though it couldn't see a thing. The sand penetrated the fabric of their gutrahs and stung the backs of their necks and cheeks. The three were huddled atop the camel, Donatelle's head buried in her thick burnoose, Aaron and Natalie shielding their heads with their arms, when the camel suddenly stopped, dropped to its knees and they tumbled down to the sand. The camel raised its head, groaned at the screeching winds as if conceding victory to the sand gods, closed its heavy eyelids and rolled on its side. Aaron and the girls crouched beside the beast and moved close to its bristly, bony shoulder. The camel's heart was pounding hard and its warm, wild smell filled their nostrils like a protective potion. Away from the stinging sand, in the shelter of this magnificent beast, they listened to their hearts beat.

The sandstorm whirled through the sky, so loud they could barely hear each other, and it blocked the sun and stars all day and night. They shared the last bread crumbs, and then the girls slept while Aaron watched the sand blow in huge drifts nearly covering them until he pushed the mounds away from the camel and woke the girls to pull them out before it covered their shoulders. When it finally died down and they could see the stars, Aaron felt like the desert was very different—like the whole world had shifted around him.

*****

The sun came up and Aaron and the girls found themselves at the bottom of a valley between two long, steep-sloped, towering sand dunes. The camel was half-buried when Aaron found the reins and gently tugged them until the camel grunted to its knees and the three riders climbed atop and continued east, toward the red sun before them.

After the windstorm, the sands coughed up boulders that once provided shade for sunbaked travelers, blankets from caravans swallowed by the sand and bones of every size and shape. Identifying the bones was the trio's favorite pastime. It worked best with skulls. The dogs and camels were easy, but there were several skulls that may have been human, although they thought some must be monkeys. They saw more skulls in one morning than they'd seen in all their weeks in the desert, reminding Aaron and the eggplant how easily their skulls could be amongst the desert's booty.

The valley twisted like a long snake through the empty dunes with changing winds etching new patterns across the sand.

Aaron looked closely, hoping to recognize some letters, a word or maybe a fresh-carved message. The patterns were too precise, too symmetrical to be random. They looked like ancient Sumerian letters, but neither he nor the eggplant could be certain.

"Look, there's a man on top of the dune." Natalie and Donatelle pointed to a high ridge beside them, where a robed figure disappeared as soon as Aaron looked up, but he caught the scent of something sweet on the wind, like incense. They saw nothing for the next few hours, not even a single bone. Then frankincense filled the air and a half-buried, small stone building appeared directly ahead, right where the walls of the valley met to form a 100-foot sand wall blocking their route.

They rode to the front door and looked through the windows still visible above the drifted sand banks. A voice called down from the roof. "Hello, my young visitors." It was woman wearing a pure white robe and speaking very slowly in an Arabic dialect familiar to Aaron.

"Sounds like she's Egyptian," offered the eggplant, feeling excited by the familiar inflections in her voice.

"We all speak French," explained Aaron, and she began again, in French, "Bonjour, my friends. The storm must have blown you far from your route." She assessed their small, hungry frames, the blisters almost healed on the girls' faces and, of course, Aaron's purple dress jangling every time he moved.

"We lost the trail days ago." Aaron looked around as he spoke and saw what appeared to be a well inside the small building.

"Maybe weeks," added Donatelle.

"And we've no more food or water," Natalie sobbed. The sight of this woman speaking so gently, like an angel or fairy godmother, was too much for Natalie. She broke down and cried her eyes out. Donatelle tried to comfort her, but she too began wailing. The woman turned from the girls, gazed directly into Aaron's eyes and he froze with fear.

"What's wrong," asked the eggplant, but Aaron didn't answer. Not much more than half of her face was exposed, yet her tall, bird-like frame and dark, tenacious eyes looked down on Aaron and held him like the King's entire army was scrutinizing him. As soon as she looked away, he felt at ease again.

"It's all right to cry, girls. I've spilled many tears in these sands. The desert can make you cry like no other place. But it will also dry your tears faster. Come, help me clear sand from the door and I'll get water from the well," and the woman descended from the roof and they all shoveled sand from the door with their hands.

"Where are we?" Natalie was still sobbing.

"In Egypt's Western Desert."

"What are you doing here?"

"I was about to ask the three of you the same question. I'm Mina, a follower of St. Anthony, an Egyptian who lived 1,000 years ago. He was one of the first Christian monks and a Coptic, like myself.

"I've lived alone in this little shrine for almost three years. You're my first visitors, outside of a few lost camels who found my doorstep and filled my food jars." A mountain of emotion was quaking just under her calm, cool surface. The magnitude of this moment completely escaped Aaron and the girls. They couldn't understand what it was like to sit alone in the desert, day after day, nobody to share her water or listen to her imaginary visions, no passionate touches or heated arguments, nobody to ask if her hallucinations were real—just sand, sun and God, the holiest of Western Desert trinities. They had no idea what it felt like to see other human beings and speak to them after years of silence. They didn't know how they made her heart sail when they spoke to her. She had become accustomed to the voices of the wind and sand and was enraptured by the blood-and-bones in their voices. For the first time in quite a while, she was certain she was alive.

133

*****

Mina grew up in Egypt and retreated to the desert as a teenager, about the same age as Aaron. She came from a family of merchants who sold or traded camels from one end of the Nile Valley to the other. She was raised with fine clothes and jewelry, but that wasn't enough. She had a hungry soul no jewels, silk or money could satisfy.

One day, she met a Coptic monk in Cairo who explained the mystic secrets of the cross. She embraced the teachings like a long lost love, but was afraid her devout Moslem father may find out about her belief and punish her. At their next meeting, the monk told her the story of St. Anthony.

When Anthony was 18-years-old his parents died, leaving him as the guardian of his younger sister. Anthony sold 300 acres of fertile land his parents left him and gave most of the money to the poor, keeping only a little for his sister. His sister moved into a community of virgins, and Anthony took shelter in an abandoned tomb carved in the side of a mountain. He fought off the temptations of the flesh and demon's attacks for the next 20 years by working and praying. He'd stack rocks in mile-long, winding walls dividing nowhere from elsewhere, swept his cave 10 times a day, ate insects and berries and prayed for a sign from God.

His reputation attracted a modest following, some who even settled near him and copied his hermitic lifestyle. But solitude isn't quite the same when the neighborhood gets crowded, so he left the desert to visit Alexandria, where he found Didymus, a wise man who'd recently lost his eyesight. Anthony admired the blind man's legendary wisdom and asked, "You don't regret the loss of your eyes, do you?"

When Didymus admitted he truly missed his sight, and couldn't understand why God did this to him. Anthony was shocked.

"You should be happy to be wise! You have a gift of wisdom worthy of saints and apostles, yet you're unhappy? I would trade my eyes, ears and nose for your wisdom." After he finished scolding Didymus, he returned to the desert alone, like a fish returns to the stream, and remained there until he died alone and was buried in a place that was never revealed.

Mina returned home with visions of St. Anthony wandering through her head. She wanted to be as strong as him, to be grateful for her gifts and overlook her troubles. She wanted to follow St. Anthony and she was ready, but her father was waiting for her at the door when she returned. He'd arranged for her marriage to a wealthy silk merchant, and she was supposed to meet her new husband the next day. Instead, Mina left her family that night and wandered in the desert for almost a year before she found the shrine. Mina believed she'd found St. Anthony's secret grave and vowed to stay there to work and pray. She prayed for strength, redemption and an end to human suffering. Like St. Anthony, she also prayed for a sign from God.

A sign first came when she noticed footholds in the well's shaft and climbed down more than 100 feet. She lit her candle at the bottom and found a pool of cool water in a large cavern with limestone walls. There was a ridge wide enough to walk all around the edge of the cavern. Then she saw something she couldn't believe. There were two large pictures carved on opposite walls. One was a woman holding a large egg-like object, with the Arabic words, "Thunder in Baghdad," underneath. The other showed a man holding another large egg with the Hebrew words, "Lightning in Paradise," carved above it. She had no idea what the pictures meant, and prayed for an answer.

*****

Mina and Aaron pushed the remaining sand from the door and went inside. The interior was bare, except for a blanket on the floor and a dwarfish rock wall around the well in the center of the room.

Mina lowered a bucket, brought up the sweet, cool water, and told a story about an old man who lived in the desert and had just one job: to offer refreshment to any monk who entered his doorway. "One day a monk who was fasting came to his house and didn't accept the old man's water or food. The old man suffered such grief, he begged the monk to take his bread and water. The monk refused, and the man suggested they both pray to the lone fig tree standing outside his door. "Whoever causes the tree to bend," said the man, "we will follow his wishes." The monk knelt down to pray and nothing happened. Then the hospitable man prayed and at once the tree bent towards him, and the monk accepted his generosity."

"Do you have a tree for us to pray to?" asked Donatelle.

The gutrah fell from Mina's face in a slow, fluid motion and she smiled at the little girl. Her face was long and her features were sharp enough to cut hairs. "No, I have no tree. I have some melons beneath the sand outside," she raised her eyebrows and long lines stretched across her thin, weathered face. "You accepted my hospitality, and I'm grateful. Let's gather some melons, then you can tell me about your voyage."

They helped Mina dig a pit large enough to hold both girls. As they shoveled, Mina explained she was starving after her first month at the shrine. "I was eating insects and an occasional lizard. I don't know how it happened, but a seed sprouted here in the shade. I watered it every day and a melon grew. I collected its seeds, and now we have a whole patch of melons. She stretched

136

down into the pit, felt around beneath the sand and pulled up a small, green melon.

They went inside and sliced it with the Assassin's dagger Aaron found at Layla's castle, and he pulled a bar of soap from its small wooden box. "Have you ever seen soap?"

Mina gasped when she looked at the bar. Inscribed plainly on its waxy surface was an egg and the Hebrew words, "Lightning in paradise."

"I use the soap to wash my hands. Do you use soap?"

"How much of this soap did you have?"

"Six bars."

"Were there inscriptions on every one?"

"Yes. Lightning bolts and eggs. I'm not sure what else."

"Do you remember a man or woman?"

"There was a man and woman on some bars. Why?"

"Can I keep this one?"

"Sure, but that's our last soap."

"Don't worry. We'll clean ourselves like they did in the old times, without soap." She wrapped the bar in a gutrah and put it in her pouch.

After they devoured the Western Desert's juiciest, sweetest melon, including the rind, Aaron wiped the juice from his face and told Mina the tale of the Children's Crusade, with more attention paid to his march with Eunisia than Stephen's antics. He recounted their arrival at Marseilles, the storms at sea and his search for Eunisia, leaving out such details as the eggplant, black powder, mushroom tincture and the camel-stealing incidents. The eggplant taught him a valuable lesson: sometimes what you don't say is more important than what you do say. The girls, on the other hand, interjected details of their personal horrors on the slave ship and described their rescue in the desert, giving Aaron credit as a true hero.

"How did you survive in the desert?"

"Aaron stole a camel from the knights," blurted Donatelle.

"He had to do it," added Natalie.

"The knights left us a few water skins and some dried meat and bread in the supplies on the camel's side. I guess we had just enough." Aaron's face turned red and he could feel Mina glaring at him, but she wasn't angry he stole a camel, she was amazed that he and the girls survived.

*****

That night Mina didn't say her evening prayers for the first time in more than three years. Instead, she bid the children goodnight and sat in the darkness, holding the soap bar in her lap, hoping it was the missing piece that would reveal the answers she was looking for. She listened to the children sleep and said goodbye to the shrine, farewell to solitude. Tomorrow they'd fill their water skins and she'd bring her mysterious new friends to her old family home in Cairo.

They left the shrine by daybreak, Mina walking beside the camel, humming a song her mother used to sing. It was a serious song with a circular melody as simple as a child's rhyme. The end of each verse began another so it could go on forever. It was a good desert song.

There were no trails and no sign of any living thing for days. The children rode quietly atop the camel, more like weary travelers on the last leg of an impossible journey than the sign from God Mina hoped they were. Aaron asked Mina questions about Cairo, and he conferred with the eggplant about searching for Eunisia. The eggplant knew the bustling bazaars and mosques of Cairo could easily hide 1,000 camels, let alone one girl.

"When you find Eunisia, what will you do with us?" asked Donatelle.

138

Aaron had been too concerned with keeping them all alive to consider their future. "Maybe we'll all find a home and live together. Or we'll return to France. But no matter what, we won't split up. I won't leave you alone. I promise."

The girls' eyes lit up like sparkling fountains and they both hugged Aaron so hard he thought they'd choke him. Aaron looked for Mina's reaction, but she walked beside them in silence, knowing her God would reveal her connection to this trio when the time was ripe.

Aaron was strangely attracted to Mina. It was different than his infatuation with Eunisia and nothing like his friendship with Layla. Eunisia was his love and Layla was his teacher. He wasn't sure about Mina. She was content with the desert and sky providing her canvas, a single camel hair for her brush, and paint made from pure sunlight. Mina looked like a ghost with a suntan as she led the camel across the barren dunes. She was taller than Aaron and as thin as the girls, with brown, smooth skin glowing in the sunlight.

"There's something odd about Mina, odd and wonderful, as if she was waiting in the middle of the desert just for us, and the sandstorm rearranged the landscape just so we'd find her. Like she was a saint, or something."

"St. Mina the Wondrous." The eggplant didn't miss a beat. "Very weird, indeed, but no stranger than your appearance at Layla's doorstep. Whenever a timely appearance is too good to be coincidentally true, there's usually some hidden meaning just waiting to reveal itself, if we're lucky enough to see it."

After days of trudging along the high ridges of winding dunes, they came to the lush, green, flat and fruitful Nile valley. It was the first green foliage they'd seen in weeks. Aaron looked at the girls and saw their rosy cheeks shining like they'd just stepped from Layla's bathtub. Their light brown hair was tied back with little white bows Mina had fashioned from pieces of a torn gutrah. To the others, Aaron looked like a tattered prince in

139

his purple dress. He gazed down at the long, lush valley and listened to his heart pounding like a compass telling him he was on course again.

It was only three days' ride to Cairo and the whole party was in grand spirits. They drank fresh water from a village well and Aaron used his last gold piece to buy fresh mangoes at the market. Mina picked wild greens along the route and they taught each other new songs as they traveled. They camped near the pyramids in Giza and played between the Sphinx's paws. One night he told Mina and the girls the story of Layla. He described her library, laboratory and her search for the Lost Stone.

Aaron was full of surprises. First his alchemical adventures, now an ancient mystery, thought Mina. "What else did your friend Layla tell you?"

Aaron didn't want to reveal his eggplant, but he couldn't lie to this saintly woman. "Layla gave me a charm."

"Uh oh," interrupted the eggplant, "Take a deep breath and think before you…"

"It tells me stories from its past," continued Aaron, "Stories about its different keepers."

"What did it tell you?" asked Mina, with a disbelieving voice and a merciful smile. She had experienced audio and visual hallucinations in the desert. Or at least she thought she did. She'd seen stones and skulls grazing across the dunes at dawn, and then returned to their stationary position when the sun was in the sky. The dunes spoke to her more than once in what she recognized as ancient languages. Nevertheless, she was surprised when Aaron proceeded to tell the story of the Lost Stone as the eggplant told it to him, audio hallucination or not, from Lilith through Abraham, right up to Hamdan's death.

*****

The next day the party left the pyramids behind, marched passed rows of tents and merchants and entered the ancient gates of Cairo, one of the world's oldest cities and it smelled like it. European cities were dark, dirty, with odorous blends of manure, mold and rotting meat. Egypt's desert air had replaced the putrid European odors of death and feces with incense, perfumes and the rich, acidic smell of urine. Cairo seemed like a sparkling white city of glorious limestone structures that was pissed on by the entire population then baked clean by the sun. The smell grew stronger as they approached the Citadel's tall rock walls, polished golden dome and towering minarets dominating the skyline.

The quartet moved slowly through the Cairo bazaar, past carpets, silks and brocades draped from long poles that crossed the street and hung from windows. Booths decorated with bright cloth and rugs sold food, trinkets, perfumes, pets and house wares. Aaron looked for Eunisia, but saw no children anywhere. Men in striped djellabas balanced giant baskets filled with fresh bread on their heads and poured sweet cane juice from silver pots they carried at their sides. Others smoked hookahs and negotiated for better deals while cones of thick incense burned in pots and mingled with the scents of spice and dried camel dung. Everyone was selling something. Gazelle heads, pots of henna, dusty jars of horsehair and colorful rugs were spread across the ground. Women read palms and tea leaves, dentists pulled teeth with crude tools and men swallowed snakes, only to regurgitate them a few seconds later. Mina was surprised at how little anything had changed. The bazaar, the smells and the buildings all looked exactly the same as when she was a girl. They continued past Al Azhar, the university mosque, and came to a two-story limestone building with wide wooden doors.

Mina called up to an open window, and a small child's head popped out. She asked for her father and sisters by name, but the boy was silent. Finally the heavy wooden door creaked open a

141

few inches and Mina saw an old woman standing inside. Mina introduced herself and the door closed.

"This was my father's house when I left Cairo." The door opened again and a man with a red turban and thick black beard waved them in. Mina and the man stood face to face and said nothing. Aaron and the girls were amazed at the riches inside. The walls were covered with tapestries, pedestals with gold statues lined the hallway, and the rich wool carpets on the floor were as soft as feather-stuffed cushions.

"You say you are Mina, but Mina left this house when she was a child. Have you come home to Allah and your sister?"

"I have come to see my father. This is his house and I'm his daughter."

"Your father has been dead for two years. Killed by Hasheeshins sent by the Old Man of the Mountain."

"And my sisters?"

"Only one still sleeps under this roof. My wife."

"I want to see her. Please."

"Pasha!" called the man, and the child she saw earlier ran into the room. "Go get your mother. Tell her Mina has returned."

They waited in the hallway, looking at the designs in the carpets and ornate statues lining the hallway while the man leaned against a wall and stared at them. They thought they heard a little scream come from above, and then footsteps rushed down the stairs. A large woman who looked much older than Mina ran into the hallway, her eyes wide open and arms outstretched. "Mina!" she cried, and ran to her. They embraced and the woman smiled though her tears. "Is that really you? You're so thin. I thought I'd never see you again. Who are these children?"

"These are my companions, Natalie and Donatelle. Another boy, Aaron, is outside with our camel. We're looking for a young friend of theirs and we need a place to stay for a few nights."

Amira's eyes caught a glimpse of the Coptic cross around Mina's neck and the smile left her face. "You must remove the cross, Mina. Coptic heretics are being imprisoned or sent away to die in the desert."

Mina tucked her cross back into her white robe, out of sight. "I'll walk as a Moslem in your home if you'll let us stay."

"You have been gone so many years. Why did you come back now?"

"Once, my heart needed solitude. Now my heart tells me to help these children."

Amira smiled and hugged her sister. "Oh Mina. You haven't changed. Instead of stray cats now you come home with stray children. I'll have the servants prepare quarters. Come with me and I'll get you tea and cake."

Aaron tied the camel to a gate, went inside and called Mina into a small room, away from the others. "I want to give you something for helping us," he reached into his pouch and presented Mina with a ring. "It was my mother's, and now it's yours." Mina took the ring and held it to her heart and kissed Aaron on both cheeks.

Amira led them to a large room with overstuffed pillows and low tables covered with shiny inlaid stones and abalone. She brought them clean djellabas, water and soap. Aaron was happy to see soap again. In less than an hour they were transformed from crusty, sand-infested desert rats to cleansed, white-bodied adolescents. A servant brought warm tea and a silver platter covered with rolls and dates. They ate and drank while Mina and her sister talked, laughed and cried.

Amira's husband didn't appreciate visitors, especially Coptic heretics with infidel children. He refused to allow them to sleep under his roof and demanded they leave his house immediately. Amira pleaded with him, but he was a devout Moslem and feared they'd bring Allah's wrath on the household. Amira knew better. She brought them to the rooftop and gave them blankets, and made sure her husband didn't see or hear them.

*****

Aaron wasted no time and was on the streets of Cairo searching for Eunisia as the vendors set up their tents along the streets and shop owners opened their sleepy morning doors. After hours of walking and examining every female approximately the same size as Eunisia, the smell of fresh-baked bread coaxed him down an alley when a man beating a goatskin drum hard and fast, blocked Aaron's path.

"Camel-wrestling!" yelped the eggplant. "You'll love this, Aaron. Get as close as you can to the ring." The eggplant adored the spectacle of raw bestiality, two equally amazing creatures, pitted against each other in a senseless match of mutual destruction—but only if it had a stake in the outcome. "Please place a small wager for me, Aaron. Just a small wager. To make it interesting," begged the eggplant. "You know I'll repay you."

If Aaron truly knew the eggplant, he'd know it would gamble away paradise if it could. Still, Aaron paid no attention to the vegetable's request. He liked neither camel wrestling nor gambling. Violence with a purpose was barely acceptable, but this was ridiculous. He didn't understand why people or dried vegetables enjoyed watching beautiful animals destroy each other.

The drummer pounded away while two magnificent bull camels, adorned with thick, multi-hued tassels were paraded across the square with a female camel ahead of them, to keep their interest. Their handlers circled each other, camels spitting and huffing, and they let the beasts go. The camels sized each other up at first, waiting for a flinch or a wandering eye, as if neither really wanted to fight. They wanted the female and wondered where she went and how they could get to her.

144

Onlookers hollered for their favorite camel, pearls and coins were changing hands among last-minute gamblers. Children pointed and laughed and urged the beasts to battle. When the bell rang and betting stopped, the eggplant sulked and paid little attention to the fight.

The camel they called Shipwrecker put his head down and charged his opponent, Boulder Splitter. Shipwrecker was from a proud heritage, but Boulder Splitter was a solid chunk of dromedary muscle, and sent Shipwrecker reeling with a bloody lip. He barely collected himself before the Boulder piled into him broadside and Shipwrecker let out a horrible cry and slumped down to his knees.

"There's nothing more hopeless than a terrified camel," declared the eggplant, "and Shipwrecker is scared." But the Boulder had tasted blood, and he wanted more. He moved behind Shipwrecker and grumbled in deep, harsh, obscene tones. The crowd roared like hungry lions, ready for the final attack.

"I've seen enough," announced Aaron. "Why do you find pleasure in camel's blood?" He walked away from the square and continued his search for Eunisia.

"Maybe it's not for everybody," admitted the eggplant. "It's a habit I picked up even before Hamdan, and it'd been centuries since I'd seen…you understand."

Aaron walked into the first teashop they found.

"You'll never find her here," warned the eggplant. "This place is only for men. Don't waste your time."

The room was noisy, smelled of Turkish tobacco, and was filled with men smoking hookahs and drinking small cups of sweet mint tea. A Persian man with a black patch over one eye sat alone at a wobbly table, waiting silently for a man who wanted to buy a young European girl. The girl was waiting in a room above the shop. It was Eunisia and she was alone, the last of the girls whom the Arab purchased from a caravan in Al-Jahoub.

The Persian man watched as Aaron walked in the door with his blonde, curly hair glowing among the shop's sea of dark-haired patrons. He walked to the counter and said in broken Arabic, "I'm looking for a girl."

"No girls here," replied the shop owner. "Tea and smoke only."

"Yes, I understand. But I'm looking for a young European girl who may be lost."

"No girls here," and he walked away shaking his head. But the Persian heard Aaron's question and waved him closer.

"Have you seen a European girl?"

"I have seen many European girls, but they all have a price." The Persian ran his finger around the rim of his teacup as he spoke, creating a soft ringing tone that faded slowly into the room's chatter.

"Don't bother with this one, Aaron," advised the eggplant. "He's not going to help you."

"I'm looking for a girl named Eunisia." This was his second day of walking through Cairo. He'd been going into every shop and asking every man, woman and child on the street if they'd seen a young European girl, but nobody could help. This man was the first to say he'd even seen young European girls. "Have you seen a girl named Eunisia, she's French with long black hair?"

The Persian man looked into Aaron's eyes and sized him up as if he were an opponent. "How much would you be willing to pay for this Eunisia?"

"Let's go Aaron," urged the eggplant.

"I'd pay anything."

"1,000 dinar?"

Exactly 1,000 dinars more than Aaron had. "I'll work for you. I'll get the money but where is the girl?"

The Persian leaned forward so Aaron could smell fish oil on his breath, and whispered, "Bring the money tomorrow and you can see the girl."

Aaron traveled too far to let money come between him and Eunisia. The eggplant urged him to calm down, but Aaron leaped at the man, knocked his seat over backwards, wrapped his hands around the man's throat and shouted, "Tell me where she is or I'll snap your neck!" A sharp blow on the back of Aaron's head knocked him out, and he awoke in an alley as the night settled over Cairo. He ran back to the shop, but it was closed.

Aaron stood in front of the shop and looked in the window above the door and saw a girl looking towards him—he was certain it was Eunisia. He tried to open a side door, but it was locked. He tried to kick it open, but it was bolted tight, so he dashed around the other side of the building but the Persian and Eunisia were already making their way down a steep staircase, out the back door and into the darkness. By the time Aaron found a way up to the room, it was cold and empty. He searched every street and alley all around the shop, but saw nothing.

"Are you sure that was Eunisia?" asked the eggplant.

"Positive."

"If it's her, we can come back tomorrow and rescue her when the Persian goes down to the shop," suggested the eggplant. "There's nothing we can do tonight."

After another hour of following ghosts through the darkness, Aaron agreed and they returned to Amira's house. Both Eunisia and Aaron watched the same moon rise over the same Citadel as they shuffled away in opposite directions.

*****

Aaron arrived at Amira's house with new hope. That night, he joined the others to sleep on the rooftop and announced he'd seen Eunisia and knew where she was staying.

"Why aren't you with her now?" asked Natalie.

147

"There was a Persian who was holding her, and he took her away right after I saw her in the window. I know it was her."

Maybe Aaron was sincere, or maybe he was really hoping his imagination was powerful enough to create reality. Either way, the eggplant was unable to hide the fact that if it was indeed Eunisia, she was long gone with a man who wasn't going to let her go—unless Aaron could come up with 1,000 dinar.

While Aaron was thinking about what he'd say when he sees Eunisia, three boys dressed in black with red sashes moved silently towards Amira's house from the next rooftop. Each carried a long blade at his side and a dagger strapped to his leg. They climbed a low brick wall onto Amira's roof and separated. Aaron watched their shadows glide between big clay jars filled with cool drinking water. One of the figures stayed on the roof, crouching a few feet from Aaron. The other two descended the rope ladder leading into the main house. Aaron stayed completely still, but his heart was pounding and his breath echoed like bellows through the clay jars. The intruder turned towards him and Aaron heard the others climb up the ladder from the main house and back to the roof, then felt something poking his throat, and when he opened his eyes he was face-to face with a boy who looked about his age, holding a dagger to his neck. "Come with me," whispered the voice in a harsh Egyptian dialect, and withdrew the knife. Aaron gave the boy an odd look, and the boy grabbed his arm and pulled Aaron to his feet. "Emshee!" he whispered again, and pushed Aaron ahead.

Aaron cried out, "Mina, Natalie, Donatelle, wake up!"

Mina jumped to her feet and the boy charged at her with his dagger and stabbed her in the arm. "Mina!" screamed Aaron, and ran to her, but another boy brought a heavy clay pot down over Aaron's head, splashing water and knocking Aaron backwards and over the side of the roof to the ground below. He fell and crashed hard against the back of a horse, then bounced off the side of another, and landed face down in the dust, unconscious.

The invaders climbed down a long rope to the street and saw Aaron lying between their horses. Sharp screams came from inside Amira's house as the boys lifted Aaron's body onto the back of a horse and left Cairo with their mission accomplished.

They rode through the night and into the next day. Aaron's arm and ankle were swollen, badly bruised and ached more with each of the horse's strides. He tried to keep his mind off the pain and wondered why these boys came for him. He was so close to finding Eunisia in Cairo, now he'd surely miss the chance. Still, he was more concerned Mina had been killed and Donatelle and Natalie would be left alone. He'd lost a lot that night, including his goatskin pouch. He carried his mother's paper and father's knife across the world. Now they were gone. At least he had the eggplant. As soon as the swelling in his ankle went down and he could walk again, he and the vegetable would escape.

The kidnappers spoke little as they rode east over the rocky desert. Fires dotted the landscape like distant stars. They made camp more than a day away from Cairo and introduced themselves to Aaron around a small fire made from nuggets of dried camel dung. They were Hasheeshins, also known as Assassins, and they were devoted followers of Hassan i Sabbah, the Old Man of the Mountain.

*****

Back in England, Layla was busy stoking her laboratory furnace, firing up her crucibles and preparing to replenish her tinctures, poison concoctions and explosives. One thing she learned from her meetings with the Old Man, she'd need some serious alchemical assistance to level the playing field against him and his Assassins.

She worked through the night, just in case the King's men were checking the area, and devised a plan to return to Egypt, where she had contacts who knew the Old Man. During the first night, she mixed enough black powder to blow up a large band of Assassins and prepared a satchel of hallucinogenic tinctures by grinding dried psilocybin mushroom caps into a fine powder, placing them in vials of pure alcohol, and keeping them wrapped tightly in dark cloth, to become more potent with time.

Next, she prepared the Vitriol, which began by distilling an oily, green substance collected from sand and gravel containing sulfur and heating the remaining substance until it broke down into two parts—powdered rust and Vitriol. This new two-part substance was distilled several times leaving odorless, yellow Oil of Vitriol, which has several uses—from dissolving human tissue to quickly corroding a knight's mesh—and was just what Layla needed to defend against attackers, escape from difficult situations and perform more difficult operations, like creating pure sodium.

For the next three nights she slowly purified sulfuric compounds, starting with the lye she used for soap making. Extracting pure sodium required a full-blown operation, with alembics, crucibles and retorts used for hundreds of heat reductions and Oil of Vitriol distilled to extract soft, silver-white, highly reactive sodium you can cut with a butter knife. But Layla had to be very careful because any contact with water caused the sodium to explode into flames. Layla experienced more than one sodium accident in the laboratory. Fortunately, only small pieces of sodium went full flame, but she was well aware too much sodium could blow the whole laboratory sky high with just a single bead of sweat.

By inserting tiny pieces of sodium into sealed containers of black powder, or attaching a small chunk of sodium wrapped in oiled leaves to a bottle of belladonna vapors, Layla could ignite the vials by simply throwing them against a wet floor or wetting the outside of the vial before she threw it. These handy little bombs helped her escape from many unsettling situations, and gave her the confidence to face a dozen warriors without blinking.

She'd sewn pockets inside a black deer hide vest she could wear with any disguise and placed vials in each one, until they were almost full, then packed the remaining vials in an embroidered bag she carried over her shoulder, where they were protected and readily available. She could even keep the bag under her clothes, which she often did when she was wearing a vest full of loaded weapons. In addition to the bombs, she also had pockets for two small daggers, just in case the scimitar strapped to her leg was ever found.

Before Layla left, she inspected the castle and found the garden was untended and overgrown with weeds, but otherwise everything was in place. She went to her meditation room and rested on the cold stone platform. It had been too long since she was able to realign her body's metabolism with the earth's magnetic poles, and she felt like she'd aged 200 years. She picked up the hourglass, turned it on its head and watched the sand pour down the glass neck, fall into a growing pile and felt her energy returning with every passing moment.

PART TWO

"Do you think all this is a coincidence?"
—St. Mina the Wondrous

1. Two Ladies and a Lost Stone

Marseilles' gleaming white buildings and markets along Canebière, the city's main thoroughfare, were bustling in the spring, but Mina was too busy looking for Layla to notice shops selling fresh pastries, bouquets of pink, red and yellow flowers, and baskets overflowing with exotic fruits, octopus appetizers, pickled squid and fish of every size and shape.

Ever since Aaron told her about Layla, it was difficult for Mina to focus on anything else. She was drawn to Layla in the same way she was once drawn to St. Anthony and the solitude of the desert.

When Aaron disappeared and Mina recovered from the Assassin's knife wound, she left Donatelle and Natalie with her sister and began her search in Alexandria, Egypt, where Aaron said Layla had at least one associate. She asked every merchant and every camel driver about the mysterious woman with long, curly, silver-black hair who traveled alone, but found no clues. She traveled to Marseilles, committed to finding Layla, no matter how long it took. This was Mina's fate, for the time being, and once she arrived in Marseilles, her prayers were soon answered.

Standing at an intersection near a busy marketplace, Mina spied an old woman with a thick, brown burnoose, large, embroidered bag over her shoulder and band of colorful beaded necklaces dangling from her arm. The woman noticed Mina, too, and began winding gracefully through the crowd, her curly black and grey-streaked hair tucked into her hood and one arm outstretched.

"Would you like a necklace?" She held the necklaces up to the sunlight and waved the sparkling, colored beads in slow, hypnotic circles. "Any one you like, it's yours."

Mina was speechless. The woman's face appeared smooth from a distance, but as she drew closer Mina could see tiny wrinkles beginning to appear as she swayed to faraway music and smelled like a dozen fragrant oils simmering on a warm stove. This wasn't a normal merchant and she wasn't French. Before the woman pushed the necklaces any closer, Mina impulsively asked, "Is your name Layla?"

The woman pulled the necklaces away and gazed at Mina, who was visibly shaking as she waited for a reply.

"People call me by many names, the woman finally answered."

"I am Mina from Egypt. I met a boy in the desert."

Layla knew it was Aaron before Mina uttered another nervous word, and she was thrilled to hear he made it safely to northern Africa. She listened to the thin, bird-like woman's story, paying close attention to the description of their journey to Cairo and Aaron's disappearance. At the end of the tale, Layla hugged Mina like she was her long lost sister. "Thank you for helping Aaron. Now you and I can help each other."

Mina felt like she was standing before the true patron saint of all free women. There she was, just as Aaron described her, ageless and beautiful. Every motion she made was like a dance. The way she held the necklaces, the way they floated in perfect rhythm, their rich colors blending in a romantic pendulum, their arc swaying like an inverted rainbow. She walked like no other woman, swift yet flowing, confident and graceful, as if she was propelled by some invisible power. Mina quivered when Layla spoke, but not from fear—from awe.

Mina became Layla's willing companion in her quest for the Lost Stone. She was fascinated with Layla and eager to assist in every adventure. There was something about Mina's hardened innocence that reminded Layla of Aaron, but Mina wasn't a blank slate—she was older and the lines on her hands and face were already deep with experience.

They remained in Marseilles for two weeks, waiting for ships to arrive with a group of high-ranking Templars returning from Jerusalem. Layla suspected they'd have information about the Stone, but the Templars were not aboard the designated ship, nor on the next. Finally, they gave up on the knights and traveled to Layla's cottage outside Paris, where they devised a new plan.

The cottage was a stone structure built into the side of a hill. Its thatched roof was covered in thick green moss and it smelled like wet socks inside. Unlike the castle and its fine kitchen, laboratory and gardens, the cottage was a bare bones outpost with a fire pit, chimney and cobblestone floor. Layla started a fire, pulled a few carpets to serve as seats and beds from a shelf, and prepared tea as they talked.

"I thought I was very close to finding the Lost Stone on two different occasions. Once, before Aaron and I fled England, I found an old Arab alchemist who lived in London and claimed to know where the Stone was hidden, but I was captured by the Templars and returned to my castle, where I was held under house arrest for more than a month while they searched every inch of the place and questioned me for days on end."

"What did they want to know?"

"They wanted to know why I wanted the Lost Stone, what power it held and why I thought they might have it. They really didn't like my laboratory, and destroyed everything they could. Fortunately, I was able to hide a bag of tinctures and other goodies before the Templars captured me.

"Finally, they let me go and I stayed at this cottage until three months ago, when I made it inside a castle in Paris where the Templars highest command was meeting. I was certain they had the Stone, but a battalion of Templars descended upon me and I was forced to escape in a huge blast of smoke and flames that almost destroyed the castle's gatehouse.

"After that attempt, I assumed if Templars had the Stone, they'd hidden it even deeper in their network of secret members. There were even rumors it was returned to a Crusader outpost in Jerusalem."

Layla and Mina threw magic coins, read Tarot cards, conducted elaborate remote viewing sessions, paid informers and even dressed as traveling knights to infiltrate Templar meetings. After a month, Layla was beginning to doubt if the Templars were any closer to the Stone than she was. With no other leads to follow, one rumor led to another and Layla and Mina were tracking clues across Europe and before long, they were back in the deserts of northern Africa.

Layla and Mina traveled like two mermaids swimming in an open sea of sand. They navigated the dunes and looked for clues everywhere. They asked every traveler they met about knights and secret, egg-shaped stones, translated the secret language of the wind and sand—messages changing as fast as time itself—and traveled from one elusive bit of information to the next, always a few steps behind the Stone. Then they heard a story a young camel driver told about two knights who went mad at an oasis near Waddan. The driver described the knights shedding their mesh, running naked and repeating their crazed visions to everyone who stopped at their oasis.

In less than an hour, Layla and Mina were on their way. When they arrived the next day, the oasis was vacant except for one man leaning against the well. He was a beggar in a torn and soiled djellaba.

"How long have you been here?" Layla gave the man a small chunk of bread and he gazed at her as if he was confused by the question.

"I've been here since the night I saw the demons." He mumbled in the King's French and ate the bread one crumb at a time, savoring every morsel.

"What happened that night, when you saw the demons?" Layla spoke softly and smiled, while Mina stood silently beside her.

"A blonde boy in a dress joined our caravan."

Layla and Mina knew it was Aaron.

"Then there were two girls who were almost dead when we found them. They were bad omens. They brought the demons."

"What happened to the boy?"

"He stole a camel and left with the girls and *The Book*."

"What book?" They were both surprised to hear yet another twist in Aaron's incredible journey.

"We were bringing *The Book of Secrets* to Persia. It was payment for an old relic the Templars just had to have."

"What is *The Book of Secrets*?" asked Mina.

"They say it's one of the world's first books, but I've heard it may not be a book at all. It may be a statue or a painting, tablets, a scroll or a whole mountainside. What were you carrying to Persia?"

"That's the odd part. All the knights called it *The Book*, but it was only impressions cast on bars of wax. Don't ask me why. They could fit in your hand and didn't melt in the camel sacks. That's all I know."

"The soap," muttered Mina.

"What did you say?"

"When I met Aaron and the girls, Aaron had a bar of soap inscribed with a symbol and a phrase. There was an oval shape, like an egg, and the words, "Lightning in Paradise.""

"Where are the other bars of wax?"

"Aaron washed his hands with them."

Layla couldn't help but smile. Apparently he did what had to be done. He'd spiked the knights' tea with mushroom tincture, left with the girls on their camel and destroyed all but the last page of the world's oldest book, or at least a rare imprint of part of it.

"And that's not the strangest thing," continued Mina. "At the bottom of St. Anthony's well, there's a cavern with markings on its walls matching the inscription on the soap."

"Are you sure?" Layla considered the real *Book of Secrets* may be a desert well.

Mina shook her head. "I'm sorry I didn't tell you about this before, but I didn't think it had anything to do with the Lost Stone and I didn't want to..."

"No, no, no Mina. No time for blame or regrets—only appreciation and looking forward," and they hugged until Layla lifted Mina off her feet and gently returned her to the ground.

"Now, how far is this well?"

"At least three day's ride, maybe more."

Mina looked at the fallen knight, dressed in rags and thinner than a desert dog. "Why are you still here? Why don't you go home?"

"The demons won't let me go. They'll kill me if I leave this oasis. I have a wife and child in France. I think about them day and night, but I'm trapped."

Layla looked at the man and took his hands in hers. "You've helped us more than you'll ever know. In return, I'll give you more than food. I'll remove the demon's spells so you can return to your family."

"Are you a sorceress?" He moved his hands away, suddenly afraid of the women.

Layla turned to the sun and asked for the demons to release the knight from their spell then faced each of the four directions and dismembered the curse, before offering a protective incantation in its place. Next, Layla cast her eyes downward and chanted magical words she promised would clear the way for the knight's overdue departure.

158

"We're not sorceresses, we're just grateful," and Layla tossed him a hard biscuit, a chunk of dried meat, and offered him the reins of Mina's camel. Layla extended her hand and Mina grabbed it and swung to Layla's camel without touching the ground, the disoriented knight stood there with his new camel and freedom, and the grateful duo bid him farewell and left for St. Anthony's well, Mina riding on back, her arms wrapped tightly around Layla's waist.

"How could you be so sure you removed the demon's curse?"

"There was no curse to remove because there were no demons. It was all a show to make him believe his non-existent demons had been removed. Do you think he bought it?"

"You fooled me." Mina wondered how many other times she'd been fooled, and smiled. "It's hard to believe your search for the Lost Stone leads back to Aaron's soap and St. Anthony's well. Do you think this is all a coincidence?"

"There's no such thing as coincidence." And the pair set out to find some answers at the bottom of St. Anthony's well.

2. How the Old Man Found His Mountain

"If I had two devotees who would stand by me, I could bend history into any shape I desired," boasted a young Hassan i Sabbah. His classmates believed him. He was bigger than them and the only Persian in their class at Al Azhar University in Cairo. Hassan spent his days reading the Koran and studying astronomy and poetry. At night he searched for censored texts filled with recipes and incantations for calling genies, teaching subjects to fly and uncovering the secrets of sexual ecstasy. For most Moslems, these old, pre-Islamic writings were pure heresy. If a Moslem had been caught reading them by the wrong mullah, he'd have his eyes poked out in public, but the risks were worth it for Hassan.

The old Arab shamans had as many forbidden texts as their camels had fleas. Hassan could spend his whole life reading censored books, but he'd only scratch the surface, and he wanted only the greatest secrets, those that could help him extend his life, so he began with Cairo's alchemists. Hassan hoped to find wise men who solved the mysteries of nature. Instead, he found old, withered souls who worked in primitive laboratories distilling essences and creating intoxicating spirits to clean their floors and protect them from invisible enemies. They also discovered cures for diseases responsible for killing thousands in Europe and found ways to make their water fizz, but Hassan was looking for more. He wanted eternal life with no strings attached and had little interest in changing lead into silver, which a few had accomplished. In the end, none of the old alchemists could give him the one thing he wanted most—the key to immortality.

Hassan left the University after his first year and set out to discover the secret of eternal life. He visited Tibetan monks who explained life was nothing more than suffering and advised him to recite six million Green Taras and pray for a joyful death. He studied with gurus in the northern mountains of India who taught him to meditate his way to eternity. He spent months learning from Coptic sects in the Egyptian desert who prescribed a life of solitude, devotion and constant prayer. He wandered through Europe, where old Crusaders described the Holy Grail like a fountain of youth. He traveled around the world searching for shamans and secret potions, but found nothing but fanciful stories and bad advice. He learned Sanskrit incantations and intricate Sufi hand dances guaranteed to make him younger, practiced strange postures and their accompanying mantras, but nothing worked.

Then Hassan joined a small band of Hebrew mystics who lived in a cave. They studied cosmological charts and gematria, the art of divining the secret meaning of language. First, they taught him the universe actually consisted of vibrations, and these vibrations first took the form of the spoken word, and the language of that word at one of the beginnings of the universe was Hebrew. They showed him how to combine letters and create vibrations to change the landscape of reality—at least alter the way people perceived the world.

Hassan had a problem believing he could use numbers and letters to change an entire society, but he hoped the Hebrew's divine language would help him unlock the mystery of life extension. Sometimes it took days or weeks to divine the meaning of a single sacred passage with absolute accuracy, and Hassan witnessed gematria used to foretell the outcomes of battles, find buried fortunes and remove men from power. He didn't doubt it possessed tremendous visionary capabilities, but not much more.

The Hebrew mystics were glad to share their lesser secrets with a willing pupil, but they couldn't help him find the answers he wanted. They had their own agenda and agreed their Persian friend had learned enough, so they showed him to the cave door and Hassan went peacefully into the night, a gematrian warrior on a silent mission.

Hassan discovered dozens of dietary regimens promising eternal life. He drank daily tea made from fo-ti-teng, a pleasant-tasting Chinese root that purified his blood and gave him the strength of 50 goats, but also made him smell like them. He went through various stages of fasting and deprivation in hopes of adding a few years to his life. He stopped eating meats, cheese, bread and certain vegetables, including beets, broccoli and eggplant, until he feared his asshole might close up due to lack of action. He was thin as a rail, anemic, desperate and certain diet was not the key to immortality.

After years of cave-dwelling, dietary insanity and half-baked consultations, Hassan was no closer to finding a Fountain of Youth. Then, out of the blue, an old, grey-bearded, legless beggar in Rome spotted Hassan on a public street and said he could lead him to the secret of immortality in return for one bottle of wine. Hassan laughed and spit on the ground beside the beggar, who turned away without a word and used his knuckles to drag himself through the dirt and into an alley. Hassan followed the beggar to a small dome hut made from rocks, sticks, animal skins and rags, all held together with a thick coat of Roman mud. He waited, but the beggar never came out. When Hassan opened the blanket door, he saw him sitting in front of a candle, staring at its flame.

"I've been waiting for you," said the beggar. "Did you bring the wine?"

Hassan crawled inside and sat down. It was dark, even with the candle, and there was barely enough room for both of the men. Pots with half-eaten, moldy food, piles of soiled clothes and an assortment of Roman rubbish were piled from floor to ceiling, all around the hut's walls.

"I brought you something better than wine." Hassan was sitting on a pile of old chicken bones and unidentifiable green matter. "Gold," and he tossed two bright coins at the stumps that were once the beggar's legs.

He picked up the coins and stuffed them into his ragged pouch. In the candlelight, Hassan could see the beggar had a strong, noble face. His skin was dark and weathered as a nomad's. His nose and chin were classic as a marble statue, and his eyes were bright and sharp. "You're a desperate man," sneered the beggar, "Go back to Arabia and you'll find your eternal life."

Hassan drew his dagger. "You fool! I've been through every wise man's cave and secret text in the Arab world and found nothing."

"That's your mistake," began the beggar. "Find the Cult of Lilith on the island of Bahrain. They'll teach you how to live forever."

"You're a beggar. What do you know of Arab secrets and women's cults?"

"I wasn't always without legs. I joined the Crusade when I was 14-years-old. By the time I arrived in the Holy Land I knew I didn't really like my fellow pilgrims. They were pigs and I didn't want to die beside them. I left the Crusade and set out on my own through Egypt, Arabia and Persia. I was sailing in the Persian Gulf when a storm wrecked my boat and I was washed up on the shores of Bahrain. Women found me on the beach and brought me back to their sanctuary. These women were like no others. When you find them, you'll see what I mean. It was like paradise and I never wanted to leave. But as soon as I was strong enough to travel, they gave me provisions and sent me packing."

Hassan's curiosity was piqued. "And what was this cult's secret of immortality?"

"The women worshiped a living goddess named Lilith, who is centuries old, maybe older. There were others who were more

163

than 100-years-old and appeared to be no more than 30 or 40. The cult lives in an old fortress on the northwest side of the island. You won't be sorry."

A million questions ran though Hassan's mind, and they could only be satisfied by a trip to Bahrain. He left the hut and returned with a bottle of the best wine he could find, drank it with the legless beggar, and then set his course for the Persian Gulf.

*****

When Hassan arrived in Bahrain, he found the fortress located where the beggar described, and was met at the tall wooden gates by a short, stout, red-haired woman leaning against a long, heavy scimitar. "I'm afraid you've wandered down the wrong path Mohammed. What are you looking for?" she asked.

"My name is not Mohammed. I am Hassan i Sabbah and I am looking for immortality. I've come to learn from the Cult of Lilith."

The red-haired woman shook her head, stepped back and examined him from head to toe, looking for concealed weapons and wondering if she could kill him in one swipe of her blade or two.

"A friend sent me here. A man who washed up on your shore and owes his life to you," continued Hassan. "He told me you were wise women with many secrets that could help me in my search."

Hassan didn't appear dangerous, so the woman decided not to kill him right away. "Why do you want to live forever?"

"I need more time to accomplish the tasks Allah has set for me."

"And what tasks would Allah give a man he couldn't accomplish in a natural lifetime?"

164

"To move the world, to change the shape of history, to create a new paradise on earth," declared Hassan, shielding his eyes from the glaring sunlight reflecting from the woman's scimitar.

Paradise was the cult's strong suit. It was like he said the magic word. She opened the gates and Hassan stepped into a breath-taking garden filled with palm trees, lush foliage, gorgeous flowers and beautiful women. There were ladies splashing in clear, blue pools of water, women sleeping in the shade and reading books atop grassy knolls. This actually looked like a home for immortals.

Hassan was introduced to a woman named Layla, the cult's librarian. "The diary of Salimamba will show you there are many paths to eternity," and she passed him a set of handwritten Sanskrit books. Salimamba was an Indian woman and follower of Lilith who died about 500 B.C. She recorded many of her bizarre experiments and orgasmic rituals and according to Layla, some actually worked in extending Salimamba's life, and more.

Salimamba believed female orgasms were the most powerful force in the universe. She devised a routine for harnessing orgasmic energy and was certain she could use it to alter events from a distance. She started slow at first, successfully lit a candle with orgasmic visualization, and later burned an empty tent. Unfortunately, her achievements were limited to pyrotechnics. "Orgasms can create thunder and lightning, change the tides, turn statues into gold, and pay your divine taxes," wrote Salimamba. "The world comes to us during orgasms. It lies at our feet and waits for instructions. It is the moment we shake hands with our favorite god. The moment we can recreate the world." Of course, these were female orgasms she was talking about, something Hassan never knew existed, but the female cultists assured him male orgasms could be equally potent, with practice.

Salimamba's diary provided explicit instructions for her 'magic of ecstasy' and Hassan followed it to the letter. He relaxed, concentrated on his breath, then visualized, touched, smelled and tasted his immortality as if it was real. He practiced charging his sexual battery every day, coming close to ecstasy, but never actually crossing the line. He'd repeat this 10 or 15 times, then pour his orgasmic juice into his vision of immortality, like he was filling a balloon with air, but he couldn't make a spark. He learned some practitioners stored up the potential of many close calls, and because the female's orgasmic dynamo seemed to be about five times stronger than a typical male's climax, some women produced a single orgasm each year with energy equivalent to a medium-sized volcano. The more power he could store in his body, the greater Hassan's creative potential.

Hassan practiced with cultists every day. They were masters of Salimamba's techniques and taught him erotic positions helping him make love for hours without a single climax. He and his partners looked like perpetual piston machines pumping out the oldest rhythms, tangled in fleshy knots, going in and out of deep trances, connected by mystic dreams more than primitive desire. He practiced as much as 10 hours a day for a month, until it felt like the sun itself was blazing in his loins. But still no sparks.

"Perhaps you should climb your mountain one step a time," suggested Mali, his favorite partner. Mali was one of the youngest cult members. She never practiced with a man before Hassan came to the island, yet she was far more adept than he was. Hassan took her advice and waited until he had two months' worth of burning loins and was ready to explode. "This is the day," announced Hassan, and set a small cup of water beside the bed. He and Mali moved like dancers, embracing and meditating with slow, deliberate breaths as Hassan visualized a fire growing under the cup. After six hours, while twisted in the Serpent's Spoon position, he visualized flames beneath the cup growing hotter and hotter, until he could feel the heat against his face and hear the crackling flames. His partner giggled while Hassan kept his eyes closed tight, imagining the red-hot cup. When he opened

166

his eyes, the cup was shaking, the water was boiling and Mali was still laughing.

The secrets of Lilith offered more hope than any other teachings he found, but Hassan wasn't getting any younger. After six months, grey hairs appeared in his moustache. By the end of a year, his beard had more silver hairs than black and he wrenched his back attempting an acrobatic position called the Flying Camel, forcing him to walk with a cane. Something was wrong. He went back to Salimamba's texts and poured over every word, looking for an answer until he found a small passage he missed earlier. "The body is a vessel that stores energy. Sex expends more than its fair share of our energy, and erotic rituals can be very expensive. For some, celibacy seems to be a more certain way to extend one's life." How did he miss it? He scoured through all of the writings they'd allow him to read, but this was the only allusion to life extension or celibacy. It wasn't much, but it was the best he had after 20 years of searching, and he'd gladly trade his virility for even a few decades of extra life.

There was one big problem with this celibacy prescription. He'd met shamans, priests and monks who claimed to be virgins, but many of them died young. Either they weren't celibate or more than simple celibacy was required. Hassan needed to know more. He needed to speak with Lilith, whom he'd never seen since arriving in Bahrain. He wondered if she was even real.

But it was too late for questions. The cult's elders decided Mali no longer required his services and it was time for him to go. Hassan pleaded with Layla, the librarian, for just a few more months at the sanctuary.

"This really isn't the place for a man." Layla was stern and held a heavy scimitar at her side. "You've read our books and tasted our fruits. We've offered all we can and we want you to leave now."

"Can I speak with Lilith before I go?"

"Lilith is away from the island. I don't know when she'll be back."

"Look at me. I've been here less than a year, but I look 10 years older than when I arrived. How do I get the years back? How does Lilith do it? How do you do it?"

"Women's work and children's songs, Hassan. It's as easy as that." She wasn't kidding.

"Don't send me away without something. Please."

Layla sighed and understood some truths are less appreciated than extravagant lies. She whispered three words, "The Lost Stone."

"What?"

"The Kabba Stone has a sibling. Another Stone was left with Lilith in the Garden of Eden and stolen centuries ago. If you find the Lost Stone and hold it as your own, you'll find your immortality."

In all of the secret teachings, Hassan had never heard of a Lost Stone. How could these women know? Was it possible the Stone was sitting in some amir's parlor or Crusaders chest?

"Where is it? You must tell me. I'll give you anything. I'll see no harm ever comes to you. You have my word."

Layla shrugged. "I have no idea where it is. Be patient, Hassan and the Stone will come to you." Then she added, "I will accept your protection, and your promise never to harm me. But if you ever return to this place, I'll personally cut off both of your legs," and she closed the tall wooden gates behind him.

*****

Hassan returned to Cairo with both of his legs and a plan. He preached his "all is permitted" sermon to students outside the University in Cairo, where groups gathered to hear his revolutionary ideas, but Moslem authorities soon squashed the gatherings wherever they sprang up and forced Hassan into exile with two other suspected heretics. The three boarded a fishing boat sailing for Palestine and Hassan fed them a steady diet of hashish and amazing stories. When the shores were in sight he stepped out of the boat and walked on water, an illusion he'd learned from Hebrew mystics. When they docked, Hassan had his first two loyal followers, and they stepped off the boat and into a new world.

Hassan didn't waste any time trying to change the old world—and find the Lost Stone along the way. In a few months he had more than 100 young fedawis ready for their first assignment. It wasn't long before he placed spies among selected caliphs, amirs, soldiers and merchants from Baghdad to Cairo. He even had informers inside the Templars, who kept him abreast of the Crusaders command lines, leader's habits and juicy rumors. Hassan guaranteed his spies handsome rewards for information about the Stone, and before long he learned of an Ishmaelite sect secluded in the Persian Mountains. Nobody knew exactly what the sect was doing there, but Hassan was suspicious. He sent several scouts but only one returned and described a magnificent mountaintop castle guarded by armored men with crossbows. Hassan thought the Stone must be there. If not, the fortress offered Hassan and his Assassins an ideal new home.

He called all of his fedawis together, almost 400 teenage boys and a few dozen 20-year-olds, organized them in teams and prepared a plan of attack. In addition to their scimitars and cross bows, Hassan's army had long leather whips, razor-sharp steel stars and kegs of black powder. They traveled at night, dressed in black and were ready to take on any foe. When they arrived at Alamut in Persia, they hid among the gnarled trees and thorn bushes halfway up the 8,000-foot mountain. The ascent was difficult by day and no right-minded goat would try it under the stars. But the fedawis preferred the cover of darkness, so they started at midnight and crept silently up the jagged incline in groups, trying not to move a rock or wake a snake. In the hours before dawn, the first wave of Assassins reached the gate.

The fortress at Alamut was built into the mountain and protected by sheer, 1,000-foot crags on three sides with a smooth, more accessible south face that concealed its single entrance. The guards positioned outside the gates were the first victims. Hassan's Assassins killed them silently with arrows, while another crept to the gate and tried to swing the door open, but it wouldn't budge.

"Hey! Who..." the guard's voice was silenced in mid-question by 10 arrows and a throwing star. Three more boys shuffled to the gates and were met by a throng of sleepy guards with bulky armor breastplates and sabers. They fought in the dark, sparks flying from scimitars, armor and mesh. More boys joined the fight until the guards dropped their weapons and ran for their lives.

Most of the Ishmaelites inside the fortress were still sleeping, and their 40 guards couldn't stop 400 crazed boys with deadly intentions. In less than one hour, all the guards and Ishmaelites were killed, including dozens of white-haired men and women who had only their canes to protect them when the boys slit their throats. Not a single person was spared.

Hassan climbed to the entrance of Alamut at dawn and arrived while his fedawis were going through each room in the castle, collecting valuables and removing dead bodies. There were more than 50 rooms inside the stone walls, a few large enough to host a party for all of the camel drivers in Cairo. Its stonework was impeccable, probably carved by slaves during the last century, and there were Persian tapestries, colorful cosmological diagrams and sacred ceramics from Central Asia in every room. There was a six-armed golden Hindu goddess, elephant-headed gods, Buddha's of all sizes and forms, including a row of laughing, meditating and angry Buddhas lining one hallway, pre-Islamic artifacts sitting on tables, and life-size Babylonian statues of Baal standing in corners like embalmed sentinels. It was hard to believe Hassan's boys would be calling this castle home.

There was nothing but rock, thorns and twisted, stunted trees from the base of the mountain to its peak, yet inside Alamut's walls was a lush, high altitude garden fed by year-round springs and protected by towering, jagged walls. The isolated, exotic environment was surely one of the secret wonders of the world. Peacocks roamed amidst fruit trees and carp-filled ponds. Manicured walkways led to marble mosques. And what Hassan liked most, it was all hidden from the world like a private paradise behind impassable walls.

Hassan stood on the castle's parapet and listened to the wind. He was at the edge of the Fertile Crescent, looking over the land where agriculture and civilization first arose, the birthplace of the alphabet, the home of Hammurabi, Zeno the Stoic, Dido, Hannibal, Pygmalion, six Roman Emperors, five Popes and the great Umayyad and Abbasid civilizations. Hassan could hear their spirits whispering around him, gently persuading him to give the world its first lesson in chaos theory.

Hassan and his fedawis would control the world from this headquarters. There would be no economic or political takeovers. No organized battles or head-to-head confrontation with armies. Hassan would launch an ongoing extermination of individual leaders from both sides—Christian and Moslem—leaving great voids of power in the lands around him, creating some very strange and wonderful struggles in the ensuing imbroglio. He imagined thousands of fedawis infiltrating the highest places in Persia, Egypt, Greece and Rome. To attract that many followers would take more than money. It would take more than anything a young man could imagine. It would take nothing less than paradise.

"I found it! I found it!" yelped a voice from inside the fortress. Soon a swarm of boys ran to meet Hassan, one holding a shining, grey stone. Hassan's eyes opened wide when he saw it. He took the Lost Stone from the boy and held it as if it were a newborn prophet, his eyes shining and his heart filling with pride as his fedawis watched their master greet his new companion. Its cloudy surface was smooth and polished so perfectly it reflected every detail of the room around it. Hassan rubbed his hands across the Stone and was surprised how much it looked and felt like a large, pale eggplant.

"Where did you find it?" asked Hassan, and the boy led him to a grand room big enough to hold 40 men at a long table, except this room had only one pedestal in its center. Its walls were covered with deep blue tapestries adorned with hand-sewn constellations and magic symbols. Hassan suspected this castle was built to protect the Stone. Now it would protect paradise.

Hassan immediately fortified his mountain fortress, which he named Eagle's Nest. First, he removed the wooden gate and filled in the space with granite blocks. Next, he created hidden passages and escape routes leading from Eagle's Nest to outlets located much lower on the mountainside. The fedawis chiseled a stairway leading from the tree line, 2,000-feet below, to the front of the castle so Hassan could climb more easily, day or night. And the garden was made even more beautiful with fresh plantings of exotic flowers, grasses and fruit trees. Finally, a harem of young, experienced seductresses from India, all well versed in the Kama Sutra, was imported to complete the perfect paradise for any red-blooded Moslem boy.

With his fortress strong and his paradise impeccable, Hassan began building his army of followers. He sent half of the fedawis to recruit Arab and Persian boys who were between 12- and 16-years-old. They traveled through villages, set up recruitment centers on the outskirts of Damascus, Cairo, and Baghdad and returned with a new team of young orphans and runaways every week. The fedawis who stayed back guarded the fort, welcomed recruits to Eagle's Nest with a feast of food, wine and sweet hashish biscuits laced with opium for dessert. When new recruits fell asleep or passed out, they were carried into the garden, where they always woke up happy. After a few days in paradise, they were fed more hashish biscuits and brought inside the hall once reserved for the Lost Stone. Hassan marched before them like a wise old sorcerer and offered every boy eternal paradise in exchange for their loyalty, a proposition Hassan's teenage troops found hard to resist. He promised them wild, sexy, religious anarchy and a family of young outlaws in place of uptight Islamic submission and arranged marriages. He provided for all of their needs and taught them basic skills like reading, writing and martial arts, while training for their assignments.

Each of the recruits spent their first three months learning to kill their opponents with terrible precision. They also read the Koran and poetry of Hassan's childhood friend, Omar Khayyam. Then they'd leave Eagle's Nest for a month of recruiting or kidnapping more boys. In less than a year, Hassan had a formidable army of the world's first Assassins waiting for his orders.

The Old Man of the Mountain and his Assassins were soon feared by every Moslem leader and Crusader within 1,000 miles of Eagle's Nest. Their motto, "Nothing is true and all is permitted," was emblazoned in white on their black banners, and they meant every word. The Assassins were wild cards in a land founded on ancient family lines and severe Islamic law. Hassan followed no rules, befriended Crusaders when they served his purpose, battled with sultans and amirs and killed those who cheated him. From the beginning, he chose his victims wisely.

His first victim was Nizam al Mulk, the minister of the Seljuks. His death led to the breakup of their empire. Amirs and sultans from other families declared war on the Old Man and ordered his fedawis killed on sight. The morning after the orders were given, the sultans and amirs who'd declared war were found with Assassin's dark stilettos in their hearts. One survived, and he woke up with razor-edged Assassin's blades stuck in his pillow on either side his head, just close enough to draw blood if he should move too quickly. This sultan withdrew the orders to attack Hassan, and sent his sincere apology to Eagle's Nest.

*****

The Old Man never forgot his days with the Cult of Lilith. The castle at Eagle's Nest was furnished with a vast library when Hassan arrived, but he was intent on making it the best in the world. His scouts were sent to collect mystical texts from every library they could find. Some were even sent to China and India to retrieve books, scrolls and tablets. He knew the Cult of Lilith had an incredible library, and he couldn't wait to read the texts they kept from him. He sent a team of spies to Bahrain, but they found the old fortress abandoned and dilapidated beyond repair, with cracking stone blocks, broken parapets, overgrown weeds where pools once sparkled and huge piles of shit with a nasty smell making it difficult for even the lowliest vermin to stay near the place long.

The stench resulted from local villagers using the fortress's once beautiful rooms to empty their shit pots, forcing the Old Man's spies to soak their gutrahs in rose water and wrap them around their noses and mouths to navigate the castle's sewage-filled halls in search of a book, an amulet—something to bring back for Hassan. After finding nothing but piles of poop in the broken buildings, the boys left the fortress and traveled to nearby villages and looked for someone who knew of the Cult of Lilith, but nobody remembered the fortress being occupied by anything but shit.

*****

When Aaron arrived at Eagle's Nest, Hassan's network of spies and Assassins was at its peak. His domain extended beyond the fortress to include the surrounding valleys, whose farmers grew food and cannabis for the Assassins, and their families alerted the Old Man with smoky fires if anyone they didn't know wandered onto the mountainside. In return, Hassan paid them generously and protected them from outlaws.

The young Assassins who captured Aaron in Cairo were trained at Eagle's Nest. Aaron learned during their trip the boys waited in Cairo for weeks before their orders came to kill Amira's husband, Abdul Fakir. Abdul had sold him 10 sick camels, and Hassan lost 200 more camels to their disease. When Abdul refused to compensate Hassan for even the 10 sick camels, he made a big mistake.

As far as the young Assassins were concerned, Abdul was public enemy number one and a deranged man who wanted to molest their mothers. It was easy for the oldest, 16-year-old Driss, to creep into the dark room and thrust his sword into Abdul as he slept. The second killer slipped in after Driss and drove his black-handled stiletto into Abdul's heart, leaving him lifeless with the knife standing in his chest like a stiff, dark flower.

When they spoke to Aaron, the Assassins described their deeds with soft, cryptic voices, as if they were holy soldiers in a secret war. Murder was a duty they performed for their master, like sweeping the floor or tending to the garden, but it was a way of life for these boys.

When they saw Aaron, they knew they had to bring him back to Eagle's Nest. They'd never seen a boy with blonde hair before and they knew Hassan would be pleased. They shared their biscuits and water, helped him with Arabic slang and gave him a blanket at night. The fedawis smelled like olive oil and musk, grew their black hair long and washed their hands before they ate. He tried to tell them about Eunisia, but they couldn't understand why he wanted to follow a girl.

The route to Eagle's Nest crossed from Egypt to Syria, then north to the Persian Mountains. They followed goat trails over steep passes and stayed away from villages and main roads connecting the valleys. When they came to a bleak, ashen mountain with a massive, craggy rock at its summit, they left their horses tied beneath the last stand of sycamore trees and started to climb. Aaron's ankle was still badly swollen and he was unable to put any pressure on it to walk. The boys held Aaron between them, his arms over their shoulders, and they marched one step at a time up a lifeless path winding through fields of jagged rocks. They came to a dead tree, and Aaron hobbled along a thin stone stairway carved into the mountainside, putting his weight on his good leg as he moved slowly up the sand-covered, rough-hewn stone. The steps were tall and crossed the mountain's stony face like a thin scar barely perceptible from below. The Arab boys bounced up the stairway like young mountain goats, holding Aaron between them until they reached a sheer 100-foot stone wall, smooth as a blanket of ice. The boys made their way across the bottom of the wall, and then disappeared into a small cave no more than a shadow between two grey boulders. Aaron followed on his hands and knees in total darkness, until the cold stone grew warmer and the light and laughter from a room at the end of the passage became brighter. As he crawled out of the passage and into the light of oil lamps, he found himself in a banquet room, greeted by a pack of smiling fedawis and a feast of roast lamb, fresh fruits, curried rice and wine.

Aaron ate and laughed with the others as if they were old friends. It was hard to believe these same boys kidnapped him and tried to kill Mina.

"What are you going to do with me?" asked Aaron.

"You're one of us now," answered one of the boys, and the others laughed and slapped Aaron on the back.

These boys did seem a lot like him, except they were all Arabs and Persians. Aaron washed down a few hashish biscuits with a tall glass of sweet wine and was soon wobbling in his seat, watching the fedawis' smiles grow and the candlelight stretch from the floor to the stars.

*****

Aaron didn't remember falling asleep. He awoke to the sound of water falling and splashing into a nearby pool and gentle birdsongs all ending with a question mark. Then he smelled the soft perfume of flowers all around and felt someone rubbing his feet and arms. He opened his eyes and sunlight trickled through the lush green canopy of leaves and palms above him. Three dark-skinned women wearing sheer white gowns and jewels on their foreheads massaged his feet and legs, all smiling and working together to gently relax every muscle in his lower extremities. He tried to recall the details of the night before, but could only remember feeling lighter than air and happy, very happy. Now his head felt like it was doubling in size every few minutes and his body was becoming lighter again. He felt almost weightless, feared he may float away and grasped one of the young women's arms, just to be safe.

He sat up and found himself on a soft bed of clover with a pillow under his head and lush, vivid green foliage all around him. Beside him were platters brimming with dates and figs the size of his thumb and sweet pastries stuffed with fruit and berries. Everything he tasted and touched was a new sensation, as if he was experiencing a new world for the first time. The stones

177

glowed in the sunlight, trees were laden with strange, fragrant fruit and leaves rustled like musical instruments.

The young ladies covered his body with smooth, warm palm oil, ran their fingers slowly over every inch of his skin and lightly rubbed his swollen, black-and-blue ankle with cannabis salve. They massaged his back and arms until they were soft cakes of fresh dough, then burned spiced incense and anointed their bodies with coriander and sage oils. Aaron knew this must be paradise.

When the young women helped him to his feet, he saw he was in a vast, beautiful garden lined with trees, plants and vines. There were mango, persimmon, warm pink roses, shafts of violet tulips, fragrant silvery shrubs, gigantic fan-leafed foliage and exotic blooms everywhere. Ornate carpets were spread like painted gardens on the lush green lawn. Four shining white palaces were spread across the grounds, each with broad columns at their entrance. There was a small waterfall in the center of the garden spilling into a long pool filled with lily pads. From there, a thin creek bobbed and gurgled over green-blue rocks to form an aquamarine vein through the center of the valley.

"It's a beautiful day." She spoke with a thick Hindi accent as they walked along the creek. "The sun so high and the sky so dazzling blue." To Aaron, her voice was wise and sincere as a goddess and she smelled like bouquets of lavender.

"Do you want to learn a Hindi love song?" And both women laughed as they walked with his arms over their shoulders, singing an old song about a woman catching her man with another lover, and another and another. They stopped singing and sat down under a sycamore tree, and shared wine and spoonfuls of honey, then sucked every drop of juice from rosy pomegranates.

At the end of the day, one of the young women gave Aaron a cane she'd fashioned from a fallen sycamore branch to help him walk, and led him inside the smallest palace. It was very clean and simple, with dark blue walls and a painting of an old man taking a shining white stone from a muscular angel with feathery wings. The young woman guided him to a bed covered with piles of huge silk pillows. She danced across the room, looking into his eyes and removing her clothes until she was perfectly naked. She kneeled at the end of the pillows, kissed his entire body, starting with his toes and ending with the little diamond-shaped scar on the tip of his nose, when he dozed off and dreamed of waking with Eunisia by his side.

The young women enjoyed their lives in paradise. It was much better than the poverty they knew as orphans in India and the bordellos in Calcutta, where they once lived like slaves for fat old sheiks with hairy backs. The boys were pleasant diversions whom they played like emerald ouds. In return, Hassan treated the ladies like royal concubines and provided them with private quarters and a safe haven. They could leave Eagle's Nest anytime, but they all stayed until they were too old for the demands of the garden, then moved to another Assassin castle or returned to a peaceful retirement in India.

*****

When Aaron awoke, he was in a large, dark chamber on a cold slab of stone. He reached for his eggplant, but it was gone and he couldn't remember when he'd lost it. He sat up and wondered where he was.

"You're not dreaming. You've returned to the world," said the Old Man. He was standing in a dark corner, speaking perfect English, with a deep, rattling voice giving Aaron the chills. "How does it feel to be evicted from paradise?"

The eggplant hadn't made a peep since it left Aaron's neck, trying to block out the Old Man's horrible thoughts and prevent

179

him from discovering the amulet in his pocket could communicate with him.

The Old Man waited, but Aaron looked for his reflection in the polished stone floor and didn't answer. "You're one of the child Crusaders, aren't you?" asked the Old Man. "All the way from Paris to Persia." He lit an oil lamp and came closer. "I'm the Old Man of the Mountain, prophet of Allah and keeper of the keys of paradise. I can give you all the delights you tasted in the garden and more. I can offer an eternity of ecstasy in return for your loyalty."

Then Aaron recognized him. "You're the Old Man who gave Stephen his instructions at Vendome and Marseilles. Some of us made it but most died at sea or were captured as soon as we landed. We never found the Holy Land."

The Old Man nodded as though this was old news making no difference to anyone. "You were never intended to find the Holy Land. You were my prize stock of European orphans, sold or given to good houses. Some went to castles in the mountains, but every one of the child Crusaders will be happier and live longer under Allah's roof than dying alone in the filthy streets of Paris."

Aaron couldn't believe slavery under Allah was better than being a free orphan in Europe. He wished he had his eggplant. "I'd rather be with a girl named Eunisia," said Aaron. "Do you know where she is?"

"We hope she's somewhere this side of the Mediterranean," said the Old Man, then he pulled the eggplant from his pocket and asked, "Where did you find this charm?"

The eggplant was silent. One word and this old creep might keep it.

"I've seen charms like this before," Hassan scowled and paced slowly around Aaron. "Does this one have any power?"

"It reminds me of an old friend," replied Aaron. "That's it."

"Where did you get it?" asked Hassan.

"Layla," blurted Aaron, and Hassan stopped pacing. "When I left her outside Paris."

"I knew a woman named Layla," recalled the Old Man. "The last time I saw her she was closing the gates behind me in Bahrain. Tell me more about your Layla."

Aaron may be an unintentionally accomplished thief, but he was compulsively honest. Before Hassan was finished with his questions, he knew Layla was an alchemist, a bomb maker, meditation expert, teacher and dancer. Hassan thought it was either a great coincidence this Layla shared similarities with the librarian in Bahrain, or she was the librarian. In either case, he wondered why she was looking for the Lost Stone. After all, it was Layla who first told him about the Stone. He also learned Aaron could read and write more languages than Hassan himself, and knew the recipe for black powder and how to use it. Aaron had many assets and Hassan was very happy to have him among his fedawis.

"Here, take your amulet. Maybe it will bring more memories of your Layla." Hassan returned the eggplant to Aaron, and the little vegetable was overjoyed.

3. The Assassins

Aaron was assigned to a group of 22 teenagers who were training in the high plateaus behind Eagle's Nest. Until his ankle and arm healed, Aaron still used his cane and sling when he watched the young fedawis scattered across the hills, practicing in teams, wrestling and fighting with wooden knives, stabbing stuffed bags with scimitars and running obstacle courses while blindfolded. He could walk on his own in a few weeks but a large bump remained on his left arm, giving him a small handicap against the other boys. Still, he trained night and day with them, always in silence. As they progressed, they became even quieter, until you could barely hear their footsteps. Before long, they could split camel hairs with their scimitars and quietly and instantly kill a man in any one of 15 different ways. They studied specific locations of vital organs, methods of strangulation, lethal and non-lethal doses of poisons, the use of black powder as a diversion and as a weapon, the art of disguise and most important, techniques for invisibility.

Aaron was happy at Eagle's Nest. During summer, he had his own cell in the castle with walls covered with star-maps and piles of books from the Old Man. He slept on the same rug every night, had plenty of food and many friends among the fedawis. It was a good home for Aaron, despite the purpose of the fortress.

They were Assassins, yet trained to have more compassion than many country's diplomats. The Assassins were always to be polite and courteous, especially to women and children. The assassinations were supposed to be quick and painless for victims.

Hassan taught them to never take murder for granted. "Kill your victim as if he was your best friend," he preached.

Hassan created a fully autonomous zone in which the boys were unleashed from social restrictions and taboos like nowhere else in the world. Being an Assassin was like playing a very serious game for these boys—a game testing social theories and stretching the power of their imaginations. A game in which everything was permitted. The fedawis played very hard and became more dangerous every day.

The Old Man made sure his boys had plenty of food, water and hashish. Aaron carved his own pipe from a goat horn and kept his hashish rations in a small tin the Old Man gave him. Smoking hashish made Aaron feel like he was in a soft, warm cloud that made it easy to dream of Eunisia. The eggplant approved, and enjoyed its own dreams of wind, sun, rain and warm, rich soil.

Aaron had become very handy with Arabic and Persian, but the eggplant preferred English. They were still best friends, but they didn't speak as much. They'd reached a point in their relationship where it wasn't necessary to talk all the time. The eggplant was content to lay back and take in the show with only occasional comments, which Aaron often mistook for his own thoughts.

If Eunisia was here, Aaron's life at Eagle's Nest would've been almost perfect. He still thought about her every day, but felt the hope of actually seeing her fading away. He considered escaping to find her, but where would he go? He had almost convinced himself she was not the girl with the Persian in Cairo. The eggplant reminded him if she survived the sea and desert, she could be anywhere between Baghdad and Blois. Aaron was tired of chasing an invisible memory. Tired of thirst and hunger following him wherever he searched. Living at Eagle's Nest was easier than searching for Eunisia, who may no longer exist.

The eggplant was thinking about Eunisia one day when it had the vegetable equivalent of a brainstorm. "What if Layla, Eunisia and Mina were all connected? If you could figure out what they have in common, you might find Eunisia."

"How can they be connected? They have nothing in common except me!"

"There's more," cautioned the eggplant. "One thing I've learned in 600 years, relationships and circumstances are rarely accidental. There's a big web of unseen connections too complex to perceive, but they usually expose the secret meaning of things. Think about it. You're intimately related to three people on this planet: a sorceress, saint and goddess."

"I found Layla and Eunisia by chance. Mina may have been something else."

"What do you mean?" asked the eggplant. "Some kind of divine intervention? And are the circumstances that led you to Layla and Eunisia so different from whatever led you to Mina?"

Aaron didn't answer, but the eggplant never felt quite right about the one-way road to Mina's well. Finding Mina's well was like being guided by an invisible hand, like they were in a stranger's game. As the weeks passed, Aaron and the eggplant still wondered about the strange occurrences in the desert and if they'd ever see any of their lady friends again.

*****

When cold weather turned Eagle's Nest into a virtual icebox, the boys moved outside the castle. They ate daily rations of opium to battle the cold, ripping winds and blankets of snow covering the mountain. Wood was only used for cooking, heating Hassan's quarters and making tent frames. They bundled up in burnooses in the day, and constructed wood frames two-feet high, six-feet wide, and long enough to accommodate 30 or 40 boys during the coldest days and nights. The fedawis would cover the frame with dozens of layers of wool rugs, strip naked and climb inside the dark box. Their warm bodies and ensuing connubial activities heated the box like a bed of warm embers. During bad storms, they'd stay in the box for days at a time, steam rising from the low, wool rooftops like smoke from hash pipes, melting the snow on the roof.

In early spring, when the boys returned to the castle, training was more intense. Languages, astronomy, map making and Eastern martial arts were added to each day's schedule. The boys studied in small groups, helping each other learn the material with games and stories. It was the closest thing to a family Aaron had ever known.

Aaron had grown much stronger since he arrived at Eagle's Nest. His hands and face were dark, weathered and prematurely wrinkled from months in the desert sun and wind. His eyes were still half-hidden in their shadowy sockets, but his smile was true, his shoulders were wide and his legs were firm. His long blonde hair had lost its springy curl, and he wore it in a single braid stretching halfway down his back.

By mid-summer, Hassan called Aaron and two other boys into his chambers. It was only the second time Aaron met with the Old Man since he arrived. "I understand you're my finest fedawis." He spoke to all three boys at once as he unrolled a map on a marble table in the center of the room and called them closer. An oil lamp cast a dull orange glow making the map look even older than it was.

"A Crusader has become too interested in Persian treasure," began the Old Man. "He knows of Eagle's Nest and may be planning an attack. He's a knight named Sir Gillian." The boys examined the map's details, looking for routes around mountains and pointing out water holes. "He's staying in an isolated desert outpost and is an adept swordsman," cautioned Hassan, opening another small map. The boys instinctively knew they'd kill him as he slept and return to Eagle's Nest before his body was discovered.

"Remember, you leave here as Allah's soldiers. Paradise awaits you when you return. And if you should die in the course of this mission, my angels will come to retrieve your souls." The Old Man became completely still as he spoke, his eyes fixed on an imperceptible script on the stone wall as he listened to a voice mumbling in tones only dogs and insects could hear. It was an ultra-high-pitched quasi-syllabic hum, like a voice waking you in the middle of the night to tell you something is terribly wrong. Hassan stood there for minutes, trying to decipher the message but the sounds were not clear enough to distinguish words. This had happened to him before. It was as if he was experiencing another man's dream. The boys watched him, waiting for a signal to leave. Finally, Hassan turned to the boys and said, "Sir Gillian must die as soon as possible, and you're the Assassins who will send him back to his God," then left the room without saying another word.

After chattering about killing the knight like murder was a game, the two Arab boys returned to their cells. They were younger than Aaron and even though this was their first mission, they seemed eager and confident they'd succeed. This was also Aaron's first assignment, but he wasn't ready. He may never be ready to kill for someone else. It was one thing to kill in self-defense, but this was quite different. Completely different.

Sleep didn't come easy for Aaron, who was glad to be the third Assassin on this mission. He may not have to kill anybody, just watch out for his friends. Anyway, this knight must be pretty bad if Hassan has marked him for death.

"I remember the Templars were chasing Layla, but I don't recall much about them."

"Sure you do. Kings would pay Templars to protect their Crusaders on their journey to the Holy Land, and they'd even get

186

a few coins from the pilgrims in return for chasing away thieves," reminded the eggplant. "After a few decades of collecting fees, Templars started the first banks in Europe and loaned money to everybody else, including King Philip."

"I thought money-lending was against the law?"

"It is," answered the eggplant. "For everybody except the Templars. What's worse, once the Templars were rich, they'd only help pilgrims who had socks full of gold."

"That explains why we never saw them," and Aaron felt better about their plans to change Sir Gillian's existential status.

*****

The boys left Eagle's Nest and rode for two days and nights, sleeping beside their horses and discussing the finer points of paradise. When they arrived at the ridge overlooking Sir Gillian's outpost, they saw only a small, one-room hut with thick, clay walls and no windows. Outside, a camel was tied to a twisted, dead tree and a well stood about 100 feet from the building. Otherwise, there was no sign of life for miles.

They slipped into their black harem pants and tunics and waited until the moonless hours before dawn, when the knight was in his deepest sleep. Aaron was first to advance, hunched over low to the ground and hustling silently to his position by the well, listening for any disturbance and waving his accomplices down the hill when he was certain it was safe. The other two boys crept slowly, like wayward sheep, one behind the other, until the first was inside the hut. A woman screamed as soon as he entered and a deep voice exploded, "Damn you Assassins! Damn you all!" The second Assassin moved in and there was a loud crash, then an oil lamp was lit inside, and the woman shrieked again and again.

Aaron crept from behind the well to the hut's entrance, trying to imagine how he'd overtake the knight.

"Don't outwit the knight," suggested the eggplant, "Outwit the Old Man."

"What do you mean outwit the Old Man?"

"Get on your horse and ride. You're free, Aaron."

"Ride where? My friends might be hurt. I have to go inside. I gave them my word. Do vegetables believe in honor?"

"This one does," replied the eggplant. "And there's nothing honorable about murdering knights in their sleep or an allegiance to Hassan and his Assassins."

"I don't like Hassan, either. But I like Eagle's Nest and the fedawis." Aaron crawled on all fours to the side of the hut and waited to hear another voice inside—maybe a knight's growl or an Assassin's cry for help—but there were only a woman's sobs. He dropped close to the ground, slid like a serpent inside the hut's doorway and saw a low bed and a pile of camel hair blankets. He raised his head slowly and there was a young woman sitting on the bed. He stood and she turned sharply. The front of her robe was covered with blood and she squeezed a dagger in her small, shaking hand. Three still, bloody bodies were twisted on the floor between Aaron and the woman.

"I'm not here to hurt you." Aaron looked into her eyes and thought she was Eunisia. Through the tears and short, dyed hair and weathered face, he wasn't sure at first, but then he knew it was her. "Eunisia! It's me, Aaron!" He reached for her hand, but she thrust the dagger towards him.

"Kill me, if that's what you're going to do, but please don't torture me," she tried to speak through tears and heavy sobs, but Aaron could barely understand her.

He dropped his scimitar and pulled off his hood. "Look at the scar on my nose. Don't you remember?" Eunisia glanced up at Aaron's face then turned away. "We met outside Paris and were separated on different ships in Marseilles. You must remember me!"

Aaron still appeared like a stranger to Eunisia. She was naked, except for the bloody robe, and quivering like a cold, wet dog. She looked different with short reddish hair and a painted face—and those weren't the only changes. She was a girl when he saw her last and now her hips were wider, her ears were pierced and her breasts bulged beneath her stained robe. She was a woman. But she was no longer the most beautiful woman he'd ever seen.

"Not exactly a goddess," noted the eggplant, as Eunisia sobbed in a heap at the edge of the bed, her face buried in her dirty hands and short red hair poking out of her scalp like bloody needles.

Aaron was at once thrilled to see her alive, sad to see her condition, and shattered she didn't remember him. "I never stopped thinking about you, Eunisia. I tried to find you, but I was kidnapped in Cairo by Assassins."

She never glanced up. Aaron sat on the bed beside her. He reached out to touch her, but she jumped away and went to the other side of the bed, still holding the dagger.

"Why did you kill Sir Gillian?" she demanded.

Aaron didn't understand why she was so hurt by Sir Gillian's death. "The Old Man of the Mountain—the same Old Man that gave your brother his orders—sent us here. We were doing what we were told."

"We were awake," she cried. "He was telling me about Baghdad when someone sneaked into the room, Sir Gillian shouted, then he leaped from bed and stabbed the attacker. Then the other one appeared from nowhere and killed Sir Gillian," she pointed to the Assassin who was on top the funereal pile on the floor. "I grabbed a dagger from the shelf and jabbed it into the darkness. When I lit the oil lamp, I saw the bodies. Two boys dressed in black, like you, and Sir Gillian. All dead."

"What were you doing with him?" Aaron noticed the dead knight at the bottom of the pile was naked, and the eggplant decided to remain silent on the issue.

Eunisia looked Aaron in the eye for the first time. "I was lucky. He saved me from slave traders in Cairo months ago. Most of the girls were sold into Arab harems or killed by camel drivers in the desert."

Aaron said nothing for a long time. Both he and the eggplant knew exactly what she was doing with the knight when the Assassins arrived. They just didn't believe it could be true. Aaron didn't want it to be true. He desperately wanted another explanation and would have settled for angelic or demonic intervention, if Eunisia had only implied it. This moment when they finally reunited was supposed to paint the sky with colored lights and fill Aaron with unlimited bliss. Instead, he felt empty and lost. Not physically lost, just spiritually disoriented. His compass had always pointed to Eunisia, now it was spinning so fast it made his bones feel brittle as thin ice.

"How could she do it?"

"The same way you did it, my friend," reminded the eggplant.

"What do you mean?"

"You weren't just hand-dancing with those girls in Hassan's garden."

"But how could she forget me?"

"Who knows what this poor girl has been through, before or after you met her," cautioned the eggplant. "Since you were apart she may have known 100 men in more ways than we dare to imagine, and she may not want to remember any of them."

The eggplant was right. Aaron realized he was a complete fool from the beginning of his imaginary romance, but it didn't seem to matter—he still felt connected to Eunisia, and wanted to protect her above all else.

"Ahhh!" There was a sharp pain pressing in his side and before he saw the dagger he shoved Eunisia away with such force she bounced off of the wall and fell atop the dead bodies already piled on the floor. Aaron jumped to his feet, stopped the bleeding with his hand and grabbed the dagger from Eunisia. While he bandaged his cut Aaron suddenly saw the world in a brand new light. It was as if someone had sucked the wind out of him and sewed him up so no air and no light could get in. Just darkness. He was silent for a long time, too weak and disappointed to cry, waiting for his pain and sorrow to subside.

"The love of your life just killed your friend and stabbed you," reminded the vegetable. "As for her friend Sir Gillian, he was nothing more than a filthy pig who owned a teenage sex slave and deserved to die. I wouldn't hold on to this bad memory. Not worth it."

"You're right." Aaron conceded. "Those are the facts. The truth."

The eggplant was pleased Aaron was finally starting to smell the real world.

It was true. Aaron understood that Eunisia enjoyed being with the knight and she didn't even remember him. These were real, intelligent insights and they made him feel completely stupid. He began to doubt everything, from a return to Eagle's Nest to ever returning to England. What difference does it make? She didn't do this to him, but still he was shattered. And he still felt guilty for leaving Eunisia in Marseilles. There wasn't much emotion left in him when he asked her, "Why did you stab me? Did you want to kill me?"

She looked up, as if surprised by the question. "I can't take being used by another man. No more," she shook her head slowly back and forth and cried as she gazed at some distant darkness, as if her horrors had stolen the stars once burning inside of her. "Sir Gillian never hurt me. He made me feel safe. Maybe I was as happy as I'll ever be."

"Not much different from your arrangement with Hassan," noted the eggplant. "He doesn't hurt you, provides some shelter and security, and you call it happiness."

"The lesser of many evils, at best," said Aaron.

"He was a saint compared to the others," replied Eunisia.

"But happiness has to be more than safety" added the eggplant.

Happiness or not, sex slave or not, stab-wound or not, Aaron couldn't leave Eunisia here in the desert for the first camel driver or castaway to have his way with her. "I'll do everything I can to find a safe home for you, and I won't hurt you."

Her eyes were cast down as he spoke, towards the knight's body. Eunisia knew she had no choice. "I'll go with you, but I don't expect anything but transportation, and you must expect nothing from me," she declared, and gathered her belongings for the ride while Aaron inspected the tiny outpost and debated whether to thank the gods for sparing Eunisia.

Finding a tattered Eunisia who didn't remember him was better than finding no Eunisia at all, he thought, and collected the few maps the knight had rolled up in long leather tubes and a small book open on the desk. The book had an old, worn leather jacket and no title. It was written in Hebrew and looked like a book Layla would have in her library. It even smelled a little like Layla, he thought, and tucked it under his arm.

Aaron pulled the bodies outside, buried them all under the same pile of rocks, and helped Eunisia fill her saddlebags with clothes and gifts from Sir Gillian. Her silver necklace with shield and cross, his last gift, twinkled in the morning sun. She tried to hide her tears as they untied the camel from the twisted, bleached tree and watched it plod away, west, to Egypt. Aaron remembered Natalie and Donatelle, and considered following the camel to Cairo, but he was afraid running would only bring more troubles, and the eggplant concurred.

"Hassan will send Assassins for you and kill whomever rides with you or gives you shelter. You know he's ruthless. Do you want to bring death to Eunisia and the girls in Cairo? Save yourself!" demanded the eggplant. "Take this lady to a safe haven and you should ride away to Damascus, Jerusalem or even Bahrain as fast as you can."

They mounted their stallions but did not ride to freedom. Aaron knew Hassan's fedawis would find him if he didn't return and he didn't want to wait for an Assassin's blade. He'd have to settle his account with Hassan first. Today, Aaron and Eunisia traveled to the only safe haven outside of Layla's castle Aaron had known, the only place in the world where friends welcomed him. They started back to Eagle's Nest.

By mid-afternoon, Aaron had described everything about the mountain fortress to Eunisia, omitting his erotic adventures in the garden. Eunisia didn't talk much. The past two years had been hard in so many ways she was numb. Arab blades had pressed against her throat many times, and she was always prepared to die.

"Sometimes it all seems like a bad dream. Then I wake up and it's all too real." She cried most of the way to Eagle's Nest. There was nothing he could do, and he feared she'd never be happy again.

*****

When they arrived, Hassan made sure they had a powerful dose of opium-laced wine waiting, and separated Aaron and Eunisia as soon as they passed out. It didn't matter that he walked across Europe with her and chased her across half of northern Africa. The Old Man had no heart for romance. His heart was devoted entirely to power, and he still needed Aaron for more important work.

Aaron awoke in the garden and frantically began looking for Eunisia—not because he still loved her—but he promised to keep her safe and feared she was taken to the harem. Hassan knew there was no place for a broken Eunisia at Eagle's Nest and he already moved her far away. Still, Aaron stumbled inside the castle and marched directly to the Old Man's quarters and demanded to see her.

"She's gone," said the Old Man, without looking up. He was leaning over a table, comparing maps and trying to ignore Aaron.

"You sent her away while I was in the garden?" Aaron was on the verge of tears and nodding from the opium hangover. "Where is she?"

"Eagle's Nest is no place for a young woman like her. We train killers here. There are hundreds of boys inside this fortress and camped in these valleys. I sent her to a woman's castle for care. They'll treat her well," assured Hassan, but he could see Aaron was bitter.

"I'll find her again. I'll find her and I'll give her the freedom she deserves."

A fragment of a smile crept across the Old Man's lips and raised his cheeks ever so slightly. "I believe you'll find your Eunisia. Months from now, or maybe years, but not today. Today you will survive. Today you will not forget you have lost two fedawis."

Aaron dropped his head, ashamed he hardly thought of his friends since he buried them. "I'm sorry, for them. They were good friends, but they were both dead when I entered the outpost, and so was Sir Gillian. I would have sacrificed myself to save them, but it was too late." Other fedawis killed themselves or were shunned by the others if they returned without all three Assassins safe. Aaron felt horrible he couldn't save his friends, but he would not take his own life.

194

"Don't worry. You won't have to pay for their deaths. Today you'll begin a new life at Eagle's Nest. From now on, you'll be my personal scribe. You'll live in the castle and you alone will work in my library and transcribe the secrets."

Aaron was surprised, but not grateful. Maybe he spared his life and Eunisia really was safe, but the Old Man had taken her away against her will, and Aaron would never forgive him.

He vowed to escape from Eagle's Nest. It may take months, but he'd do whatever it took to leave this place alive and find Eunisia. He'd obey the Old Man and work in the library, for now. But when the chance arose, he'd be gone.

*****

The Old Man's library was spectacular. It occupied two large rooms in Eagle's Nest and its walls were lined with books, scrolls, tablets and plates that had been stolen, traded or purchased from every corner of the world. Before it was destroyed, Alexandria's library held texts from deep antiquity, beyond the ancient Egyptians, Phoenicians and Sumerians—some predating the biblical account of creation, among its many literary and historic masterpieces. Hassan's library was quite different. It contained the unsavory underbelly of history, rejected by mullah's, priests and tribal leaders as either foul heresies or just too wild and wicked to be worthy of their hallowed shelves. In fact, the writings kept at Eagle's Nest were less contaminated than the soft, revised versions of history burned at Alexandria. Hassan had retrieved sacred and profane writings from caves in Northern India, maps, diagrams, sketches and lewd drawings from the undiscovered pyramids in the Mongolian desert, emerald tablets recovered from beneath the sphinx, medical treatises from Babylonian surgeons operating in 1,000 B.C., Plato's original writings on divine deviance, sex manuals from Pacific islands, homosexual time-travel rituals of the ancient Greeks, sadomasochistic practices in Sumeria, astrologic projections from Persia's most decorated star watchers and assorted alchemical cures for the clap, all neatly stacked on tall, hand-carved, wooden shelves. Hassan had the sour cream of ancient literature in his library, and he spent hours each day with the rare manuscripts.

Aaron loved it, too. The library was an amusement park for intellectual daredevils. It was so overwhelming, Aaron almost forgot about Sir Gillian's book. When he finally pulled it out, he didn't understand why a knight would be interested in the strange Hebrew writings it contained. He thought the Templars were supposed to be the ideal Christians.

The book had only twelve pages. Its paper was thick, as if made from chunks of manzanita bark. The symbols and Hebrew words were written in dark brown ink that looked like dried blood. The word, "Paradise" was on the first page, along with a small, rough map of an island and a compass symbol. The remaining pages were filled with short, nonsensical verses. He set the book aside and wondered what Sir Gillian was really doing in the Persian desert, and if Eunisia was more than just the knight's lover.

"Would it make you feel happier if she was a spy?" asked the eggplant. "Or a female Assassin?"

Aaron and the eggplant often wondered if true happiness was possible. The eggplant thought happiness was a state of mind interrupted by suffering, or vice-versa. For vegetables, it's black and white. You're either happily fulfilling your existential potential, or you're suffering in putrefied, fermented and decomposed denial. It's either Eggplant Paradise or Compost City. Aaron saw a lot more on his menu. He learned there were many flavors of happiness in this world.

"Laughing with my fedawis, kissing girls in the garden and devouring ancient texts in the library are just a few ingredients for gourmet happiness."

"Sure, that's happiness. Until the girls forget you and find other lovers, the fedawis betray you and the ancient texts turn out to be lies," said the eggplant, who still preferred its salt-and-pepper view.

"Do you think that'll happen?"

"It always does, one way or the other," sighed the vegetable.

Aaron was happy in the library. It was like he was in his own world. He began transcribing the oldest texts first. The Old Man provided sheets of smooth hemp paper, specially mixed Persian ink, a large wooden desk and two oil lamps. Aaron didn't need a chair. He preferred to stand as he copied the faded, yellow, crumbling originals onto fresh paper in his finest Farsi lettering.

His first manuscript was a long Hebrew passage from the *Book of Adam*. It described Adam's first wife, Lilith, who was already one of Aaron's favorites. The passage began, "God formed Lilith, the first woman, just as He had formed Adam. Adam and Lilith never found peace together, for when he wished to lie with her, she took offense at the position he demanded."

"Why must I lie beneath you?" she asked. "I was made from dust, just as you. You will lie beneath me and I will ride atop you like a master over her beast," proclaimed Lilith.

"Adam tried to take Lilith by force, like the lion takes the lioness, like the steed takes the mare or the sun takes the sky. But before he could have her, she uttered the magic name of God, rose into the air and left him forever."

Aaron became very familiar with Lilith. Over the next few months he transcribed six different versions of her tale. In ancient Sumeria she was the left hand of the goddess who coaxed men to Ianna's temple for ritual orgies. To Mesopotamia's Semitic-speaking people, she was a goddess of destructive winds and storms. Near East natives called her Lamashtu, and believed she was a wise, clever and seductive demon who collected seed from sleeping men and masturbators. And in the Talmud, she was a winged demon who only killed uncircumcised boys and girls who were under 20 days old.

One text described the Garden of Eden like an eyewitness account. This book never mentioned Lilith, but Aaron liked to think she wrote it herself, and he kept it by his bed. It was more of a diary than a book, and contained everything from pictures of trees and fruit to a map of an island titled, "Paradise." There was one eight-pointed star on the map, at the top of the island. Beside the star was the word, "Eden." The map looked just like the one in Sir Gillian's book.

Then he found the *Black Book of Genesis*. This Lilith story was similar to the first, except Lilith was a beautiful, voluptuous woman who left the Garden with a large, egg-shaped Stone made from a fallen star.

Aaron closed the book and whispered, "Layla."

If the eggplant had shoulders, it would have shrugged them.

The longer he worked in the library, the more Aaron appreciated it. The old books each had their own subtle aroma and he often imagined the noses they'd pleased each time they were read. He handled every text as if it were made from thin, delicate sheets of glass and read them like they were clues in a marvelous, four-dimensional puzzle. He transcribed texts revealing everything from parlor tricks to the secrets of transmuting lead into silver. One magic diagram illustrated the shape and motion of the sun and moon, with the earth a medium ball circled by a small round moon, both of them traveling around a huge spherical sun.

He copied tantric books filled with explicit illustrations of sexual positions, some requiring the ability to hover several feet above the ground. No matter which way he looked at the pages, he couldn't tell which way was up, so he copied them as they were, mostly variations on arms and legs tangled in exotic formations, each position with its own name and particular attraction.

Hassan's library contained the world's largest and oldest collection of homosexual manuals, treatises, scrolls and tablets in the known universe. His spies had scoured the secret libraries and private collections in dozens of countries and returned with the authoritative history of homosexual activity among the world's earliest civilizations, greatest thinkers and heroes. There were six-foot reliefs from the tomb of Niankhknum and Khnumhotep, two male lovers whose embrace had lasted almost 4,000 years. Homoerotic poems of Nebuchadnezzar. Erotic tales of Alexander the Great, Aristotle and Caesar. Aaron even transcribed the original Gnostic Gospel of St. Thomas claiming Jesus was an over-sexed hermaphrodite.

From erotica, Aaron moved to the life extension texts. These books documented the lives of men and women who'd discovered the secrets of immortality. There was Enoch, seventh-generation descendant of Adam, Thoth the Atlantean, and Uzume, the eternal Japanese shaman goddess. There were recipes for adding hundreds of years to a life with herbs, meditation and incantations. Aaron was surprised more people didn't live forever with so many potions available.

He copied star charts and maps of Druid longevity shrines stretching across Europe. He found the story of Abraham and the Kabba on a Sumerian tablet, which was identical to the story the eggplant heard in Bahrain 300 years ago. Aaron transcribed texts each day until his fingers were ink-stained and sore, all the time discussing the stories with the eggplant. Before long, they knew more about sacred mysteries than the holy men in Cairo, Mecca and the Vatican combined. One of his most interesting revelations came when he was transcribing original Kabbalistic texts from decayed Hebrew scrolls listing the secret names of angels and the three mother letters used to create the universe. It was good to know the names of angels and what they did, but the three mother

199

Hebrew letters—mem, aleph and shin—were the same as the English letters his mother had written on the piece of paper he carried across the world to Cairo. Aaron wondered how his mother could have known what these letters meant, or if it was just another coincidence.

Still, Aaron was amazed at how many of the stories he'd already read or heard while he stayed at Layla's. There was even one book, called *The Rape of Mecca,* which recounted the ending of the Hamdan Karmat tale Layla and the eggplant started. *The Rape of Mecca* began in the courtyard of Hamdan's son, Tahir, where he was confronting a magician:

"Allah has given your Karmation armies many victories," said Falukki Babazini, the magician. "But your greatest is yet to come. When the Lost Stone is found, a Karmation will hold it as his own and become the leader of the Moslem world."

The words rang through the courtyard like a golden prophecy. Tahir bowed his head to conceal his grin. He savored the idea of being a powerful holy man. He imagined holding the Lost Stone in his hands and felt immortality was within his grasp. Yes, this was his destiny, he thought, and smoothed his thin, greasy moustache with his hand then wiped beads of sweat from his forehead with his sleeve. "Tell me the rest," and he continued to pace around the room, now slowly twisting his mustache.

"The magician sighed deeply and said the Prince will march on Mecca before the kumquats are ripe on the trees. You should also know layers of secrets protect the Stone. Only certain incantations can unlock its powers."

"What do you mean?"

"To possess the Stone is not enough. It's like a lamp without oil and only correct incantations can make it shine. It's been sleeping for centuries and may be difficult to awaken."

"Can a magician like you perform the incantations?"

"The old mullah taught me the words and showed me the night sky that must accompany them."

200

In fact, the magician was never taught anything about the Lost Stone. He never even knew it existed until he found it amongst a thief's booty at the back of a cave near the Dead Sea. Babazini was hiding from the Sultan al-Adil, who sent several warriors to bring back his head after the magician disappeared with one of the Sultan's prize horses and never returned. Babazini rode the horse for days, then sent it away to divert the warriors and traveled by foot through the dry, barren hills around the Dead Sea with no supplies, except a half-filled skin of water. He was starving and explored caves, looking for crumbs left behind— scraps of bread or rotten meats, bird bones, grease from old pots—anything even slightly edible. When he smelled something really bad coming from the darkness at the back of one particularly deep, low-roofed cave he crawled to investigate and found the bodies of what appeared to be two heavily armed female warriors and three male Persians, who were also armed with swords. It looked like there was an awful fight in the darkness, leaving everyone dead. When he searched through the women's clothes, he found one of them was wearing a pouch under her blouse that held a peculiar large, egg-shaped stone. It was the Lost Stone. Combined with the dried food supplies from the women's pouches, two small daggers and a long, shining scimitar, the magician was back in business to set the stage to destroy the Karmations, who had killed his family in a raid two years earlier.

*****

With Hamdan Karmat dead, Tahir was the Karmations lone ruler. Tahir sent his highest guards and berserkers all across the island and into the Arabian Desert to search for Babazini, but they never found him.

Tahir's appetite for longevity grew stronger. If he couldn't have the Lost Stone, he'd take the Kabba Stone—surely it had the same powers. His advisers were shocked to hear his plan to attack Mecca. They never thought of him as either religious or a warrior. Yet Tahir claimed the caliph of Mecca was an idol worshipper who conspired to destroy the Karmations, and commanded his army to take the sacred city for all Moslems.

The Kabba was in the center of the Mosque, located at the eastern end of the sacred territory in Mecca, with mountains on two sides. The Karmations attacked after midnight with more than 1,000 half-drunk warriors and berserkers who slashed and chopped the mullahs, pilgrims, and merchants as they rode through the narrow streets then went right for the city's heart, descending on the Great Mosque like an unnatural disaster in almost total darkness. Only a few lamps burned and there was barely enough light to see the carnage. Holy men who'd devoted their lives to this shrine tried to protect the Kabba with their bare hands, but the berserkers would lop off their arm before the poor men could reconsider their bravery. The moaning and cries rang like shattered bells in a sandstorm.

Thunder rumbled and boomed overhead while bolts of lightning ripped through the sky to illuminate a surreal, mutilated landscape of men running blindly with knives in each hand, slashing the air around them with steel scimitars. It was a bloody battle, both sides Moslem, both sides fighting for the same God, one side praying this is a bad dream, the other side wide awake and ready to thank their God for victory.

Tahir saw the Kabba and went for the Stone. Thunder shook the ground beneath his feet. Lightning flashed from all directions, illuminating the tall, square sides of the Kabba and casting long shadows across the square. He plunged his dagger behind the Stone and tried to pry it from its nest in the wall, but it wouldn't budge. He used his blade to attack the stubborn Stone from all angles but it fit so tightly in its groove in the wall of the Kabba he couldn't find a weak point.

Tahir forced his dagger into the space at the edge of the Stone and twisted it until a small piece of the wall broke away, he wedged the blade behind the Stone and ripped it from the Kabba. He rubbed the cold black rock with bloodstained hands, pressed it to his heart and sneaked away, like a common thief.

Tahir returned to Bahrain with the Kabba Stone, and wore it close to his body, tied in a shoulder harness under his djellaba. He wanted to feel the Stone against his skin, where it reminded him he was the amir who was destined to rule the Moslem world.

The omnipotent mood left Tahir the moment he stepped into his private courtyard and saw Falukki Babazini waiting there with the headless body of the Karmation's top general, sitting upright against a potted palm tree. Before he could ask a question or call for a guard, the magician barred the door behind Tahir and pulled out a long, curved dagger.

"What do you want? Money? Gold? Slaves? I'll give you all of them," offered Tahir.

"I'm here for the Kabba Stone," whispered Babazini.

Tahir could hear his heart pounding against the Stone. He only held the Kabba Stone for one week and already he was infatuated with its dark allure. As long as he kept the Stone, he was important, and he was desperate to be historic. Maybe even epic. Breathing hard, trying to focus on emergency options, the best Tahir could muster was to threaten the magician with 1,000 Karmation soldiers and berserkers who'd find him and kill him if he stole the Stone.

"Just like they found me last time?" Babazini walked to Tahir with his dagger drawn, patted him on the shoulder and cut a long strip across Tahir's djellaba, leaving a thin line of blood on his chest. Even after battle, Tahir still feared the smallest wound, and the sight of his own blood made him queasy, so he didn't look. The magician smiled and wrapped his arms around him, squeezed him lightly, snatched the Kabba Stone and kissed his cheek. When the magician released him, Tahir felt his chest and demanded the magician return the Stone or be hunted for the rest of his life.

Babazini continued to smile, and promised Tahir he'd return the Kabba Stone—after he introduced it to the Lost Stone, which he pulled from a pouch in his vest. He examined the two Stones closely, comparing their size, shape and weight, and found only one difference: unlike the Kabba Stone, the Lost Stone was more cloudy grey than black.

"You're a fool, Tahir. The Kabba Stone belongs in Mecca. You should never have taken it. I only came here long ago because your father's army killed my family and I wanted revenge. I knew he had the resources to find and capture the Lost Stone, and I knew my story would interest him. It's easy to kill people, once inside their bedroom. And it would be easy for me to kill you now. But stealing the Kabba Stone should bring you plenty of suffering and infamy, unless you do the right thing and return the Kabba Stone to Mecca."

Before Tahir opened his mouth to strike a final bargain, he saw only a flash of blue smoke and was left alone with the Kabba Stone at his feet, broken into seven pieces.

Tahir's metal smiths banded the Stone back together, and he struck a bargain with the mullahs in Mecca, demanding nothing less than the absolute sovereignty of Bahrain for its return. The arguments lasted for 23 years—mostly because the mullahs and caliph didn't like the idea of accepting a broken, banded Stone— when a grey-haired Tahir finally won sovereignty for his people in Bahrain, and the Kabba Stone was returned to its rightful place.

The Kabba Stone was once again adored and kissed by thousands of Moslem pilgrims, giving it plenty of staying power. It could be destroyed or plundered or cracked into a million tiny fragments and sold to the highest bidders, the Kabba Stone would still come back to its rightful place in Mecca. The Kabba Stone was bigger than truth or religion—it was a direct connection with another world—the world of gods.

The true Lost Stone offered the same connection, but in a more intimate setting. For one thing, the Lost Stone is only important for the few who knew of its existence, and Babazini overestimated those who knew or even heard of the Stone. But the moment the magician left the island with the Stone, he suspected everyone around him was conspiring against him. In just a few months, he'd killed most of his adversaries and allies. The magician wandered aimlessly, obsessed with the Stone, trying to unlock its secrets with incantations and tempering his growing madness with solitude. He spent weeks at a time in caves eating bugs and contemplating the Stone. He tried to connect the Stone to stars in the endless desert night. He used every magic phrase he'd ever learned and developed new incantations by rearranging words in the Koran. He meditated for days and prayed to Allah for assistance, but nothing seemed to make a difference. There was no sign the Stone had any power at all. He was able to enter the fortress of a ruthless Karmation army, kill their leader and leave right under their noses without a scratch. Now he couldn't get the Stone to do anything but sit there and shine. He sat in the sun, on the side of a cliff near the Dead Sea, polishing the Stone with a corner of his djellaba until he could see his reflection on its smooth, grey surface. He looked old and tired. He knew he was running out of time.

Finally, the magician returned to Cairo old and weak and used his magic to attract a small group of impressionable young Ishmaelites who surrounded him day and night, protecting him and the Stone. Then one of the boys surprised the magician with an early pot of tea and saw the Stone on the magician's chest as he changed his robe. This was the first time anyone had seen the Stone since he'd taken it from Tahir. To protect his secret, the magician left Cairo before the tea was cool, but it was too late.

A dancer from the court of Hamdan, named Samar, knew of the magician's plan to take the Lost Stone and recognized him before he left Cairo. The dancer's brother was a devoted Ishmaelite, and he followed the magician, killed him and took the Stone, which stayed in the hands of a secret Ishmaelite sect for the next 250 years, hidden in a fortress in the Persian Mountains, protected by a small army and unknown to the world at large.

According to this legend, the Stone waits in this mountain fortress for a single person who is destined to be its true keeper, a person possessed with compassion and suffering and the insatiable pursuit of the highest ecstasy, a person whose pure innocence outweighs all the sands of the deserts.

"I don't believe it," started the eggplant. "The Lost Stone was here all along? I wish we knew where Layla was right now. She sure would like to know we found her Stone."

"Not so fast. We don't know it's here."

"C'mon. You and I both know it's probably hanging across Hassan's chest right now."

*****

Hassan visited Aaron daily. They usually smoked a bowl of hashish, looked over the texts Aaron was working on, and after a few months, Hassan brought associates from outside Eagle's Nest to the library. One afternoon Hassan appeared with a guru from the high mountains of India and asked Aaron to help him locate a lost chapter from the Kama Sutra. Aaron enjoyed the guru's company and his ideas about the world. Their conversations always started at the top of the mountain and worked their way slowly down the ice-coated slopes. The first question Aaron asked the guru was, "Do you think a man can ever be free?"

The guru was eating rice with his hand from a clay bowl. "No," he said, and never looked up. He continued eating without saying a word. Aaron waited politely, and after several minutes the guru continued, "A man may think he's free to choose, free to wander, free to laugh and cry, but it's only an illusion. We're all slaves trapped in a magnificent web. Look closely and you'll see it all around you."

Aaron looked around and held up his hands. "I'm free."

The guru laughed. "Did you choose to come to Eagle's Nest? Did you decide to transcribe these texts? Did you arrange for me to sleep and eat beside you in this library? No, my friend. You're not free. No man is truly free."

Aaron agreed with the guru, up to a point. "I could change it all at any time. I enjoy your company, so I stay. The texts are rare gems, so I happily transcribe them. Eagle's Nest suits me well and I love the library, so I make it my home. I make my choices."

"Our choices are like sheep finding different paths on the mountainside. The sheep may wander but the mountain never changes," preached the guru.

"Goats are much brighter than sheep," added the eggplant, unclear if freedom was a concept vegetables even consider. Establishing its existence with any certainty was enough trouble—trying to wrestle with the question of one's own free will was simply too much, even for most humans.

The next week the guru departed and Hassan returned with a Tibetan monk. They transcribed texts together for almost six weeks. Next, Hassan had an astronomer and physician kidnapped from Cairo to instruct Aaron. They stayed for six months before Hassan released them. Aaron's last visitor was a Templar who introduced himself as Jacques DeMolay, then rarely spoke again. Aaron wondered if he knew about Sir Gillian.

Jacques paged through piles of manuscripts with his greasy fingers, taking notes and shuffling fragile clay tablets as if they were made from bronze, spilling his food and drink and taking most of Aaron's valuable light. Aaron protected his newly transcribed texts beneath his desk, and kept his distance from the foul-smelling knight. Jacques copied nearly every lethal recipe in the library, along with notes on antidotes. There were thousands of beautiful books revealing amazing secrets, but like most visitors to the library, he was obsessed with murder. Magicians, knights or priests, it made no difference—most preferred death to ecstasy.

Climbing atop a wobbly ladder, Aaron discovered a wooden box pushed to the back of the top shelf. He opened it and found lists of the Old Man's victims arranged by year, country and crime. He counted more than 700 assassinations Hassan had ordered over the past 30 years. There were tyrants, thieves, monks, mullahs, sultans, caliphs, amirs, merchants, Crusaders and even one pope, Celestine III, who condemned sexual deviants to death while abusing his own harem of young boys. Hassan's victims had beaten women, obstructed freedom, destroyed art, stolen ancient treasures, cheated friends and relatives, imposed ridiculous taxes and committed the high crimes of greed and arrogance. The Old Man appeared to be eliminating some real bad guys, but there were also good-hearted victims whose only crime was cursing the Assassins.

Beneath the victims' names was a list of those whom Hassan had granted lifetime immunity from the Assassin's blades. There were 13 on this list. Most earned their immunity by aiding Assassins or providing goods or services. But the first name on the list had no year by its side and no reason for her special dispensation. It was Layla.

"Layla?" echoed the eggplant. Then it remembered. Layla helped a man many years ago when she was a librarian in Bahrain—he must've been Hassan. He was searching for the secret of eternal life and when he left, he promised to always protect her. The eggplant even recalled Layla accepting the offer.

Aaron couldn't believe Hassan and Layla were connected. He was afraid the guru was right. For the first time, he could see the web really was everywhere.

4. St. Anthony's Well

Mina warned Layla they wouldn't find St. Anthony's well unless they were lost, and she was right. It took them 16 days to stumble onto the shrine, including three days spent wandering in circles. There was neither a miraculous sandstorm nor any landmarks to assist Mina's navigation, only her keen sense of desert intuition. When they finally spotted the building, it looked more like a fallen birdhouse than a shrine. Only the very peak of the stone roof poked up like a tiny A-frame in the sand, yet Mina recognized it, and they spent half the day digging before they could go inside. When they crawled in the door and stood beside the well, its little wall and tiny circumference appeared much smaller than Layla had imagined. She peered down the dark hole and knew she'd never fit. She didn't see how Mina could squeeze down the thin passage, but she did.

The well's shaft was no more than 20 inches wide with limestone walls for all 100 feet, straight down. The original chisel marks were still visible in the walls and there were grooves for hands and feet carved every 12 inches. Mina descended one-step at a time, she and Layla counting them together, until their voices sounded like distant echoes. Mina stopped at step number 98 and Layla lowered a small, lit torch down the shaft.

"Hold the torch right there," called Mina, and she held her nose and dropped into the water with a splash resounding from the walls for minutes. The water was cool and delicious after weeks on a camel in the desert. Mina bobbed to the top, cleaner and more refreshed than she could remember. She felt like a child as she climbed to the walkway around the edge of the pool, dripping wet, the torch illuminating the cavern's wall with dancing sepia light.

"Are you all right?" Layla's voice was small and far away. The splashing water still echoed in the cavern, as if making up for centuries of silence.

"Yes." Mina gazed at the figures carved on opposite walls, glowing with warm yellow and orange torchlight. "I didn't remember how beautiful it was down here."

"What? I can't hear you."

"It's beautiful!" she hollered up the shaft, "I wish you could see it!" They weren't sure they'd find anything at the bottom of this well, but Mina had never looked far beyond the figures before. She went to the wall with the woman's body first and rubbed her hands all over the lines carved on the cool, moist limestone. She pressed against the figure with all her strength, but it didn't budge.

"What are you doing?" called Layla.

"I'm pushing against the woman who's carved in the wall."

"Say the words carved in the wall when you push."

Mina pushed again. She put her thin shoulder into the center of the egg the woman was holding and said, "Thunder in Baghdad," then started to shove. The words echoed around the cavern. She repeated them again and again, and the volume seemed to double each time, until the walls shook and the carving of the woman moved just enough so Mina could grab its edges and pry it away from the wall, like a thick, heavy puzzle-piece. Inside the shallow cavity was an old, decayed pouch. Mina pulled it out and opened it.

"I found a map! I'm going to see what's behind the egg on the other wall." Mina made her way around the edge of the pool and stood face to face with the man. He was holding a Stone that was positioned perfectly even with Mina's ass, and about the same size. She turned around, put her backside to the carving, then pushed against it and repeated, "Lightning in paradise,"

211

louder each time. The words rang like giant bells and Mina pushed the wall with more force, but nothing moved. Then she bent down pushed her shoulder hard against the egg carved in the wall and said the words again, "Lightning in paradise," louder than before. On the third shout the egg cracked and left a deep indentation in the wall. She pulled away enough loose, crumbling limestone to reach behind and touch something on the other side. When she realized what it was, she pulled her hand away and screamed.

"Mina! Are you all right? What's happening?"

"There's a naked man behind the picture!" Mina called back. She wanted to add she just grabbed his penis, but couldn't believe it herself.

"Leave him there. We'll come back if we need him. Just be very careful and don't drop the map." Layla's voice was like a sea gull calling from a faraway shore, reminding Mina which way was up.

But Mina couldn't just leave him there. She broke away a few more chunks of limestone and pulled the torch closer to see the face. He was brown and hard as stone. His eyes were closed. He looked like an Arab, but she couldn't be sure. She'd seen mummies before, but never one like this. He was unbound and had been preserved with all of his parts intact, including a fully erect penis. This was the first time she'd ever seen an erection and she wasn't sure what to make of it. There was something spooky about it, as though it was alive on his petrified body.

Layla paced around like a wise man waiting for a virgin birth. She wondered what a map was doing here, hidden in a remote desert well. Who could have put it here? And when? She knew those questions may never be answered, but she was pretty sure she could identify the petrified man behind the wall.

Mina climbed out of the well exhausted, dripping wet with face, hands and bare feet red with scrapes from the shaft's rough-sided walls. Still, she couldn't help but make little laughing bird sounds as she presented the map to Layla.

"Thank you, Mina. Thank you for finding me in Marseilles, being my friend and bringing me to your shrine." Layla was on the verge of tears as she looked at the map. It was written in Hebrew and pointed to the Stone of Eden. The accompanying note made it clear—the Stone was at a fortress in the Persian Mountains, until one pure and innocent soul could set it free. "The Old Man had it all along."

They hugged and laughed and filled their water skins with fresh water from the secret well. Mina was still thinking about the first penis she'd ever touched, and she wanted to know more about its owner, even if she'd never see him again. "Who do you think the man behind the wall could be?"

"There's an old Ishmaelite legend claiming *The Book of Secrets* accompanies the body of Adam. If the bottom of this well is *The Book of Secrets*, then you just touched the actual body of the world's first man.

Mina's mouth fell open. "Do you mean Adam as in Adam and Eve?"

Layla nodded.

Mina looked at her hands. A moment ago they felt filthy touching the repulsively stiff genitalia. Now that she knew it was Adam's penis she held, she felt much better about herself. After all, he was the first man, his staff delivered the seed starting humanity, and he was her first man, too. Her hands seemed suddenly sanctified, perhaps even capable of wondrous acts, since she had touched the holy staff.

"What did he look like, Mina?"

"Short, brown and hard as a rock."

"Mummified?"

"That's not all," said Mina, looking down at her dusty feet. "He was kind of cute."

5. Seeds, Bones and Runaway Stones

Harsh missions had taken their toll on the fedawis. Of the original 23 boys in Aaron's old training brigade, 13 survived. Recruits still came easy from the Arabic and Persian orphans who were eager for adventure with the Assassins, and new teams of young boys quickly replaced the dwindling 17-year-old elders.

Still restricted to the library, Aaron was eager to learn about the outside world. One evening at dinner he met a boy named Majid who was transferred from one of Hassan's fortresses 200 miles south. Majid worked in the aviary, feeding pigeons and dispatching messages to and from spies and outposts. He said there was a castle in the south occupied by almost all women. This news sent a warm breeze over the embers in Aaron's heart still glowing for Eunisia. Aaron returned to the library, pulled every map he could find, located every castle to the south and reduced the field to three possible sites. It may take a while, but he knew he'd find Eunisia in one of these castles.

"Are you kidding me? That ship sailed, don't you remember? See the scar on your side? She tried to kill you," reminded the eggplant. "She didn't even remember you!"

"That doesn't mean I can't take care of her—rescue her if she needs it." Then another map caught Aaron's eye. It was much larger and included the Persian Gulf. There, halfway down the Gulf, was Bahrain. He opened Sir Gillian's book and found the two maps were identical. "Paradise is in Bahrain?" asked the eggplant. "I lived in Bahrain for more than 100 years, but had no idea."

At the end of Aaron's first year in the library, Hassan called him to his private chamber. Hassan never called anyone to his chamber unless he had an assignment for him, and Aaron feared he was being sent to kill someone.

"You're an excellent scribe, but I have another job for you."

The wind rushed from Aaron's sails and he felt sick.

"I've procured a laboratory from Damascus. I want you to conduct some simple experiments."

Aaron was partially relieved, but he really didn't want to leave the library. "I haven't been in a laboratory for years. You should probably kidnap a professional."

Hassan had considered kidnapping, but a proficient alchemist may just turn the tables on the Old Man. He knew of potions that could drive a man mad with just a few drops in his water. Having an angry alchemist at Eagle's Nest was too risky, even for Hassan.

"Surely you remember working with Layla," reminded the Old Man.

"I just measured her tests and took notes. I'm no alchemist."

"You'll do fine. I have books that'll guide you through each operation," assured the Old Man, and led Aaron into a room that looked almost identical to Layla's laboratory. Shelves ran from floor to ceiling, each lined with clay jars filled with metals, minerals and dried plants, a large oven occupied almost an entire wall, water tanks, condensers, crucibles and retorts with long, pointed necks and stout, round bottoms were scattered on thick, wood tables and a large ventilation fan overhead was operated with a long rope that dangled in the middle of the room.

"Do all these laboratories look alike?" wondered the eggplant.

From then on, Aaron divided his time between the library and laboratory. He transcribed alchemical books filled with symbols and recipes in the morning and practiced simple operations the rest of the day. He enjoyed the hands-on process of mixing different substances to create something new. In the beginning, most operations were over Aaron's head, so he peeled bark from young trees, dug roots and gathered blossoms from medicinal plants for tinctures, extracts and salts.

His first concoction was a hashish elixir. He started with the fresh buds from cannabis plants grown in Alamut Valley, chopped them, soaked them in water for an entire day, cooked them, and then condensed the blend into a potent, alcohol-based tincture. But he made it stronger by evaporating the tincture in a dish, and then used the remaining grains for an elixir that packed an incredible wallop. In addition to giving him the vision of canaries in a silver mine, just a few grains in a glass of tea helped him forget his problems and focus on work.

The Old Man gave Aaron a long list of operations to perform. There were recipes with exotic ingredients like Andovian tree hair, underground water-foam and ostrich milk for curing warts, baldness and immunizing against most sexually transmitted diseases. He found various recipes for black powder, but none for making bombs, like he and Layla had done. He even found directions for "shrinking a full-size vegetable into a bright little amulet to provide its keeper with a lifetime of good fortune."

"I had no idea that I could have relatives," said the eggplant. It wondered how many others there were out there in the world, trapped in life-long dialogues with a species unable to understand the trials and tribulations of the vegetable kingdom. Then the eggplant remembered one sniff of roasted garlic made inter-species dialogue a pretty sweet alternative. It would be nice to speak with another intelligent vegetable someday, especially if it was an eggplant.

Aaron's biggest challenge came after his first weeks in the lab. Hassan asked him to extract seeds from metals, a preliminary stage in creating a Philosopher's Stone. He studied for days, and then fired up the oven. He mixed distilled sulfur and mercury and heated them until they melted into a sublime yellow ball called "paradisiacal fruit." He sealed the fruit in a flask, cooked it in the oven for three days until the last vapors broke the surface and it looked like coal in a smoldering fire, bubbling and resting at the bottom of his vial. This was the blackness of black, the head of the crow and the moonless night. It was the perfect putrefaction of the seed and it smelled like a dead cat. It was only the Black Seed, but he was halfway there.

He stoked the oven's fire again—this time on the first night of the new moon—and kept it blazing as glorious colors appeared on his Black Seed's surface. Hours passed. The colors faded then turned as green as a fresh water lily before the seed ripened to pure white. This was the White Tincture used to transmute metals into silver. Aaron knew he was getting close. He used more coal, opened the vents and increased the oven's heat. The seed glowed for a full day, then the White Tincture turned to pale yellow, then citron, then its bright surface changed into a glowing, blood red ball, beating like a fiery heart. This was the Red Seed and it smelled like molten steel. He was one step away from the Philosopher's Stone, yet the Seed made him feel lonely. It was beautiful, but empty. He'd worked so long, and for what? To further Hassan's power? Working in the lab was not much different than working in the blacksmith's shop. The eggplant was right. He should have left Sir Gillian's outpost and never looked back.

The work kept Aaron busy, but he was getting older. A year had passed quickly and he could never get it back. At over 6-feet, he was one of Eagle Nest's tallest inhabitants. His long braided blonde hair and thin beard made him stand out among the sea of dark-haired fedawis. He was 19-years-old and felt like he was just waking up a seeing the real world.

Hassan created a grand theater in the mountains with the Assassins as his co-stars. Eagle's Nest was a great experiment in bringing paradise back to earth, but the Old Man's paradise was nothing more than bait. The assassinations were performed for an audience of politicians, priests and peasants. His library was filled with contradictions crossing the line between sacred lies and profane misdirection. Aaron felt like an accomplice in some dark machine-driven plan already in motion. Eagle's Nest was a diversion. It was not an impenetrable Assassins' fortress, it was a theater for a great world tragedy filled with props and promises to lure young boys and its proverbial curtain concealed a frail and lonely Old Man.

Aaron felt trapped in a giant stone cage and he wanted to leave right now. He sat in his cell, watching spiders crawl across the ceiling like dark spies and wondered how he could beat the Old Man at his own game. He wished he could find a crack in the stonework and get a better look at the web woven around him.

*****

The next day, the Old Man visited the laboratory and Aaron presented the Red Seed. "Next you'll have the Philosopher's Stone," assured Hassan, and removed a soft leather pouch from his robe and placed it in Aaron's hands. It was heavy. Aaron opened it and saw a large stone, smooth and shining so the entire room reflected on its grey surface.

"Do you know what you're holding?"

"It's the Lost Stone," gasped the eggplant. It looked like the Kabba Stone, which the eggplant had seen 400 years ago, when Hamdan's grandfather made his pilgrimage to Mecca. He made it

218

a point to touch the eggplant to the Kabba Stone, after he'd kissed the Stone himself. "A Stone like that is hard to forget," said the eggplant.

The eggplant wasn't kidding. The bond between vegetables and minerals is far greater than most people might suspect. They share a common patience and self-determination animals can't appreciate. Happiness comes naturally for minerals and vegetables. Even stones originating in deep space and mummified eggplants born in the Arabian Desert have a smile on their invisible faces. It's no accident ancient trees become petrified and turn to stone. Not many mammals earn that honor.

"Is this the Lost Stone?" Aaron ran his hands over its warm, smooth surface.

The Old Man was surprised Aaron heard of the Lost Stone, but then again, he was learning new secrets every day in the library. "I first held the Stone the day we captured Alamut," began Hassan. "I've carried it with me ever since and believe this Stone is capable of transmuting the entire world. It can turn heretics into saints and saints into demons. It can lead men into cages like sheep. Kings and caliphs have forfeited their freedom and lost their souls for this Stone." The Old Man watched Aaron stroke it like he was petting a sleeping puppy. "The Stone demands activity, savors the moment of attack and lives for nothing less than the onslaught of unbearable ecstasy. This Stone is an angel of chaos changing the world from a swamp of oppression to a mountaintop of unlimited potential."

Aaron wasn't impressed. "You think you can use this Stone to change the world? How many more attacks? How much chaos? How much terror will it take?"

"My goal is not to change the world with terror. I want to remove humanity from its downward spiral and stop the premeditated enslavement of its soul," said the Old Man. "I want to remove guilt and replace it with ecstasy, one assassination, one uprising and one revolution at a time. With the Stone, anything is possible. I can have the world at my feet."

"Nobody will let you take the world. Leaders have armies. They make the rules."

"I'll remake the rules," said the Old Man. "One Assassin is worth 100 knights. I'll unleash psychic armies and rewrite history one day at a time. I'll give the world the freedom it's never known."

"Whose idea of freedom, Hassan?"

"Freedom is greater than one man or an entire country. Freedom is the true natural order, unbridled as a storm cloud rumbling across the sky or a river carving a path through rock and sand. Freedom is the wind, whipping the Assassin's black banners as they ride towards the sound of clashing scimitars. Neither the laws of caliphs nor the bonds of Mohammed can stop history's wheels from turning. The Assassins will be the apostles of the New World."

"You want to create chaos? That's your big plan for freedom? That's your New World? "

"No man can impose order on others," explained the Old Man. "Assassins only enforce nature's will and break history's cruel chains. I will extend Eagle's Nest across the seas."

The Old Man's world used to make sense, but now it all seemed crazy. "I've seen chaos and it's far more cruel than history. It's the great destroyer blowing away old roads. It's giant waves swallowing ships filled with children and rocks that crush their bodies. It takes parents from their families with invisible disease, tears people apart and destroys hope. Chaos is like a fever spreading and killing at random."

"History is a disease spread by lies," answered the Old Man.

"What if we all want to rewrite history and change the world?"

"There would be beautiful chaos and much misery," replied Hassan. "Like the weather or disease, history is too large for most souls to challenge. It's a hungry beast rolling entire populations under its hooves. It consumes piles of tragic dreams, devours genealogical oceans, laps up heroic centuries and gnaws at progress like a blind dog chewing on a bone the size of Africa. It's the judge who never leaves the courtroom, the big mirror in the sky, the maker of shadows, the first and final ancestral epitaph. History is the invisible beast demanding submission."

"You demand submission, Old Man. You bring more misery and suffering, just like history."

"I carry misery like 1,000 motherless children," the Old Man scowled. "I devour mouthfuls of misery and wash them down with innocent suffering. I turn misery upside down and shake it until its pockets are empty. I wipe my ass with misery," answered the Old Man, growing angry at Aaron's arguments.

"Sounds like some pretty nasty misery," whispered the eggplant. Aaron wrapped the Lost Stone in its soft leather pouch and passed it back to the Old Man. "Has the Stone ever been miserable?"

Hassan shook his head. "The Stone is boundless. Its power is limited only by our imaginations. It's like a marvelous book in the hands of small children. I've only explored the pictures on the cover, and they are sublime." The Old Man opened the pouch and gazed into the Stone. "Sometimes I sense paradise just beneath its surface. Preserved like a seed. I want you to help me solve the puzzle of this strange fruit."

"And the world will become even more miserable," scoffed the eggplant.

Aaron was ready to take his chances in the desert when the Old Man made his final offer. "I've given you the world's greatest secrets. Now, I ask you to help me unlock the secrets of the Stone. If you find the keys, you can have your freedom and my protection. The choice is yours."

Aaron began the experiments with the Stone like a reluctant camel starting a 1,000-mile journey. He wondered if it had any power at all. Aaron and the Old Man worked together some days, dropping salts, sulfurs and herbal essences onto a minute section of the Stone's surface, recording every subtle change. When they tried to collect some shavings from the Stone it shattered all of their instruments, except raw diamonds. After weeks they shaved less than one-tenth gram of the heavenly substance into a small pile of black dust. Again, they poked and prodded, distilled and putrefied whatever fragments from the Stone they could. It appeared the Stone was distinct, but not spectacular.

*****

The Old Man spent hours each day alone in his chamber with the Stone. If the eggplant was Aaron's best friend, the Stone was Hasan's great benefactor, teacher, healer and source of power. The Stone had never spoken to Hassan, yet he felt it was trying to tell him something. He waited years for the Stone to offer a command, symbol, anecdote or even a little rumble. He'd spend days at a time in a dreamy, opiated state somewhere between wakefulness and sleep, mumbling to the Stone.

This day, Hassan was asleep on his bed, fully clothed, loaded on a ball of raw opium the size of a scarab and dreaming of a ship sailing high in the sky over foggy, green mountains, him looking over the ship's rails, watching ant-size people in the world below. Whichever way the ship sailed, so sailed human destiny. Stormy weather produced wars and plagues. Warm trade winds and calm seas beget creativity and beauty. The ship could take a conservative path towards a safe harbor or cut through the hard winds and rain and risk its cargo. The Old Man witnessed all sorts of weather in his recurring opium dreams—waterspouts, hurricanes and hailstones the size of melons. This dream was different. This time his ship was nose-diving straight for a crash

222

landing on the ground, the big wooden steering wheel spinning wild on the main deck and the lower world burning below him. He tried to hold the wheel steady and steer the ship out of its terminal dive, but it was no use.

Hassan usually opened his eyes at this point, rose from his bed, quenched his thirst with a cup of tea and studied gematria in the garden for the rest of the afternoon. Today, when he opened his eyes he was lying on his bed with three men looking down on him. He closed his eyes and opened them again, but the men were still there. "What are you doing in my chamber?"

"We've come to meet the Old Man of the Mountain," said a short, Arab man with a gigantic nose and high-pitched voice. "I am Hamdan Karmat. You may remember me. I too tried to change the world. I once believed the Karmation's pursuit of euphoric pleasure would change the world, but nothing changed. Then my son led an attack on Mecca and ripped the Stone from the Kabba with his own dagger. He was a fool who thought the world would change and he'd be a great prince, but the Stone remains in the Kabba and he died in his lonely fortress, a disgrace to all Moslems."

"I once lived in a beautiful paradise and was feared by all," continued Hamdan. "But history forgot my paradise just as it will forget your Garden. You won't change the world, Hassan. You'll die like a beggar with no legs."

Next, a knight whom the Old Man recruited during the 1st Crusade, Gerard de Rodefort, stepped forward and said, "You gave me many secrets, Old Man. You led our knights to the true cross and Solomon's treasures. Then you sent your Assassins to kill my brothers. We all suffered for our deeds. I lost my existence, but you'll find more misery in death than in 10,000 lives."

Hassan tried to respond, but couldn't find his voice. He tried to get up and leave the room, but he was frozen on the bed.

A bearded, longhaired man in a white robe looked at the Old Man as if he was his hero. It was Jesus, the Hebrew prophet. "You have so much wisdom, so much courage and have solved mysteries of life itself, yet you bind yourself to fear. It's not too late to change, Hassan. Look at me. Apparently I changed the world and I never killed anybody. You have the freedom to choose. I only had a dozen apostles. You have thousands of fedawis, all children of God. They can bring the world to your feet, if you guide them with light. Guide them with darkness and you'll all die together like blind men falling from the cliffs of Masada."

A fourth being appeared and it was neither a man nor a familiar beast. It moved closer to Hassan like a great serpent, its breathe as hot and foul as fresh excrement, its scaly body oozing with sickly green bile. It had dozens of feet like lion's paws and a bearded, half-human face with the rubbery lips of a carp. Its hair was white and curly, like a statesman, except for its pubic hair, which looked like a burning red bush growing from its scaly crotch.

"You have no idea how much we have in common," began the creature. "I walked this earth for thousands of years, turning over every rule, opening every cage and transforming otherwise orderly events into affairs of glorious panic. I wanted to open the gates of paradise and release its wonders to the world. I wanted to steal the keys of history and have a million copies made. I wanted people to be free to create their own misery or happiness. What do you want, Hassan?"

"I want immortality," said the Old Man, surprised to hear his own voice.

The creature laughed and spewed oily bile over Hassan's robe.

"Do you think murder brings eternal life? Do you think the more misery you create, the more life will follow?"

"Some things are necessary," said Hassan. "There will be suffering with or without me,"

"Exactly. Do you think fear and misery give you power? They don't. They give you a horrible ache in your belly, a sharp pain behind your eyes, a tickle in your throat and stinky feet. You can't control a mad world. You may poke at history's cheeks, but you'll never get it to bend over for you. It's bigger than you think," warned the creature.

"And I am more patient than you suspect," added Hassan.

"Patience is a powerful virtue," encouraged Jesus, and the beast drooled a great pile of green slime on his shoulder.

The creature grunted and moved closer to the Old Man. "Listen, pal. Nobody is exempt from judgment. You've broken the greatest rules of heaven and earth and I commend you. But you've built your imaginary empire on misery and you'll reap your consequences from all sides. No land will hide you, no mountain will protect you, no drug will ease your pain and no Stone will keep your cold heart beating. Your patience won't help you. Not in a million years."

"What should I do?" asked Hassan. There was no answer. He stared at the ceiling of his chamber and swallowed hard. The visitors were gone but the sour smell of bile remained. His mouth was dry and cold sweat dripped from his brow. It didn't matter what these ghosts said, Hassan would move the world from the shadows. He'd remain in his mountaintop paradise, protected by his Assassins.

*****

In the following days, a covey of the Old Man's spies reported Templars and three Caliphs were meeting in Damascus to form an alliance against him. Until now, the Templars were like his own warrior monks. He opened his library to their Grand Masters and they used the Assassins' model to organize the Templars years ago. Some, like Sir Gillian, had already gained too much from Hassan's generosity. He was sorry the knights were taking arms against him, but he'd make them pay. Within hours, Hassan dispatched more than 40 Assassins to eliminate the knights and sultans in Damascus. He also sent word to his European agents to kill Pope Honorius II for good measure. He'd cut the alliance's head off before it could mobilize.

But a trap awaited them in Damascus. Knights and palace guards who watched from every entrance to the city, ambushed the Assassins, paraded them into a courtyard outside the palace and all but one was beheaded, Aaron's friend Majid. Majid listened to his fellow fedawis laugh as the blades fell across their young necks and their smiling heads rolled across the dirt. Majid tried to turn away, but the knights held him and forced him to watch every beheading until there was a heap of young bodies stacked before him.

Majid returned to Alamut alone and described the massacre to Hassan, who remained silent long after the boy finished. Majid also had a message from the Caliph requesting a meeting with the Old Man. If the Old Man refused, the Caliph's army of 30,000 men along with 1,000 knights would attack the fortress and completely destroy every trace of his existence. The Old Man knew better. Still, he agreed to meet with the Caliph and the Grand Master of the Templars and ordered his Assassins to prepare for battle.

*****

Aaron was too busy to notice the increased activity at Eagle's Nest. He was with Hassan in the laboratory, aligning the

Stone according to an illustrated compass in an alchemical diagram, with ends pointing directly north and south. He uttered incantations in ancient languages, but nothing happened.

Aaron felt a huge hole growing in the center of his heart. It was big enough to hold all the gods and demons in the entire Sumerian pantheon and cavernous enough to echo for a full minute when the eggplant suggested it was time to leave Eagle's Nest, with or without Hassan's blessing. The dried vegetable was right. They were both ready for desperate measures. Aaron felt like he was at the wrong end of a hot poker and hiding from a crazy camel driver at the same time. He had to find a way to disable the Old Man long enough to get a head start. "Maybe I can drug him. If I can find some rye bread."

"It will take at least a month to make rye mold tincture," complained the eggplant, eager to leave this cold fortress.

Aaron knew he couldn't wait. He left the castle and went to the garden. It was a beautiful day and Hassan had sent the girls away, so Aaron explored parts of the garden he'd never seen before. The craggy, 50-foot tall grey walls looked down on the garden like heartless, fanged sentinels. He walked around the perimeter, hoping he might find another way out of Eagle's Nest. He looked for goat trails or even a ravine until he saw a dark opening in the stone face behind an old olive tree. He crawled inside and it opened to a taller tunnel.

"This is it!" announced the eggplant, and they followed the cold, damp sides of the tunnel through total darkness.

Aaron stepped slowly, imagining traps and deadly snakes, but there were none. He walked for almost an hour before he saw light, crawled out and found himself on a steep ledge at least 2,000 feet above a green valley with a small village of mud huts.

"Our path to nirvana," said the eggplant.

Aaron followed the tunnel back to the garden with a smile on his face and a plan under his tunic. He was unaware that just outside Eagle's Nest, packs of boys moved across the mountain, preparing tents in valleys behind the summit and stockpiling weapons.

Majid was waiting in the garden and ran to Aaron as soon as he saw him. When Majid told Aaron about the massacre in Damascus, Aaron's smile disappeared. He knew many of those boys, and the image of their headless bodies made him queasy.

"The caliph and a knight are coming to strike a deal with the Old Man. If there's no deal, they'll attack Eagle's Nest," explained Majid. "I also have good news for you. I think I found your Eunisia. She's in a castle called Fatima. It's about three days ride to the south."

Aaron hugged Majid, thanked him at least six times, then ran to the library and shuffled through his maps until he found Fatima. It was about 100 miles south and would be the easiest ride of his life, until he felt a shadow pressing over his shoulder. He turned and saw a strange man who introduced himself as Farouk, commander of Hassan's southern fortresses. He was big, burly and reminded Aaron of the blacksmith he knew in England. "Hassan would like to speak with you," said the commander, and he followed Aaron to the Old Man's chambers.

"Don't worry. I'm sure he doesn't suspect anything," assured the eggplant, and Aaron's chest pounded like a nervous hammer against a rubbery anvil. "Don't let your foolish heart get the best of you. Just breathe and relax." Aaron closed his eyes and inhaled a long, slow breath through his nostrils, then exhaled the unruliness in his heart into the void before entering the Old Man's chambers.

Hassan was seated behind a long table, surrounded by unfamiliar faces. "Hello, Aaron. I won't be in the laboratory for the next few days and I wanted my commanders to meet you," then he turned to the other men. "This is Aaron, my personal scribe and alchemist. He can assist you in certain magical matters."

Aaron was embarrassed by Hassan's announcement.

"See, I told you it would be all right," comforted the eggplant.

"He'll prepare the black powder for your fedawis. We may not need any firepower tomorrow, but be prepared," advised the Old Man. "I'll be meeting our guests at daybreak. Keep the stone steps surrounded by Assassins. I don't want our guests inside Eagle's Nest."

Hassan stood and his commanders hurried from the room. Before Aaron could follow, Hassan stopped him.

"Uh-oh," muttered the eggplant.

"We'll continue our work with the Stone after this matter is settled," said Hassan. "The caliph and Templar who beheaded my Assassins will be here in the morning and you need to produce a small mountain of powder by then." Aaron turned to leave and Hassan added, "Be careful. We want to save the explosions for our enemies."

Aaron knew the survival of Eagle's Nest might depend on the black powder. As much has he'd like to see Hassan destroyed, he also wanted to save the fedawis' heads. He gathered ingredients in the laboratory and began mixing. He worked through the day and night making bombs of all shapes and sizes. Cigar bombs, holy-cross bombs, Lost Stone bombs and crescent-shaped bombs. He and the eggplant gave the bombs names like Eunisia's Revenge, the Non-Existent Bomb and his favorite, Layla's Special—voluptuous, shapely, small-waisted bombs packed with double-strong powder and lit with long black and silver horsehair wicks treated with mucus from murex snail glands to emit bright blue smoke as they burned. He even painted smiling faces and slogans on some. The eggplant's favorite was, "Nothing is true, except this bomb." He wrapped the black powder in several layers of thin rice paper, and then wound them with cloth. Some bombs were packed tight for explosive effects, others were loosely filled with powder to maximize their smoke and flash.

The bombs were collected in baskets and distributed to fedawis all along the watchtower. The teenage boys looked at the little balls of fabric and long paper cigars like they were magical objects delivered by angels. Assassins hid behind boulders, in crevices and under piles of rocks waiting for the caliph and his army all morning, but they never came. Instead, two men rode on horseback along the steep paths to Eagle's Nest without anyone to assist them. Six Assassins met the guests and led them to the stone steps, where the Old Man was waiting. The caliph and Templar sent their representatives—a skinny mullah with a high voice and thin moustache, and a short, stout, old knight from Jerusalem, to negotiate the agreement. Hassan stood on the steps, towering over both the mullah and the knight.

"You're very brave to come here without an army," said Hassan.

"I'm not the first Templar to stand on the steps of Eagle's Nest," said the knight, his voice dry and wispy, like an old insect. "My order knows you well, Old Man."

Hassan studied the knight and wondered if he'd seen him before, but his mesh hood was raised over his head and his bearded face was covered in shadows. "You don't know me as well as you may think, considering your alliance with the caliph," replied Hassan. "Tell me, what do you want? Do you want immunity from my Assassins?"

"We want more. We want the Lost Stone."

High above, watching through a thin-slit window in Hassan's chambers, Aaron wondered what they were saying. He was surprised Hassan had left the fortress. Aaron moved away from the window and heard a hollow sound beneath the carpet. He rolled the carpet back and found a loose piece of stone in the floor. He used a dagger to wedge the large square stone from its place and pulled a heavy wooden box from the hole in the floor. It was locked. Aaron looked out the window again.

Hassan was still far below, talking to the mullah and knight, when he pointed up, towards the tower. Aaron saw Majid standing on a parapet, looking down to his master. "Majid!" cried Aaron, but it was too late. Hassan lowered his arm and Majid jumped from his perch into the void, sailed like a rudderless ship sinking into the stiff clutches of unforgiving gravity, and left his body the precise moment it hit the cold, grey rocks 1,000 feet below.

Hassan looked up at the slit window Aaron had called from, but saw nothing. "Tell you're caliph and Templars there are 5,000 others just like him. They will all give their lives to keep you from these steps. Now go with my blessing," and he turned to walk away.

"If there were 5,000 who could fly, we'd be very impressed," started the knight. "We didn't come here to watch your fedawis kill themselves."

"And we didn't come here for your blessing," added the mullah.

"We want the Stone, Old Man," wheezed the knight.

"I don't know what you're talking about," and he stopped and looked at the pair. "Nothing is true," he said, and raised his arm, but the two leaped and grabbed him before his arm started to fall. The mullah pointed a dagger under the Old Man's arm, the knight pulled a scimitar from his burnoose and held it across Hassan's neck.

"If anyone attacks, we'll kill your master!" shouted the knight. "We've come for our Stone, and we'll leave in peace when we have it."

"Kill them!" yelled the Old Man. In an instant, an Assassin's bomb exploded with a bright flash leaving half of the stairway engulfed by a thick cloud of orange smoke. When it cleared, all three had vanished. The knight and mullah clung together and followed close behind the Old Man, who led them to a hidden passage into the mountain. Once inside, Layla crept silently but very close to the Old Man, making sure she didn't lose him, while Mina stayed close.

Aaron ran to the window when he heard the explosion and knew he had to act fast. He smashed the lock on the box and found the Lost Stone, wrapped comfortably as a newborn babe in its fur-lined, soft leather pouch. Aaron slipped the holy pouch over his shoulder, ran into the library, stuffed his maps, the book from Sir Gillian, four large bombs coated with thick wax at the insistence of the eggplant, glass vials of powder for smoke bombs, a dagger and a few gold pieces into his sack. The eggplant urged him to take more powder, wax and gold, but Aaron was already running for the garden.

He was in the tunnel before the mullah and knight reached Hassan's chambers. The Stone was heavy and warm on his chest and he could hear the eggplant speaking to the Stone in hushed, reverent Arabic. Proceeding through the tunnel one small step at a time, Aaron made his way down the mountainside, crossed the valley and was exchanging his first gold piece for a horse in the village before nightfall.

*****

The Assassins searched the mountainside, looking for their master, but he was already inside the fortress, pinned to his chamber wall by the mullah's blade while the knight questioned him. "Where's the Stone? We're not afraid to start cutting your fingers off. Isn't that what you'd do, Hassan?"

Hassan saw the empty, broken box on the floor and began to shake. "The Stone is gone," and he pointed to the empty box on the floor. "It was taken while we were below."

"Who took it?"

"I believe it was a young Englishman," said Hassan.

"Aaron," replied the mullah.

"How do you know this name?" The Old Man was suddenly suspicious. "Was he a spy? Was he working for you?"

The knight ignored his questions. "The caliph's army and 1,000 Templars are marching here as we speak. You'll need all your demons to defend this rock. And they may not be enough," warned the knight.

A brigade of Assassins crashed into the outer chamber and was ready to charge into the room when the knight growled, "One more step and his arm comes off." The knight lobbed a small glass vial that shattered in the middle of the boys and released a steaming gas that burned their mouths and eyes. The pair of invaders covered their faces with bright scarves and left Hassan and his boys rubbing their eyes and coughing in a steamy yellow cloud of stinging belladonna vapors.

The knight and mullah had one more stop inside Eagle's Nest before they left. They scaled the rock wall outside the living quarters and climbed towards the spring above the garden. When they arrived at the spring and saw the garden, they were amazed. "Oh my. It is beautiful," said the knight.

"It's like paradise," agreed the mullah.

The knight removed the heavy mesh hood and long, curly salt-and-pepper hair cascaded down the back of the burnoose. This was not a male knight. It was a woman. She removed her breastplate and heaved a sigh of mammary relief. It was Layla. "My breasts felt like stale pancakes in there," she whispered. "They've never fallen asleep and started tingling before," and she shimmied enough to wake them, then filled her water skin and took a long drink. "Well Mina, it was easier than I thought, even though we don't have the Stone."

Mina removed her mullah's hood and twisted her slender neck and petite, pointed face to the west and watched the approaching Caliph's army kicking up a line of dust stretching across the landscape like a long brown rope heading for Hassan's neck. They were both happy to be women again, and eager to leave Eagle's Nest before the real knights arrived.

*****

The battle at Eagle's Nest was brutal. Once the Old Man's generals saw the size of the opposing army, they knew the teenage boys had no chance and left the mountain with their tails between their legs. The Assassins were trained to attack in darkness, with three armed boys going after one sleeping victim. Facing a fully conscious enemy was a different matter. The boys rushed from boulders with suicidal ecstasy sparkling in their eyes—sometimes 20 at a time ran for the knights, howling like packs of jackals, swinging their scimitars in great circles overhead, tracing the paths of vultures gathering for the feast. The knight's shields deflected Assassin's blows and their swords and arrows dropped them, while the caliph's soldiers skewered the boys on long spears and sliced them with scimitars. It was a bloodbath.

Some black-powder bombs fell from the tower, but never came near the battle, most exploded in the hands of the fedawis, at their bare feet or in the air over their heads. The young Assassins ignited their bombs at random. There were a few explosions atop boulders and flashes under bushes, but none posed a threat to the attacking army. The soldiers, knights and Assassins all marveled at the noise and smoke. The knights were certain this was some sort of magic at work, and grateful the Assassins couldn't control their noisy concoctions.

Inside the fortress, Hassan collected his gold, amulets and magic stones, draped a hood over his head and made his way down a steep passage to the garden. Boys were wailing outside, crying out for their mothers, grunting like animals and bleeding on the barren mountainside. Hassan ignored the sounds as he hustled into the garden and walked in long strides, determined to retrieve the Stone and make Aaron, the knight and mullah pay with their lives. He vowed to get the Stone back and kill all three before the next new moon as he made his way around the garden's perimeter, to a tunnel hidden in the trees. When he arrived, the tunnel's entrance was blocked by a large rock. Atop the rock was a small scroll tied with a bright purple ribbon. It was a message from Aaron.

Greetings Hassan. If you find this note, you're probably running for your life, just like me. You stole freedom from Eunisia, the fedawis and me and now it is time to give it all back. If you hunt me, I'll hide the Stone where no Assassin will find it. If you kill me, you'll never find the Stone. I don't intend to use it or trade it to another soul. The Stone is still yours, Hassan. I'm only borrowing it. Try to remember—all is permitted and my words are true. Aaron.

The Old Man wasn't surprised. If he had 1,000 Assassins like Aaron, the world would've been changed long ago.

*****

Layla and Mina drank tea by a small fire at the edge of the village behind the Eagle's Nest fortress. Layla was dressed in layers of rich-colored skirts, blouses, sashes, belts and scarves. Mina wore a simple white djellaba with her hair clipped very short. In the firelight, they looked like mother and son, engaged in a serious family matter.

"I'm certain he'll go to find the girl named Eunisia," insisted Mina. "He was searching for her when I met him and he talked about her every day."

235

"The question is, where will the Stone take him?" asked Layla. "Is he riding to an old flame or a new destiny?"

"Maybe they're one and the same," suggested Mina.

Layla pulled her big, embroidered bag of tricks close and looked inside. "We have just enough weapons to get through another skirmish," she said. "And plenty of tinctures. We may need to get our hands on more black powder, if Hassan has any Assassins left to chase us."

"What about Greek fire?" asked Mina.

"What do you know about Greek fire?"

"I heard stories about Byzantines beating Arab attackers with their magic Greek fire. What makes it so special?"

Layla smiled. "It burns very hot and when it touches water, the quicklime makes it burn even hotter," she said, then stood and gazed toward a small stand of trees to the south. "We'll need lots of pine resin."

*****

Aaron galloped along ridge tops under a crescent moon. He was alone again in this world, except for the eggplant and Stone. He had no family, home, old dog or cozy fire to return to. No more camaraderie to greet him and no place to be greeted. He wasn't even sure if he really wanted to see Eunisia again. It still hurt to know she never loved him.

"I think she liked you, Aaron," consoled the eggplant.

Sure, she liked him. Maybe. Aaron was free to go anywhere. Back to Eunisia. Back to Europe and Layla. Maybe Marseilles.

"Go deeper into Africa," offered the eggplant. Aaron's mind was racing, but it was nothing compared to the eggplant's excitement. Its proximity to the Stone made the eggplant so ecstatic it could barely contain itself. It was still trying to strike

236

up a conversation with the Stone, but to no avail. The eggplant wasn't sure if it was being snubbed, if the Stone was sleeping, or if it was just plain dumb.

If the Lost Stone had spoken to the eggplant, it thought it would sound like a burning bush or faraway thunder commanding leaves of grass to grow. It would probably rattle like thousands of dry bones shaking inside a hollow moon untethered for just one night.

"There's an old vegetable saying," began the eggplant, "A peanut and camel are the same if judged only by their humps."

"What does it mean?"

"It means there are a lot of ways to use language that have many meanings to different people," replied the eggplant. "What do you think it means?"

"I don't know." They shivered in the crisp night air as they bounced over the Timar Pass and followed Aaron's wounded heart south, to Eunisia. Even if she didn't remember him, he felt responsible for her fate since Marseilles. And when Hassan sent her to Fatima, Aaron felt even more responsible for anything that may happen to her.

"What if she's happy?" asked the eggplant. Aaron didn't answer, but the eggplant knew it was Aaron's second biggest fear.

Aaron rode day and night, sleeping no more than an hour at a time, stealing or trading horses as they traveled.

"You've become quite an accomplished thief," noted the eggplant." In fact, you're the first I've ever known."

Aaron blushed with shame. "I'm no thief."

"What do you call taking horses, camels, a dress and priceless religious icons that don't belong to you?" asked the eggplant.

Aaron thought for a moment and remembered what the non-existent knight told him before he stole his first horse. Morality is not always black and white, especially where survival was concerned. "I'm exercising my right to survive. And survival outweighs thievery, making my actions perfectly acceptable."

"Would you want someone to steal your horse?" asked the eggplant.

"Only if they needed it to survive."

"Maybe you can use your moral argument to get into the fortress at Fatima," joked the eggplant, and the pair began arguing about the proper methods of entry into an enemy fortress.

"I'll start with the biggest bomb and save the others for emergencies."

"Not a good idea," countered the vegetable. "Don't blow your biggest wad in the beginning. Save it for the big finale."

"I want to make a good first impression."

"Do you want to make an impression, or rescue Eunisia?"

By the time they arrived at Fatima, the plan had not progressed past the question of when to blow the big wad. He dressed in black, rubbed charcoal all over his face and scaled the wall with his sack tied around his waist, digging his toes and fingers into the sharp cracks between the rough blocks. He pulled his body over the top of the wall and lowered himself inside the fortress. Only a few lamps burned in the rooms. Aaron moved invisibly in the darkness, looking into windows at sleeping faces for a hint of Eunisia. He peeked into the first lamp-lit room and saw three young women, all naked, shining with oil, stretched across the bed. Then one of the ladies called out and Aaron ducked out of sight, thinking the voice sounded familiar. He peered over the windowsill and there was Eunisia, naked and reaching for another man, an Arab wearing nothing but his red-checked gutrah on his head. Eunisia kissed him and wrapped her arms around him.

Aaron's heart deflated. If he was holding a bouquet of Shirazi roses, the blooms would have wilted in his hand, the petals would have turned brown and fallen to the ground, leaving Aaron with a handful of thorns. His breath was sucked from his chest and he felt like a shell that lost its soul. He wanted to scream or cry or curse the sky, but he couldn't. He was frozen there, squatting beneath her window, listening to her laugh as she fell to the bed and joined the others.

"This feeling will pass, Aaron," comforted the eggplant. "Leave here before you forget your good memories of Eunisia. Get out of here before someone finds you!"

"Go where? What's left? Why?" asked Aaron. "I have the Lost Stone but I feel like I just lost everything! I've dreamed of being with Eunisia for years and I've failed her in every way. Now I'll spend the rest of my life trying to forget her."

"We could bring the Stone to Layla," suggested the eggplant.

"We'll never find Layla," said Aaron. "I should never have left her. Now she'll never know I loved her, too." Before the eggplant could stop him, Aaron jumped to his feet and rushed into the room with his scimitar drawn and the women screaming, pulling blankets over their bodies. The Arab man grabbed the gutrah from his head and used it to cover his crotch.

"Eunisia, it's me, Aaron."

She looked at him as if he was a stranger.

"Don't you remember me?"

"Who is this man?" demanded the Arab.

Aaron held the point of the blade to Arab's chest.

"That's my husband! Let him go!" ordered Eunisia, running to the Arab's side. Aaron took the blade from the Arab's chest, and felt like cutting his own throat.

"This is Abufazil, my husband, and these are his other wives. They're like my sisters. This is my family now. I have a son sleeping next door."

"She has a son," whispered the eggplant, the words echoing and mingling with footsteps approaching outside the room. It was like a bad dream.

"No time for melancholy, my friend. Let's get moving fast!" The eggplant tried to hurry him out of the room, but it was too

239

late. Five men rushed in and before they grabbed Aaron, he looked at Eunisia but neither had anything else to say. Aaron pulled a glass vial from his pocket, made a weary face and threw the vial on the ground, where it exploded in a cloud of sad blue smoke giving Aaron just enough time to slip away.

He left the fortress swallowing his pride and his hope, rode to the top of the nearest ridge without stopping, and then looked back at the fortress one last time. Lamps were burning inside and he could see people moving between huts, otherwise there was darkness wherever they looked. "Well, my trusty eggplant and fearless Stone, shall we proceed to paradise?"

"Yes, Aaron Sloopshire, it's time to leave this unfortunate circumstance behind us," replied the eggplant, and they headed south, to the Persian Gulf.

At the same time, two riders were approaching the fortress from the north, surprised to see so many lamps burning so late. It was Mina and Layla, only an hour behind Aaron.

PART THREE

"It can't end like this. Tell them I said something marvelous."
—The last words of Hassan i Sabbah

Paradise Waits

Heaven on earth. Abode of the blessed. Kingdom of terrestrial bliss. The original state of affairs before Lilith ran off to independent pastures, before Eve bit the fateful fruit, before man's first disobedience to his God. Before the first trio knew the difference between good and evil, before they realized energy and mass were related to time and death, before they considered the fragility of their existence, woke up and splashed the first graffiti on heaven's walls. Before the world became messy, there was paradise.

Aaron sat on the beach gazing out over the water, wondering if paradise was really on the horizon. And if the Garden of Eden was on the island, would it still feel like paradise, or had it turned into some snake-infested, overgrown swamp?

"Does it matter?" asked the eggplant.

"Maybe not. I've lost everyone I ever loved and most of my friends. I might as well lose paradise."

"That's not what I meant," sighed the eggplant. "It doesn't matter if it's a swamp or a botanical masterpiece. Paradise is vast, it contains multitudes, remember?"

"Like you said a long time ago, my absurd dream of Eunisia made everything look a lot better than it really was. The hope of holding her hand and hearing her voice made the desert seem like Dover beach. But it was never more than a childish dream."

"Another fantasy missed its interlude with fate," lamented the eggplant.

Aaron paused for a long time, picturing Eunisia with the Arab at Fatima and remembering the musky, sour scent of the

242

room. "Can you believe she's married and has a son?" Aaron shook his head and wiped his eyes. "What good is paradise without anyone who cares?"

"I care," replied the eggplant, "If a vegetable counts."

Aaron smiled. "Dried vegetables count triple—once for nobility and twice for longevity. And it doesn't matter if the Garden of Eden is on the island, does it?"

"Here's another old vegetable saying," offered the eggplant, "If one sees only shapes, the sun and moon are one and the same." This time, Aaron understood. There's more to paradise than a few preconceived notions, and that's why he really didn't want to find paradise on Bahrain. He didn't want paradise to be located in any specific place. He wished paradise was a state-of-mind accompanying true love, the cosmic glow surrounding beauty or the eternal magnetism unconditionally attracting, embracing and pressing its soft, warm belly across your skin like sunlight on a fig leaf.

He listened to the sea splashing on the shore, its long, liquid fingers scratching at the sand, tossing up tangled weeds, a lost sandal, broken shells and colonies of invisible creatures reproducing and dying in small pools that disappear before the next high tide.

"How many non-existent knights do you think are still wandering the forests and streets of Europe? How many Assassins are lost in the desert or forgotten in Cairo?"

"I don't know," answered the eggplant. "But there are probably dried, shrunken vegetables talking to themselves at the bottom of jewelry boxes."

"I've tried to make the right choices since my parents died. Why do I feel like my destiny's always been in someone else's hands? It seems like paradise is at the end of all my roads. But it's never *my* paradise. Never *my* dream."

"There are more people with their own paradise than you once believed," replied the eggplant. "Anyway, paradise isn't such a horrible destination. You could've ended up in other people's hell."

"Maybe I've been guided to paradise, like a pigeon flying to its home." Aaron wasn't joking. "Except I feel more like a puppet than a pigeon."

"Come on, Aaron. It's not so bad, compared to what we've been through together. With the Old Man behind us and paradise ahead, the good times are just beginning," predicted the eggplant.

"Hassan was right about two things: nothing is true and everything really is permitted."

The eggplant agreed. "Truth is what happens. History is what people said happened. But that's all we have. Roses fade, songbirds die, eggplants talk and bad guys walk away smiling," it pondered. "And the periwinkles and fireflies still come back."

These things were easy for Aaron to accept. He'd seen, heard, smelled and even tasted some of them. But his troubled feeling grew and became one big invisible hand tightening around his neck. Aaron knew this feeling. Like something smothering his face and body with a giant pillow that smelled like mushrooms and sour cheese. He smelled it when he learned Hassan knew Layla. There were just too many connections to be pure coincidence. Now he sat on the shore of the Persian Gulf, gazing at boats sailing to and from Bahrain, holding the Lost Stone in his hands and the secrets of antiquity in his head. He could feel the strings pulling him across the water like a spider tugging on its web. "Should we follow the web to the end, or break the strings and start a new life?"

"Do you think you'll ever be happy if you don't play the last piece of this puzzle?" replied the eggplant.

"Or is another coincidence waiting to confuse me. If I go to Bahrain, I'll probably have to face the Old Man someday, and a part of me wants to get far away from here as soon as possible. I've traveled too far to go back to Europe. I could ride to India,

244

change my name and find a wife. I could go anyplace. My horse is rested and my water skins full. What d'ya say, old friend?"

"It's a tough choice," summed up the eggplant. "Easy-living in the Southern Hemisphere or adventures in paradise."

Aaron picked up Sir Gillian's book. "Do you think this is part of the plan, too? Was I sent to kill the knight to get this book so I would travel to Bahrain?"

"That sounds about right," muttered the eggplant.

He opened the book and looked at the map of Bahrain again. For an instant, he considered throwing the Lost Stone and the book into the Gulf. Instead, he slapped his horse on the ass and watched it gallop away with an empty saddle, took a deep breath, smelled mango blooms mixed with the salty mist and set out to discover his destiny in Bahrain.

Boats of all sizes were tied and anchored along the shore, some with sleeping sailors aboard, others rocked like empty cradles. Aaron spotted a group of young pearl divers on the beach, grabbed his sack and met them at their boat. They looked like brothers, all sun-bronzed with black, oily hair and wearing only loincloths. They were suspicious the moment they saw the strange blonde-haired European.

"No pearls. No pearls today," they repeated.

"I don't want pearls. I want a ride to the island," explained Aaron in Farsi.

"No pearls," clarified the oldest, who looked no more than 14-years-old, then invited Aaron aboard. They crowded on the small boat and headed the 20-odd miles across the Gulf. The boys took turns rowing two sets of oars. Aaron sat in the front of the boat, watching the sea birds dip in and out of the water, sometimes catching fish twice their size. He hadn't been on water since the Crusader's crossing and had forgotten the effects of rolling waves on his stomach. He stared at the horizon to regain his balance, grateful for the gentle waters.

The eggplant was nervous on the water, as usual. "You know me. I like the good old terra firma. The more firma, the less terror," joked the vegetable, despite its growing fear as they rowed farther from land.

When they weren't rowing, the boys clamored around Aaron, offering their largest, most lustrous pearls in exchange for his sandals. Aaron gave them his sandals and refused their pearls, but they wanted more. One of the boys reached into Aaron's sack and Aaron automatically pulled a dagger and held it to the boy's throat. The others stopped rowing and pulled their own knives. The boy slowly removed his hand from Aaron's sack.

The eggplant was more alarmed than anyone. "Take it easy now, Aaron. We're in a boat. In very deep water. You're outnumbered. It doesn't look good."

Aaron was in a fighting stance with his stiletto drawn when two boys lunged at him with oyster knives. Aaron booted both attackers over the side with two smooth kicks across their bare chests. Three more came at him and Aaron flipped them over the side like pups. That left one diver, the one who reached in the bag, the boy with Aaron's sandals. He didn't pull a knife, didn't charge and didn't jump over the side. Instead, he shrugged, returned Aaron's sandals, sat down and began to row. Aaron sat behind him and their boat bobbed slowly towards Bahrain.

"I don't believe you did that," gasped the eggplant. "We could have both gone overboard, or you could have been killed!"

"It was just like Assassin's training at Eagle's Nest, but those boys were very slow."

*****

Layla and Mina were stepping onto a fishing boat not far behind Aaron. They were rowing for Bahrain when they saw five

246

boys in the water, waving for help. When Layla pulled the boat closer, the boys began babbling about a yellow-haired mad man with a dagger who threw them off their boat and kept their friend as a hostage. Layla and Mina looked at each other and shook their heads. They may be less than an hour away from a surprise rendezvous with their old friend. Layla hadn't seen him since he was 15-years-old, and she hoped she'd recognize him.

Mina grinned like a swan near the end of a long migration. She saw Aaron in 1,000 dreams since he disappeared from Cairo. She replayed the night over and over, and knew he wouldn't have been kidnapped if she hadn't brought him to her sister's house. She had many regrets. She should've gone after him. But what can one woman do? She hoped he'd forgive her, and clenched his mother's ring, still hanging around her neck.

When their boat landed on the island, Layla and Mina bought horses at the first village and rode straight for Eden's spring. Along the way, olive groves, fig plants and date palms covered the shallow valleys, and pools of cool water teeming with schools of sparkling goldfish dotted the countryside.

The Karmations surrendered to attackers centuries ago, not long after Tahir's death, and were dispersed across Arabia and Persia. Their fortress in Bahrain was occupied by a procession of sheiks, each fighting for control of the island, until they too were driven away by stronger leaders with more warriors. Finally, the peaceful Cult of Lilith returned the castle to its finest days, but after almost a century, they abandoned the fortress and left Bahrain for continents near and far.

Hamdan's fortress had been unoccupied for almost 100 years, except for mountains of excrement everywhere inside its old, crumbling walls. The once-glorious compound was used as a steaming, stinking depository ever since. Hamdan's private quarters were the first to fill. Animals traveled miles to lay their waste atop another specie's pile. Women and children hiked from villages with their steaming pots full of a day or week's worth of

247

their family's feces. There were foothills of petrified shit, shit sculpted into busts of various sheiks, long brown loaves arranged to spell out obscene words in beautiful Persian scripts, scatological landscapes inhabited by colonies of rats surviving for generations, creating dynasties of rodent rulers fighting over turdish territories with constipated ideologies. The place reeked from a mile away. Nobody remembered how it all started and there were plenty of other places to dump waste, but excrement was drawn to this broken castle like dying elephants to their graveyard or crows to a murder.

Layla smiled under layers of scented scarves as they passed her old stomping ground. She remembered showing Hassan the door many years ago, when the cult of Lilith tended its gardens and filled its halls with sweet, feminine fragrances. The cult disbanded after Hassan's visit. They knew he'd return one day to pillage their library, or worse. Before they left, they used the last of their collective sorcery to cast a spell and leave something special for Hassan, something with a lot of flies. She had no idea their incantation had worked so well.

Layla and Mina escaped the fortress's stench and followed an inland path that bypassed the beach. They arrived at Eden Spring by dusk and stretched out beneath the first starlight.

*****

Aaron walked along the edge of Bahrain, where the sea rolls its relentless brow over the earth's skin, grains of sand fall between your toes and invisible stars poke holes in an infinite blue bowl. This is where birds still sing the world's first songs and the scent of paradise is on every breeze. It was all here, beneath his feet, over his head and in his face. He wandered barefoot between misery and magnificence, in no hurry to reach a point on anybody's map. Then Aaron smelled something so horrible he stopped in his tracks and started to gag.

"What's going on?" asked the eggplant. "Did we find the swamp pits of Bahrain or is this what paradise smells like?"

Aaron dipped his shirt in the water and wrapped it around his face, but it barely helped. He considered turning back. Then, without warning, he dove straight in and swam with his head underwater to escape the terrible, choking smell. He swam until he was exhausted and beyond the wall of odor, then he floated to the beach and crawled to rest between two precarious boulders the natives called Adam and Eve, when there was a sudden vacancy inside him—something important was missing.

His sack was beside him and the Lost Stone was still on his chest, but the eggplant was gone. He searched the sand beneath him and started to panic. There was no trace of his little friend. When he realized he lost the eggplant in the water he fell into a bottomless pit of grief and could barely breathe. He ran to the shore and tried to retrace his path, feeling along the sandy bottom with his feet, reaching down to bring up little rocks and threads of seaweed. He searched for hours, sobbing and half-frantic, thinking about his friend alone on the bottom.

Aaron sat on the beach and cried until the sun went down. He could barely sleep. He listened for its little vegetable voice and prayed to every god whose name he'd ever transcribed. Aaron knew this was the eggplant's worst nightmare. He prayed it would wash up on the shore in the morning. He prayed it would forgive him. He even offered his own life for the eggplant's safe return, but there were no takers. The next morning at dawn, he combed the shoreline and went back in the water, hoping for a miracle.

*****

By mid-afternoon, Aaron was discouraged. He vowed to stay on the island and walk the beach every day until he found his friend. He wouldn't leave the eggplant here without hope. He couldn't. Aaron marked the spot with a long row of sticks, remembered the leaning boulders named Adam and Eve, and followed deer trails through low bushes leading to Eden Spring.

He walked for hours, wishing there was some incantation for recovering an object lost at sea, when he came to a large clearing enclosed by cypress trees and filled with long grass, sweet flowers, and two nude women dancing in the meadow. He thought he was hallucinating, until he recognized Mina, who looked even more bird-like without clothes, and Layla, who was more bountiful and gorgeous and silver-haired than ever.

Was this his paradise? He stepped from the bushes, stared and waited for them to disappear like the hazy mirages he'd seen so many times in the desert. But they didn't vanish. They looked right at him and ran to him with scarves floating behind them like colored wings. Aaron was a one-man audience watching ghost actors running across an organic stage, over the proscenium, into his lap, and wrapping their arms around him until he knew they were real.

"Aaron, Aaron oh Aaron!" Mina repeated his name, louder each time, holding his hands and pedaling her feet in-place, like she was still dancing.

Layla was a proud mother, grateful for the return of her prodigal son. There he was, tall and strong with long braided hair, pants rolled up over his knees and a soiled camel skin sack over his shoulder. "How are you, Aaron?"

He looked up at her, the sun in the sky behind her, her voice smooth and kind and deep enough to hold an ocean of orphan's tears. Aaron reached for the eggplant, but it wasn't there. "I've been better. But you look too good to be true." He hugged them both at the same time. "I can't believe you're here in Bahrain. Why now?"

"Mina and I learned Hassan i Sabbah had the Stone and we knew it would take a huge diversion to get it from him, so we formed an alliance with the Caliph in Baghdad and Templars, who both wanted to stop the Old Man. We went to Alamut before the caliphs and Templars attacked, but learned you already took the Stone from the Old Man. We thought you may come here, to Bahrain." After a long pause she finally asked, "Do you have the Lost Stone?"

Aaron was surprised to see them here and shocked when he realized they were expecting him. He pulled Sir Gillian's book from his pouch. It had been soaked when he dived into the water, and most of its pages were falling from their binding and ruined. "I found this in Persia. This is why I came to Bahrain." Then he stuffed the wet pages back in place and passed the book to Layla. "I'm sorry it's so wet, but you may still want this."

Layla smiled. "I wrote this book, Aaron. I needed something powerful to trade for information about the Stone. I used my oldest paper and goat's blood to make it look real."

"But why did you put a map of Bahrain and a star to mark this place?"

"I wanted to give the Templars something, for the sake of my own integrity, even if they didn't know what it was. The verses were just one of my songs. The names the Templars gave me in return for the book were equally useless." Layla shrugged and then quickly crouched down. "Shhh, I hear something."

A black-handled stiletto flew from the bushes and pierced Mina's thin neck. She dropped to the ground and more daggers flew over their heads. Aaron spotted the red sashes of Assassins all around them. He lifted Mina into his arms and ran for cover, trying to stay low and keep his balance as they shifted and swerved through the heavy underbrush. Layla grabbed her clothes and bag of potions then stayed behind, breaking vials of poison

251

gas in the Assassins' path. Dozens of fedawis were closing in. Layla could hear them rushing through the brush, some coughing and choking, unable to penetrate the invisible wall of short-lasting poison.

"I'll take care of Mina." Layla broke more vials behind her and rushed ahead to Aaron.

"What about the Assassins?"

"You take care of them, Aaron. Use your powder." Layla collected large green leaves from a bush beside them, pulled the dagger from Mina's neck and her slender, avian frame jerked like she fell from a low branch. Layla wrapped leaves all around the wound then wrapped her scarves around and around Mina's neck, and the bleeding stopped.

Aaron watched Assassins dodging behind trees as he prepared his small arsenal. He had only three bombs left, all soaked in wax so they'd still explode, so long as he could stuff dried grass in place of the old fuses.

"There's no time—set the bushes afire! Quickly!" Layla lit balls of pine resin packed in wax, threw them towards the water and they exploded in a fast-spreading flames.

Aaron couldn't believe it. He'd just found paradise, now he was going to burn it down. He cracked open a bomb with a sharp rock and spread the black powder across the ground and lit it, stood back and watched the flames grow. In a few seconds they were surrounded by thick white smoke and crackling fire. Assassins charged through the smoke like cats after invisible mice, leaping over flames, swinging scimitars and chopping the air with their daggers.

With Mina over her shoulder, Layla clutched Aaron's hand and pulled him into the open. They ran as fast as they could, leaving the Assassin's coughing in the blinding smoke. Then Aaron heard a voice calling above the mayhem, "Aaron! Aaron!" It sounded like a frightened woman. It sounded like Eunisia. He stopped and listened. The woods were suddenly quiet, except for

252

snapping flames and her voice, haunting as a broken angel. "Aaron! Come back!" He had no choice. He could never leave while Eunisia was calling his name. He turned back and was immediately surrounded by 20 Assassins. Aaron raised his hands and the fedawis led him into the meadow, where Eunisia was tied to a stake with a pile of wood beneath her. Hassan i Sabbah was standing beside Eunisia, strutting back and forth like a tethered serpent.

Without a word, Aaron bolted to free Eunisia from the stake.

"Not so fast," ordered the Old Man, and jabbed his scimitar between Aaron and Eunisia. "You didn't think I'd let you get very far, young scribe?" Hassan pulled his blade away and never met Aaron's glare. Instead, Hassan stared at Eunisia as if evaluating her predicament.

"I'll give you the Stone when you set Eunisia free."

"It's never that easy. There's also the price of betrayal. I'd say that's worth another 100 years of servitude from you, plus the girl's life."

"I'll work for you, but only when she's safe." He moved closer to Eunisia.

"Then she burns." Hassan threw a black-powder bomb that instantly burst in a flash of roaring flames. Eunisia screamed from the center of the fire. She cried and prayed and begged for mercy.

Aaron pulled his burnoose over his head and dashed to Eunisia. He cut the ropes with his dagger, picked her up on his shoulder and carried her outside the ring of the fire, where they both fell to the ground and he brushed the burning embers from her djellaba. Her legs and arms were already blistered and she sobbed and shivered as Aaron held her close. He coughed, wiped ashes from her face, then looked up and saw Hassan standing over them with his raised scimitar.

"No!" Aaron jumped in front of Eunisia and the Old Man's blade flashed down like a bolt of lightning and landed squarely in the center of his chest. Sparks flew and the Old Man was thrown backwards and onto the ground, his sword's blade broken in pieces by the Lost Stone Aaron was still wearing beneath his clothes.

"There's no honor in killing an innocent woman in cold blood." Aaron was standing and speaking beyond the Old Man, to the Assassins all around him, who were silently watching one of their own brothers challenge their master.

"Kill them! Kill them both now!" The Old Man called out the order, but the Assassins didn't move. They knew Aaron was right. There was no dignity in chasing their brother and burning this island. They'd all seen Aaron rush into the flames to save the woman. That was nobility. He was one of them, an Assassin, and those who didn't know him personally, heard Aaron was always the first to fix broken bones, mend wounds and help the boys. If you came to Eagle's Nest sick, he tended to you until you were well. He was a friend to all, especially new recruits who needed extra attention. Some of the boys dropped their swords and walked away after Aaron spoke, never to return to Eagle's Nest. Others just watched, too confused to judge anyone.

"The game is over. Give me the Stone or I'll kill the girl first," demanded Hassan, holding a stiletto to Eunisia's throat.

"It's not that easy for you either, Old Man." Aaron grabbed a sharp rock from the ground, lunged towards Hassan and smashed the rock across Hassan's ankle, sending him to the ground writhing in pain, then smashed the rock against his other ankle, and again the Old Man screamed out in agony. A small group of young Assassins rushed forward, but Aaron grabbed the Old Man's dagger and warned he'd kill Hassan if they moved a step closer.

"This is between the Old Man and me." The young Assassins relaxed their daggers. They wanted to trust Aaron, but the Old Man was like their grandfather.

"You betrayed me Hassan. How did it feel when you found your precious Stone was gone? Did it feel like someone ripped your heart out and left you with nothing to live for? Now you know how I felt when you sent Eunisia away. You've gone too far this time, Hassan. You shouldn't have brought her here. All is permitted. You made the rules. And your rules will make you pay. Today, the Stone is mine to give or keep."

Paradise was ablaze. Flames crackled and jumped from bush to tree. The ground was already charred black and shafts of smoke rose from hot spots. Aaron stood in the center of the last remaining Assassins, a smudged and blistered Eunisia shaking and sobbing at his side. Hassan was sitting up, grimacing with pain, and wrapping his cut and swollen ankles in strips of cotton he'd torn from his robe. Aaron held the blade against the Old Man's neck and spoke to the Assassins all around him.

"You're my brothers, my fedawis. I was kidnapped and carried to Eagle's Nest, like many of you. I trained with you and worked at Hassan's side. I believed in the Old Man. I believed he was wise and generous. I even believed he was a holy man, but he is no holier than you or me. He used us for his own selfish dream, and we got nothing but empty hopes of paradise. Paradise is not for Hassan to give or take. This is only a regular old man, like any other. Today he is an old, selfish man who turns paradise into a burning hell." The flames and smoke were closing in, making it difficult to see and forcing the Assassins to disperse before Aaron was finished.

Aaron lifted Eunisia and walked towards the spring. Hassan tried to stand and stop them, but his ankles were too painful and he fell back on the smoking ground, crying out in pain until a few fedawis rushed to the Old Man and carried him to safety.

Aaron washed Eunisia in spring water, rinsed her burns then wrapped them in soaking wet strips from his burnoose. Her eyes were glazed like balls of soft pastry and her lips still trembled. Aaron asked if she was cold, but she didn't answer. She closed her eyes and tried to hold back the tears. He kissed her forehead and could feel her whole body shaking. This was all his fault. He remembered her child and husband at Fatima, this time with pity for the loneliness they'd feel if they lost Eunisia. He stayed and cried beside her for a long time. He cried for her husband and child. He cried for his own parents, for the non-existent knight, for all the children who died or were sold as slaves in the Crusade, he cried for Majid and Mina, but he wept the most for the eggplant.

Aaron was kneeling beside her in a clearing when Hassan reappeared with two Assassins helping him stand. "It's time to give me the Stone," he grumbled.

Eyes red and weary and his face streaked with tears, Aaron whirled around and looked at the Old Man through the smoke. "It's time for your Assassins to leave Bahrain, then I'll give you the Stone."

The Old Man turned away and raised his arm. The two fedawis took their positions with daggers in hand, prepared to kill Eunisia and Aaron.

"Wait!" Layla called out from atop Eden Spring, holding a long, slender log in her arms with smoke pouring from its back end. It was a makeshift cannon, loaded and ready to fire. The Assassins froze in place. Before Hassan could lower his arm the log exploded and a flurry of rocks shot out, hitting one Assassin and knocking him to the ground, and sending the other running away before Layla could reload.

"Old Man! Leave Aaron and his girl alone. Take your boys and return to Alamut before your own Assassins turn their blades on you," demanded Layla.

The Old Man was weak. He leaned against a tree and smiled as if he knew something the others didn't, and disappeared in a cloud of black smoke.

The garden looked like a demon's battleground. Deep, smoking burns cut across its center like infected wounds. Many palm trees and bushes were charred or burnt to the ground, birds were silent and a cloud of pain and smoke hung over the meadow.

Aaron and Layla searched for injured fedawis and found Hassan in the bushes, lying on his back, looking at the sky and unable to stand. They stood above him, looking down like grand inquisitors. Aaron removed the soft leather pouch tied over his shoulder. "Here, the Stone is yours. Just leave us alone. We're no danger to you and I don't want to kill you." He dropped the pouch in Hassan's lap.

Layla was shocked. "How can you give it back to him?"

"He'd haunt me until he took the Stone back. It's not worth it. Nothing is." Then he turned to the Old Man, who smiled as he cradled the Stone close to his chest. "I never want to see you after this day. If I do, I'll kill you." Aaron was calm and clear as he spoke to the Old Man, looking right in his eyes. "You brought more than 100 Assassins this time. What next? A whole army to kill me in my sleep?"

The Old Man put the Stone in its pouch and looked away, towards Eagle's Nest. "I'll give you immunity."

"And immunity for Layla, Mina and Eunisia," added Aaron.

The Old Man was in no position to argue. Only a handful of the youngest Assassins remained, and only because they had no place to go.

Aaron escorted the Old Man's dark procession to the shore. They carried him on a makeshift stretcher, with Aaron walking at his side. Before Hassan boarded his boat, he turned to Aaron and said, "Our business is not finished."

"Yes Hassan. We're finished. You tried to change the world, but this is how the world will remember you. A broken old man carried back to Eagle's Nest by boys." Aaron watched their boat pull away from the shore and disappear into the mist like a poison snake crawling back to its pit.

*****

Layla was with Mina and Eunisia when Aaron returned, her robe rustling in the breeze as she cleaned their cuts and burns. She had already mixed a special blend of opium and herbs to soothe their pain, and was preparing a batch of salve from comfrey leaves and lavender flowers to protect their wounds from infection.

"Will Mina be alright?"

"She'll live, but the scars will probably raise her voice an octave or two." They were both grateful the ladies survived. Eunisia cried out more than once and Aaron was there to hold her hand. She was trembling with her eyes closed, wincing with pain and he felt helpless.

"Do you think Eunisia's burns will heal soon?"

Layla nodded and smiled. "You saved her, Aaron. You pulled her out before the flames could really do their damage. She'll hardly have any scars, if my salve does its job."

When Layla's opium tea kicked in and Mina and Eunisia rested peacefully beside them, Aaron applauded Layla's aim with her cannon. "We owe you our lives."

Layla looked surprised. "You did your share, my friend. Going toe-to-toe with Hassan was impressive."

"I have to know one thing: How'd you get the hollow log to shoot on such short notice?"

Layla laughed. "I knew Hassan would come for the Stone, so I found a hollow log and had it ready to shoot even before you arrived."

"I'm glad the log didn't blow up, like the first time we tried to use a cannon at your castle."

Smoke covered the sky and small flames still burned along the edge of the meadow. "I don't believe I thought this might be paradise. It's been more like hell. You know before I crossed the Gulf, I almost went to India, instead."

258

"Why would you go to India?"

"I wanted to reclaim my life. I wanted to go someplace and do something on my own. I almost threw the Stone in the Gulf and rode away forever."

"Don't be foolish! Nothing could've stopped Hassan from sending his Assassins here. He would've held Eunisia if you were here or in Calcutta. It seems like something else is bothering you. What is it?"

"I lost the eggplant."

Layla was startled, but didn't want Aaron to see how badly she felt for the vegetable. "Where did you lose it?"

"In the water. It's worst fear."

"It's only a charm. There'll be others." They both knew it was much more than a charm and there would never be another, but she could see he was terribly hurt.

Aaron shook his head. "It was my best friend. We were always together. Now it's at the bottom of the Gulf. It really doesn't like to be alone."

"Remember, it's a vegetable. I'm sure it'll survive the quiet until it washes up on shore."

"Do you think it will?"

"The sea gives up everything, one way or another." She reached for a goatskin sack. "Remember this?" It was Aaron's old sack, the one he carried from England. "Mina kept it for you." Layla pulled out the paper and knife he'd carried for so long, plus his journal of Layla's hallucinogenic voyages, *Messages from Paradise*. Aaron took his keepsakes and held them like they were the most sacred objects in the world. He gently ran his fingers across the paper on which his mother had written the three letters of the alphabet—M, A and S—and he could smell the faraway memory of her gentle hands. He picked up his father's trusty old dagger, still sharp and strong, and knew this knife and paper were still his most valuable possessions.

"We found some pretty interesting keepsakes at the bottom of St. Anthony's well, too." Layla explained how they chased the Old Man across Europe and back to Africa, where they met a knight at an oasis who told them about a young European who stole his camel and cargo. They also learned that knights, outlaws and fedawis were all hunting for *The Book of Secrets* you'd stolen."

"Really? What *Book of Secrets*?"

"Mina told me about the soap. Those bars of lye in the camel's bags were impressions from *The Book of Secrets*."

"The soap was a book?"

"Almost. The Templars found impressions of *The Book*, but never found *The Book*. They didn't know what the impressions meant. The knights you met were bringing them to Alamut, hoping the Old Man would help them. Then you relieved them of their precious treasure." Layla explained how the soap led them to Eagle's Nest and the Lost Stone, and Aaron felt the web tightening around him again.

Aaron looked at his hands. "I washed with *The Book of Secrets*?"

Layla patted him on the back. "Now we'll get the Stone back from Hassan."

Aaron looked at the ground.

"I'm just joking. The Stone will come back in its own time."

"Its time has come." Aaron pulled the Lost Stone from beneath a pile of leaves and displayed it like a trophy.

"That's the Stone! You still have it! Then what does the Old Man have?"

"When I found a smooth, grey rock on the beach almost identical to the Lost Stone, I got an idea. I knew Hassan wouldn't leave without the Stone so I gave him the real one at first, and switched them while it was in the pouch, right before he sailed. He'll probably come back, but it'll take his ankles a long time to heal. And now he'll have to take the Stone from you. I have a feeling that's why I'm here. Now you have the Lost Stone and my destiny is fulfilled."

Layla looked confused. "Why so somber? You be should be happier than ever. You're in paradise with people who care for you, free from the Old Man, free to find a new adventure with the whole world stretched out before you. Why do you seem so sad?"

"I'm happy the Stone is in your hands. I know I'm lucky to be here with you now. But look at Eunisia and Mina. They barely escaped with their lives. My eggplant is gone. Is that lucky? There's no such thing as coincidence, is there? Everything in my life has happened for a reason. It's been planned and plotted like a ship's course, but I couldn't see the destination until I arrived."

Layla looked concerned. "Do you feel alright, Aaron?"

"I feel like I've been chasing this Stone all my life, whether I knew it or not. Yet I wasn't chasing it for me. Not for success or nobility or love. I was chasing it for you, right?"

"Of course not! You may've been chasing the Stone, but only you can tell why. You followed Eunisia to Marseilles and you boarded the ship to Algiers. You stole the camel with the *Book of Secrets* and stayed with the Old Man. You'll choose many more destinations. Don't stop to look over your shoulder every time you arrive. Go further. You're just beginning, Aaron."

"I feel like the race is over and I should be grateful I survived. Somebody else got the girl, the Stone and even the eggplant is elsewhere. Everything seemed so connected, now it's all gone. How could I be so lucky and always end up with nothing?"

"You've done and seen things in this world nobody could believe and you'll always have those experiences and the lessons you learned. And the connections in your life are still connected, whether coincidence or not."

"Huh?" Now Aaron was even more confused.

"Isn't it impossible for thousands of children to march across Europe to try to save the Holy Land? Or for Assassins to rule half

261

of Arabia from a mountain hideaway? Or for an English orphan to end up with the Lost Stone? They may be impossible, but they happened. Truth is always more fantastic than history. The things you call coincidence are really signposts to greater secrets."

"What kind of signposts?"

"When a sparrow flaps its wings in Baghdad, there's lightning in paradise. The world is very complicated, but not impossible. You're right about the course of your life. There was nothing random about you finding me in the forest, no chance was involved when you found Mina in the desert, being kidnapped by the Old Man's Assassins had to be planned, my books must've been planted along with Eunisia at Sir Gillian's outpost, and speaking of Eunisia, there's nothing haphazard about she and her husband being awake when you arrived at Fatima. And nothing at all accidental about the four of us here now. Do you think invisible angels or legions of secret knights arranged all of this?" Aaron didn't answer. "Do you really believe someone planned this? It would take dozens of operatives and thousands of actors for such a grand conspiracy."

"How would you explain it? Why am I here in the center of this cyclone?"

"Sparrows in Baghdad!" Layla pointed as two yellow butterflies passed between her and Aaron.

"I suppose it's no coincidence these two butterflies appeared here now? Have their parents crossed our paths before? Will they affect the weather in London 100 years from now?"

"Yes, yes and yes," answered Layla. "Everything is connected. Nothing is coincidence. The past and future are all contained right here, in this meadow. These butterflies have come together by chance, flown on a random path and they both found us by chance. It's true. It's also true this random path was their destiny. They're living proof of random beauty. Signals from other worlds. Clues to your existence. Watch them closely. They're like windows into the secret meaning of things."

Aaron looked at Eunisia and Mina, lying in a bed of soft green clover, sleeping in the shade of the tree, safe from the flames. "What's the secret meaning of innocent women harmed by trained killers? Does it all just end in suffering?"

"I'm sorry, Aaron. I don't know why the world isn't fair. I don't know why mean people are rewarded with wealth and power. That's the way the world is. It's up to us to find our own strengths and use them wisely to make it better for everybody. Try to balance the darkness with a little light."

"Are you going to use the Stone to spread some light?"

"I hope so." She looked down at the treasure nestled in her lap again. "I've been waiting for you a long, long time." Layla was speaking to the Stone like she was seducing her long lost paramour under an eclipsed moon, like they were midnight lovers destined to be together, waiting for the perfect moment to embrace. Aaron couldn't recall seeing Layla so delighted, sitting on the ground, legs folded beneath her, head swaying and a smile extending all the way to the ends of the island.

It took days for the wind to blow the charred battleground scents away and replace them with the salty, melancholy fragrance of Gulf air and fresh blooms. Birds and their songs slowly returned until there was a symphony in every tree.

It was time for Layla to bring the Stone to life. Mina and Eunisia opened their eyes and watched Layla moving about the meadow like a Hindu goddess, the Stone in her hands, weaving it through the space around her in an elaborate dance. She chanted in an ancient language that seemed almost reptilian—hissing and clicking with deep, baritone sounds gurgling from her throat, moaning and smacking her lips like a giant lizard that just finished a good meal. The whole time she swayed back and forth, moving the Stone in graceful arcs and tiny, slow motion circles cascading down from above her head as if the Stone was an acrobatic bird turning upwards just before its tail feathers touched the ground.

Aaron and the others waited for something amazing to happen at any moment, something none of them could imagine, something wonderful and glorious and heavenly and perhaps involving something far more sublime than leagues of angels, Gabriel's trumpets or even pearly gates. Aaron hoped it would instantly change the world. Something that would heal Eunisia and Mina and return the eggplant to his chest.

Layla's lip smacking gradually drifted into a song that Aaron heard before. It was a Persian lullaby that she sang in England, except she changed the words:

> *Like lightning in Baghdad,*
> *or thunder in Paradise.*
> *Like moonlight Crusaders*
> *or knights on the prowl.*
> *Like runaway camels*
> *or holy bandits.*
> *Like beats in a heart*
> *or a rose in the desert.*
> *Like Adam in a well*
> *or a Lost Stone found.*
> *Like a spider in the garden*
> *with a web to the moon.*

She repeated the verse three times, lifted the Stone over her head like the great primordial egg of infinite hope, connecting this world to another—but to her companions, it looked like she was holding a shining, grey, egg-shaped rock.

Mina and Eunisia were both smiling and Layla was in a state of pure ecstasy, humming softly with the Stone back in her lap. She knew this moment would never be recorded in the official history books. Its place was among hidden and long-forgotten legends like frogs falling from the sky, men surviving inside the corpses of whales, giant flying objects and other rare and beautiful combinations of the fantastic and real. Layla held the Stone and sang until the next morning, when she finally fell asleep. Aaron stayed up with her, watching for visitors and trying to telepathically connect with the small, lost eggplant.

*****

The eggplant was cold and scared. The water pressure made it feel unbalanced and queasy, and both were uncomfortably new sensations for the vegetable. It by far preferred Aaron's rumbling digestive tract to this infinite chamber of horrors. It rolled along the sandy gulf floor, a prisoner of tides, weeds and other bottom dwellers. It had been reduced to an insignificant object of no man's desire. It was no different than a million other discarded stones, shells and bones tumbling under the waves, buried in this sunken world. It longed for its moments in the sun, terrestrial aromas, the touch of a human and a friendly voice. It missed Aaron. It wanted to call out to him, but was afraid.

The eggplant couldn't bear it much longer. It wanted to put itself out of its misery. If it could only throw itself into an underwater volcano, or be crushed by shark's teeth. It was considering suicidal options when it sensed something cold and slimy moving across its surface. It stopped atop him, planted its lips onto a small patch of eggplant skin and started sucking, like a baby camel at its mother's teat.

"Whoa, partner! That's a bit sensitive right there. I'd appreciate it if you moved on to another meaningless, bottom-dwelling amulet." The eggplant's voice sounded different underwater, and apparently got the attention of the snail, which released its sucker and moved on, as its host suggested.

The eggplant sobbed as best it could. It sounded stuffed and raspy, like it had a bad cold. The lives of humans were blinks in

265

the Great Eye, but this immortal vegetable was going to be around for a while. It was ready to participate in giant cycles turning like big wheels, rising and falling like the sun and moon, like the four seasons, like life and death all around him. It shivered in the darkness and knew this was going to be a painfully long eternity.

*****

Aaron returned to the beach the next morning to search for the eggplant. He soaked his gutrah in oils from fresh mango blossoms, tied it over his face to combat the stench oozing from the fortress and combed every inch of the beach where he first dove into the water. He sifted sand through his fingers and poked through fresh piles of driftwood and weeds, but found nothing. He canvassed the beach again and again, but still nothing. Tomorrow may be different, he thought, and headed back to Eden as the late afternoon sun lit up the western sky.

All three ladies were drinking tea around a small fire when he walked into camp. The evening light made Layla look like she was 100-years-old. They could see Aaron was broken-hearted.

"I wish I had a magic spell to bring the eggplant back. It may be on the beach tomorrow, don't give up hope," consoled Layla.

Aside from Layla, the mood in paradise was somber. Mina was bandaged and silent, Eunisia's burns had just been re-wrapped with fresh leaves, and Layla was pouring a cup of tea for Aaron when he asked, "Do you think anything has really changed since you brought the Stone to life?"

"Yes. Absolutely. It's hard to see a round world from a flat map and it's even more difficult to see the world change from a garden in Bahrain. The change may be like a seed growing for years before it bears fruit." While she speculated on the effect of

266

the Stone, she had no way of knowing at the very moment the Stone was reactivated, an earthquake shook villages and moved rivers that would define state and national boundaries on the continent known someday as North America, three aboriginal chiefs in the South Pacific made peace for the first time in 2,000 years, the next Dali Llama was born in a tent in Kirghiz, and the seeds of a small but fruitful enlightenment were scattered across England and the European continent, bringing the Dark Ages to an official end.

"I never heard of this Stone before yesterday. It means nothing to me." Eunisia was sitting up on her knees as she spoke, her cheeks smudged, and hair knotted.

"Don't worry, Eunisia. We understand it's been hardest for you, I know you must miss your family."

"Not worrying won't bring me home," scorned Eunisia. "I don't even know why I'm here. One minute, I'm in bed with my husband, the next I'm kidnapped by three boys who brought me to this island where an old man tried to burn me alive. Why me?" Her voice grew louder and she began sobbing as she spoke. "Your lives have been devoted to this Stone, one way or the other. I'm just trying to make the best of my life, trying to find happiness without hurting anyone. I have a family who wonders where I am. Why am I here?"

"I'm so sorry. It's all my fault." Aaron glanced at Layla and Mina before he gazed shamefully into Eunisia's eyes. "You're here because I loved you."

"What?"

"The Old Man knew I'd do anything for you. He wanted to trade you for the Stone." Aaron felt as guilty as if he'd kidnapped her himself. "I'm so sorry, Eunisia. I didn't mean for you to be in the middle of this."

"I don't blame you. I blame the Stone," cried Eunisia, and gazed at Layla. It has no soul, no memories of little brothers, no sons or husbands or hopes. This rock has never suffered from

267

thirst and fear in the desert or watched its best friends die. This Stone is cold and dead."

Layla was puzzled by Eunisia's anger. "Why do you blame the Stone? It's done nothing."

"That's why I blame it. The Stone has the power to draw you and the Assassins to this island—why doesn't it help you when you need it?" Eunisia stood and brushed the leaves from her burnoose, wincing with pain as she moved. "The Stone is important because you give it meaning. You give it power. To me it's nothing more than a dumb rock. Now I want to go to Fatima and see my family. I know you've tried to protect me, Aaron. And you never asked for anything. I should be asking for your forgiveness."

"My forgiveness? For what?"

"We were so young, but I do remember you were always kind to everyone—especially me. I used to think about you every day in the boat, hoping you'd be there when we landed. But it was horrible, and after that I tried to forget everything. I'm sorry, Aaron." Tears pooled in her eyes and she sobbed, "I have to get back to my family."

*****

Aaron and Eunisia rode back to Fatima like acquaintances who grew up in the same city, filling in the years they were apart with their best memories. Aaron learned Eunisia could ride both horses and camels, speak pretty fair Farsi, perform the dance of seven veils and play the bendir. These were valuable talents for any desert bride. Her son had already spoken his first words in Farsi, Arabic and French. She'd met her husband, Abufazil, when she arrived at Fatima. He was commander of the fortress and she joined his other wives after six months.

Eunisia seemed happy as she talked, but mostly she seemed relieved she was away from Bahrain. Once the Assassins took her from her home, she was afraid she'd never see her son again. Aaron understood. They rode along the Gulf, where the air was cool, made camps on the beach, then climbed through the mountains. The view of the Gulf waters and Arabian plateau was spectacular from the ridge top trails. It was much different from their death march across France a few years earlier.

"What are you going to do, Aaron Sloopshire?"

"I'm going back to Layla and Mina. See what washes up on the beach. Maybe do some fishing and swimming."

"No more adventures?"

Aaron thought for a moment. "I'm not sure it's up to me."

They slept beside each other, under the Arabian stars and Eunisia felt safe with Aaron. He was still a young man, compared to her husband, and Aaron would protect her with his life. She knew if the world had turned a little differently, she would've known Aaron much better than she ever did.

When they came to the ridge overlooking the fortress at Fatima, Eunisia threw her arms around him. "Thank you, Aaron Sloopshire. Thank you for saving my life and bringing me home," and then she watched him vanish forever, over the hills.

*****

The ride through the mountains and down the coast with Eunisia seemed like a dream. Before Fatima was out of sight, Aaron was worrying about the eggplant. What if it had washed up while he was gone? He should have asked Layla to look for it. He rode day and night, stopping only to sleep. He traded his horse for a small boat, sailed across the Gulf to the beach where he lost the eggplant and started searching. He walked methodically back and

269

forth, first on the beach and then in the water, eyes cast downward, looking for a trace of the little charm. It felt good to be hunting for a friend again—taking action was far more satisfying than sitting and feeling miserable and helpless.

That evening he went to meet Layla and Mina. Layla had already transformed the area around the spring into her home. She constructed a tall thatched-palm roof covering a large bed of dried grass. A fire pit with several large flat stones on one side served as her kitchen. Small conduits ran from the spring to little pools around their refuge. The battle scars were still visible in some bare, blackened trees and bushes dotting the countryside, but Layla's camp was green and inviting.

Mina recovered slowly. She still couldn't speak and her neck was tightly bandaged, so she didn't move her head much. Otherwise, she was in good spirits, sitting up, drinking tea and communicating by writing words in the sand with a stick. Layla was collecting fresh plants, barks and herbs to make new salves for Mina's wound when Aaron walked into camp.

"Aaron!" How are you? Have you eaten? Come sit down. Drink some tea and I'll warm some fish." Layla put her arm gently around Aaron's shoulder.

"I'm happy for Eunisia and her family—now it's time to help the eggplant. I have to find it. I'm going to build a hut on the beach where I lost it and stay there until the Gulf gives it up."

"How far away is the beach?"

"About four hours east from here, where it smells like a sewer."

Layla served him a bowl of hot fish and fresh vegetables. "You'll find our little friend, Aaron. You'll find it soon." She sounded certain.

The next morning he walked to the beach and collected palms and driftwood for his hut. He was used to sleeping under the stars, so he didn't require anything too elaborate.

The eggplant was washed onto the shore after three weeks. It tumbled across the beach during a rare high tide on a moonless night, and wound up dangling in a ball of seaweed and bird droppings. The salt water, snails and fish droppings had turned it a grey-green color and its necklace was long gone. It felt incredibly lucky just to be dry and free from the tides. For the first time ever, the eggplant was grateful to hear bird songs and feel the warm sun. It hadn't talked in weeks and was getting used to living alone in silence.

Aaron's hut wasn't far from the eggplant. He rarely spoke, so the vegetable couldn't hear his voice. One night after Aaron cooked a big bass over the fire, a huge gull swooped down and snatched the whole fish from the embers.

"Hey! Come back here with my dinner! Please, please, please come back!"

When the eggplant heard Aaron's voice, it thought it was dreaming.

"Aaron! Aaron! Is that you?" squeaked the eggplant, in a fungus-toned, barely recognizable voice. Aaron didn't answer. "Aaron! Aaron!" it howled again.

Aaron heard it this time. His heart pounded and he followed the rattling little voice, pulling away layers of slimy green weeds, sticks and feathers until he held the sad little vegetable in his hands.

"Oh Aaron! You've no idea what happened to me. It was awful. Please, take me away from the water. Please."

"I'm so sorry this happened. I'll never take you in the water again. I promise." Aaron tried to smile so the vegetable wouldn't know just how bad it looked. "It's so good to hear your voice! We'll spend one more night on the beach, then go see Layla and

271

Mina in the morning." Tears were rolling down his red, sunburned face as he cradled the eggplant in the center of his palm and rubbed its rough, sea-stained skin with his baby finger.

"Let's go back now," begged the eggplant.

"It's hours away."

"Please, Aaron," its voice was weak and shaky. "I'd feel a lot safer away from the water. The sooner the better."

Aaron agreed and they started back. After nightfall, the wind came up and heavy rain fell. Aaron was soaked to the bone when he arrived at Layla's camp. Harsh winds had blown the roof away and the fire pit was filled with rainwater, so Aaron joined the ladies out of the rain, under a lean-to made from leafy boughs.

"You look like you just found your best friend." Layla saw the smile on Aaron's face. "How is our little vegetable?"

"It's a bit water-worn, but glad to be out of the Gulf." Aaron held out his hand and showed the charm to Layla, who sighed when she saw its pitiful condition.

"Do I look that bad?" gasped the eggplant.

*****

The next days were spent collecting building materials for a more permanent home site. This time, they built the kitchen into the side of a hill and used heavy branches and sod to fortify the walls and roof. Aaron still slept under the stars most nights, and built his own simple hut close to Layla and Mina. His hut wasn't tall enough to stand in, but there was plenty of room to sleep and write.

They made simple tools and planted a huge vegetable garden to grow enough food for a family twice their size. The eggplant offered botanical advice and visited with Mina, who could speak in whispers now, but still appreciated the vegetable's silent conversations, while Aaron fished at the beach. There was fruit to pick, fish to clean and when Layla returned with provisions from a neighboring village, there was bread to bake. Life was never boring in paradise.

"Do you think the Old Man will be back for the Stone?"

"Hassan has his hands full with other problems," said Layla. "He lost nearly half of his fedawis in the battle with the caliph and Templars. He's weaker than he's ever been, with more enemies ready to attack. I don't think we'll see him again."

"What about the Templars?"

"The knights won't be visiting Bahrain for a while. Their Crusades aren't what they used to be. They've lost almost every Christian outpost from the sea to the Saracens. Their coffers are empty and their European Lords may have the Templars heads mounted on their cathedral walls before long."

"What about you, Aaron. Are you happy here?" Mina's voice was soft and cautious, but still sweet as a meadowlark.

He remembered what Eunisia had said about happiness. "I feel safe. I'm happy to be here with both of you and the eggplant, but it just seems like there should more."

"Whatever there is, only you can find it," said Layla. The next day, while Aaron was fishing, Layla and Mina prepared a royal feast and surprised him with three young women from the closest village. The guests were dressed in their finest silk sarongs and wore fragrant oils that made Aaron's eyes water. They laughed and ate and talked about their brothers and sisters until the moon was high, then Aaron escorted them back to their village. Layla and Mina were waiting for him when he returned.

"Well, which was your favorite?"

"Favorite what?"

"Favorite young lady. Did one of them scratch your fancy?"

"None of them scratched anything. But they were all nice."

Months passed quickly in paradise. The garden's vegetables grew large, Aaron met every eligible young lady in the village, and Eden fully recovered from the Assassin's battle. Then one day Layla returned from the village with news Hassan had been killed.

Aaron wasn't sure if he should laugh or cry. He hated the Old Man, but he knew him better than he'd known his own father, better than any other man in the world. Was it possible? The Old Man was supposed to live forever. "How did he die?"

"A man who claimed to be his son killed him as he slept. The son took control, most of the Assassins left the mountain, and the Mongols moved in shortly afterwards and sacked Eagle's Nest."

"Eagle's Nest was sacked?" Aaron couldn't believe it. The immortal ruler and the impenetrable palace gone? "I need to see for myself." And Aaron left Layla, Mina and the eggplant the next day to visit his alma mater.

When he arrived he saw a few goats roaming the hillsides around Eagle's Nest like lazy graveyard guards. He walked through the garden's marble arch and saw scorched earth, fallen temples and a choked pool of thick brown mud where there was once a pristine waterfall. A long row of charred bones lined the edges of the pool like remnants from a savage party. The fresh water spring had stopped running and the lush, green paradise was gone forever. His memories of this garden shriveled into a small, dark storm cloud hanging around his heart.

Inside, the fortress was empty except for bloodstained walls and rodents. The Old Man's chambers were barren. His laboratory was smashed and trampled into an unrecognizable heap of broken ceramics and splintered wood. The library was reduced to ashes, each pile marking months of Aaron's life that would never be regained. The revolutionary eroticism, ecstatic practices and profane, ancient secrets—all gone forever.

Right here, among the ashes of his past, with the smell of death hanging in the air and the cries of boys still echoing in the halls, someone tugged on Aaron's invisible nose ring and he watched his future stretch before him like a scroll unraveling at his feet and he knew it was his fate to rewrite the texts from the Old Man's library and bring the great secrets back to life. Yes. He may not remember them all, and they may not be perfect, but he'd start at the beginning, and write the authoritative versions of every book, scroll, tablet and palimpsest plate he transcribed for the Old Man. He'd spend the rest of his life restoring the rites of antiquity, or reasonable facsimiles that would just have to pass for the real things.

Aaron set out for Bahrain composing lists of his favorite texts in his head. He remembered incantations and rituals for controlling events from a distance, mind control techniques and knockout potions. Some of the world's most powerful secrets would be resurrected from the ashes of Eagle's Nest, and new ones would have to be created.

*****

Back in Bahrain, Layla and Mina had become quite affectionate, holding hands and cooing like lovebirds. They both tended to the gardens, meditated two hours every day, their heads pointed first north then south with the eggplant keeping time, and prepared elaborate evening meals. Besides Layla and the eggplant trying to get a sign of life from the Stone, they used it every day for grinding dried herbs and mashing roots into thick pastes.

Aaron returned to camp smiling from ear to ear. He'd found his destiny and was ready to go to work. The eggplant thought it was a wonderful plan. They sat by the fire under a million twinkling stars, assured he was a terribly tiny part of this universe, as insignificant as a grain of sand yet able to change the world with the right strokes from his mighty, magic pen, like so many others before him.

Aaron spent mornings making paper and drying it in sheets in the sun, and he'd write in the afternoon with the eggplant providing advice and adding details. Aaron rewrote the great works of ancient masters for days, and then he'd take a few days off to fish and work in the garden, and rewrite more, until he completed the tales of Lilith and the Garden, reproduced Sumerian creation myths, copied the complete Emerald Tablets, and prepared charts for the authoritative Arabic alchemical standards. Of course, these texts were never exactly the same as their predecessors—in some cases only small portions of the originals made it to Aaron's manuscripts. Although philosophically sound, he injected just the right amount of inaccuracy to make it more difficult for the reader to actually achieve fruitful results from their operations. He never remembered all the exact words and inadvertently interchanged symbols here and there, sometimes adding few surreptitious zeroes. In the process, he developed new tarot decks by unknowingly changing the order of the Arcana, which kept some decks from revealing any actual insights.

One day, Layla found Aaron laughing quietly to himself as he sat with his paper and pen. She didn't know he and the eggplant just shared a joke about certain scrolls they were planning to hide in caves near the Dead Sea. "It looks like you've found it, Aaron."

"Found what?"

"What you were looking for—your happiness."

Aaron shook his head. "I guess I have. I needed to leave something behind for fellow travelers, like you suggested a long time ago."

Layla looked confused.

"We're editing history, reshaping old myths, adding a few inside jokes and saving the medical texts as best as we can remember. We're choosing which secrets will die with Eagle's Nest and which will survive. Look at these," he showed Layla a book with complete diagrams of the human body, including internal organs, and major veins, arteries and bones from skull to feet. "And here's a table with the correct herbal correspondences for every part of the body. Not bad, eh?"

*****

Aaron, Layla and Mina lived quietly in Bahrain for years. As Layla grew older she remained strong and fit, although she no longer rode a horse or camel. Mina learned that her sister Amira sold her husband's camel-trading business and her home was now an orphanage. Natalie and Donatelle turned out to be excellent nurses, and stayed with Amira to care for the sick and hungry. Aaron looked forward to seeing them again someday. They were good girls, and he was glad they found a good place in this world.

Aaron continued rewriting the great secrets and traveled to hide them in caves, mosques and shrines, where they were mysteriously discovered years later. Life was quiet in Eden, until a teenage boy appeared outside Aaron's hut.

"Are you Aaron Sloopshire?"

"Yes I am. What can I do for you?"

He looked into Aaron's eyes. "My name is Aaron, too. My mother's name was Eunisia."

The boy's words hit Aaron like a falling angel. It was hard to believe Eunisia's boy was standing here before him. He looked like her—more European than Arab. "Is your mother alright?"

"She died a month ago in Baghdad. My father died a year before."

Aaron swallowed hard. "I'm so sorry. How did she die?" Aaron whispered, as if someone had just punched him in the belly and he was trying to hide the pain.

"Lightning."

"Lightning?"

"There was a lightning storm with no rain. We went outside to watch the sky light up with thousands of bolts. It was beautiful. Then the bolts came closer and closer. We ran to shelter, but one of the bolts hit my mother. Before she died, she told me to come here, to this island and find you. She said you'd know what to do."

Aaron didn't want to cry in front of the boy, but he couldn't help it. He reached for the boy and squeezed him like he was the most beautiful thing he'd ever seen. "You came to the right place."

Aaron helped the boy build a hut and tried to convince him to change his name. "One Aaron is enough for this garden, don't you think? Did you ever consider the name Falukki?" But Eunisia's boy liked the name Aaron and decided to keep it.

Young Aaron, as he soon became known, helped Mina and Layla with daily chores, and the Elder Aaron taught him to map the stars and conjure spirits. Before long, they were rewriting books together, and devising grand schemes to keep historians and latter day mystics guessing beyond the next millennium.

At twilight, when the fireflies' dim green lights danced through the tall grass around their huts, the Elder Aaron gathered the others to hear a story he'd just finished. Before they arrived, he remembered the night his parents died. He imagined his mom and dad were there in the grass, dancing alongside of him. He imagined Eunisia, Samar, Donatelle and Natalie, the non-existent knight and his friend Majid, all right here, a galaxy of his friends and family, glowing like little stars.

When Layla, Mina and young Aaron took their seats on pillows around the fire, they were ready for his story to begin.

"What's the story about?" asked Young Aaron.

"It begins with an orphan from England who found the world's most amazing teacher, followed his heart across the sea with an existential eggplant and found a family in paradise." And the Elder Aaron slowly rubbed the contented vegetable with the tip of his finger and started to read, "It's midnight, April 30, 1211 and Layla is sealing her last vial of belladonna vapors and wondering if she'll ever return to paradise."